For a limited time only: men up for grabs!

Retail maven Carlotta Wren loves nothing better than to shop, but with her scandalous—and debt-ridden—background, she's been too busy trying to keep her head above water to have the luxury of shopping for a man! Now she has three men in her life—a sexy cop hot on the trail of her fugitive parents, a fascinating body mover who has secrets of his own, and her repentant first love who's back with his heart in his hands. Thrust into the middle of yet another crisis, the once-lonely Carlotta finds herself surrounded by lots of prime male merchandise!

One man she'll try on for size...

One man she'll save for a special occasion...

And one man will make her an offer that's hard to refuse...

STEPHANIE BOND

BODY MOVERS:
2 BODIES
FOR THE PRICE OF 1

MIRA®

MIRA

ISBN-13: 978-0-7783-2484-3
ISBN-10:   0-7783-2484-2

BODY MOVERS: 2 BODIES FOR THE PRICE OF 1

www.MIRABooks.com

Printed in U.S.A.

First Printing: August 2007
10 9 8 7 6 5 4 3 2 1

Acknowledgments

As with every book, there are certain people
who made the journey easier. First, thanks to my
editors Brenda Chin, Margaret O'Neill Marbury and
Dianne Moggy for your assistance in getting the
Body Movers series off the ground running, and for
the guarantee that as of this date, the series will
last for at least four books. Thanks, too, to my agent
Kimberly Whalen of Trident Media Group for handling
the logistics, to my critique partner, Rita Herron,
for your unflagging support and to my husband,
Christopher Hauck, for your glowing cover quote. ☺

Thanks, too, to the booksellers who have
recommended this series to your customers, and
to all of you readers who e-mailed asking when the
second book would hit the shelves—I hope you enjoy
2 Bodies for the Price of 1! Keep those e-mails coming!

Prologue

Hi, there. My name is Carlotta Wren. I'm a whisper away from being thirty years old. I work for Neiman Marcus in Atlanta. And I'm single. You're probably thinking, *Sounds pretty normal.* But let me tell you, friend, you won't believe what I've been through in the last ten years.

I was barely eighteen, a senior in a private high school, living in a mansion in a tony area of Atlanta known as Buckhead, engaged to a handsome rich young man named Peter Ashford and on my way to college when my father was charged with investment fraud. The world as I knew it crumbled around us as my family lost every worldly possession and we were forced to move into a grubby townhouse in a *less* tony part of town.

My father said he was framed but instead of staying to face down his problems, he decided to skip bail—and town—and my drunken socialite mother went with him. I haven't seen them since. And here's the kicker: They left me to raise my nine-year-old brother Wesley. Can you imagine? I was barely an adult and ill-equipped to finish raising *myself,* much less a sensitive kid with a genius IQ.

But I regrouped. College was obviously out, so I started a retail job and discovered that my life as a rich kid had at least prepared me to sell expensive things to my former friends. Yes, I said "former." As soon as my father's scandal hit the papers, my friends fled—and so did my boyfriend—Peter dumped me like last year's handbag.

But Wesley and I made it through somehow and one day I looked up to discover that he was a grown man. As you can imagine, Wesley and I are close, but we do disagree on a few things. Wesley is convinced my father is innocent and is hiding out until he can prove it…I'm convinced my father is an asshole and is hiding out on a tropical island.

Another area in which my brother and I disagree: Wesley, now nineteen, has an aversion to working a regular job—he'd rather play Texas Hold 'Em poker and hang out with the wrong sort of people. In fact, he's up to his—and my—neck in debt to two loan sharks. And recently he was arrested for hacking into the courthouse computer database to delete speeding tickets for his friends. When I went to post bail, I met the arresting officer, Detective Jack Terry, and we didn't exactly hit it off.

Wesley's arrest caught the attention of the D.A. who'd arrested our father and decided to take it out on Wesley. My dad's former attorney—and lover, sheesh—stepped in to help Wesley and he got off with probation and a fine—yay, more debt. But with the Wren family back on the radar, the D.A. decided to reopen my father's case and assign it to none other than Detective Terry.

Deciding that Wesley needed a little tough love, I told him to get a job or get out. And he got one—moving bodies for the morgue! His boss, Cooper Craft, was cuter than I expected a man who ran a funeral home and moved bodies would be, but still, it's a creepy way to make a living.

Meanwhile, I decided to crash an upscale party—I do that occasionally, but I'm not proud of it—and ran into my old flame, Peter Ashford, who had married a former friend of mine and was doing very well for himself working for the firm where my father had once worked. Problem was, Peter wasn't happy in his marriage and he felt bad about the way he'd dumped me and wanted to pick up where we left off.

Then—and this is where things get hairy—his wife was murdered and I was implicated because she and I had had a little spat. And of course none other than Detective Jack Terry led the investigation. It looked like Peter had actually murdered his wife—in fact, he confessed to it! But I knew he was innocent so I did some investigating on my own and the real killer was eventually caught—after a few bullets were exchanged and Detective Terry sort of saved my, as he put it, "ungrateful behind."

So suddenly I had three new men in my life: Peter, Jack and Cooper. Wesley swore to me that he'd given up gambling. Things were looking up. I'd even begun to think my life was getting back to normal—and then my long-lost father called.

"Sweetheart, it's me...Daddy."

Carlotta Wren stepped off the up escalator in the Atlanta Neiman Marcus department store where she worked, so shocked by the sound of the voice on the other end that she dropped her cell phone. It landed on the shiny, waxed floor with a smack, bounced and skidded away. With her heart in her stomach, she frantically scrambled after the fleeing phone, the baritone of her long-lost fugitive father ringing in her ears.

Was it really him calling after ten years of silence? Ten years during which she'd put her life on hold to finish raising herself and her younger brother Wesley after her parents had skipped bail—and town—on investment fraud charges. Ten years of feeling alone and abandoned after her friends and even her fiancé had withdrawn their affection in light of the scandal.

The tiny phone spun away like a mouse scurrying for

cover. Carlotta gulped air as she clambered after it, brushing the shoulders of people in her path, darting between racks of clothing. The foot of a striding customer struck the phone and sent it spinning in another direction. Carlotta hurtled after it, feeling her father slip farther from her grasp with every agonizing second that passed. She was practically hyperventilating when she fell to her knees, curled her fingers around the elusive phone and jammed it to her ear. "Hello? Daddy?"

Dead air. If it had been Randolph Wren on the other end of the line, he was gone.

A sob welled up in her chest. "Daddy, can you hear me?"

She couldn't bring herself to hang up, unwilling to sever the only connection she'd had with her father in over a decade. Then she realized that he might be trying to call her back and stabbed the disconnect button. Sitting under a rack of beaded bathing-suit sarongs, Carlotta stared at the phone, willing it to ring again, thinking how ridiculous she would seem to an onlooker—an almost thirty-year-old woman sitting on the floor waiting for a call back from her long-lost daddy.

Somewhere between her nonexistent career goals, her brother's legal problems, their hulking debt to loan sharks and her confused love life, she'd made the transition from pitiful to pathetic.

Suddenly she remembered the callback feature and realized with a surge of excitement that she'd at least be able to see what number he'd called from. She stabbed at buttons on the phone, but was rewarded with a rather sick-sounding tone and noticed with dismay that the display was interrupted by a hairline crack. Liquid gathered in one corner, much like when Wesley had broken his Etch-a-Sketch when he was little.

"You can't be broken," Carlotta pleaded, blinking back tears. What would she tell Wesley? That their father had finally made contact and she'd hung up on him? Wesley still believed that their father was innocent and that he and their mother would return some day to clear his name and unite their shattered family. Carlotta felt less forgiving, especially toward her mother Valerie, who hadn't been charged with a crime, yet had chosen a life on the lam over her own children.

"Ring," she whispered, hoping that only the display had been compromised. She sat on her heels for five long minutes, her thumb hovering over the answer button, perspiration wetting her forehead. A shadow fell over her. When she looked up, she winced inwardly to see the general manager, Lindy Russell, standing with her eyebrows raised.

Minus ten points.

Next to Lindy stood a tall, narrow blonde, conservatively coiffed down to her upper class hair flip and wearing a haughty expression. Carlotta recognized her from sales meetings; she was new and worked in accessories next to the shoe department where Carlotta's friend Michael Lane worked. Patricia somebody or another.

"Carlotta, is there a problem?" Lindy asked.

Carlotta pushed to her feet and straightened her clothing. During the dash for her phone she'd lost a shoe. "No."

"Glad to hear it. You know you're not supposed to be using your cell phone while you're working the floor."

"Yes," Carlotta said, her throat closing. "But this is a—an emergency."

"Oh?" Lindy crossed her arms in front of her chest. "Are you on an organ-donor list?"

"No."

"The phone-a-friend for a contestant on a national trivia show?"

"No."

"Waiting to hear back from your next employer?"

Patricia snickered and Carlotta swallowed. "N–no."

Lindy extended her hand. "Hand it over. You can pick it up at the end of your shift."

"But—"

"No buts, Carlotta. You're already skating on thin ice around here."

Carlotta bit her tongue. Lindy had been more than fair to give her a get-out-of-jail-free card for buying clothes on her employee discount, wearing them to crash upscale parties, then returning the fancy outfits for full credit. Ditto when she had been involved in a knock-down drag-out fight with a customer right here in the store—and been implicated in that customer's subsequent murder. That particular misunderstanding had since been cleared up, but Carlotta's once-stellar sales record had slipped badly in the interim. It hadn't helped that the murdered woman had been a high-volume customer.

She was lucky that she hadn't been canned weeks ago, and since she and Wesley depended on her paycheck for little things like paying the mortgage…with a shaky smile, she handed the phone to Lindy.

"Carlotta, have you met Patricia Alexander?"

"Not formally." She extended her hand to the blonde. "Hello."

The woman's hand was just as cold as her smile. "Hello."

"Patricia is number one in sales this week," Lindy said.

"Congratulations," Carlotta murmured, stinging with the knowledge that not too long ago, *she* had owned that number one spot.

"Thanks," Patricia said, then laughed—a sound that reminded Carlotta of a test of the Emergency Broadcast System. "No hard feelings, I hope."

"Why should there be?"

The woman angled her head. "Because I plan to break your sales record. Better watch your back." Her frosty smile didn't match her breezy tone.

Lindy gave Carlotta a pointed look, then dropped the phone into her jacket pocket. Carlotta watched the women walk away, along with all hopes of talking to her father today.

Had it really been him? And if so, would he think she'd hung up on him purposely, that she didn't want to talk to him? Worrying her lower lip, she wondered—*did she?*

If anyone had asked what she would do if her father called out of the blue, Carlotta would've sworn that she would hang up on him. Over the years her anger had grown into an almost tangible mass, like a tumor. Yet at the sound of his voice, she had regressed to Daddy's little girl—the entitled, spoiled teenager she'd been when he'd disappeared, the naive, young woman who couldn't conceive that her parents would desert her and her nine-year-old brother. With a mere four words uttered from his mouth, she'd been ready to accept his explanation and his apology…assuming he'd had either to offer.

She covered her mouth to suppress the aching wail that lodged in her throat. Knowing that her father still had that much power over her made her feel even less in control than usual. How dare he dive-bomb back into their lives like that?

Perilously close to losing it, Carlotta backtracked to find her shoe, but was blinded by tears of frustration. She wiped at her eyes angrily and swore under her breath.

"Is this what you're looking for?"

She winced, then turned at the unmistakable noise of Detective Jack Terry's voice. She blinked away the moisture to find him studying her red Dior stiletto-heel slide with the same intensity that she'd seen him study evidence at crime scenes. Wesley's job as a body mover had thrown her and the detective into close proximity at a couple of crime scenes, with abrasive results. Jack Terry was the one person she didn't want to see right now—the brute had recently reopened her father's case.

"Yes," she snapped, snatching the shoe out of his big hand. "What are you doing here?"

"Irritating you, apparently." Then he suddenly looked sheepish and she realized he was dressed too casually to be on duty. He cleared his throat. "If you must know, I need a monkey suit for a bigwig department dinner and I could use your…uh…help…picking out something."

Her anger receded. He had no idea what had just transpired. And wouldn't know unless she told him…or unless he'd made good on his threat to put a trace on her and Wesley's phones. He wasn't convinced that a handful of post-cards was the only contact they'd had with their missing parents.

He gestured over his shoulder. "Maybe I should just go to the place where I usually shop."

"I didn't realize that Dick's Sporting Goods sold formal wear," she said dryly.

"This was a bad idea." He turned to go.

"No, Jack. Wait." He stopped and Carlotta wondered if he realized it was the first time she'd called him anything other than Detective Terry—or one of the several unsavory nick-names she had uttered privately. But recently he—and one of her collectible Judith Leiber breastplate necklaces, circa mid-1980s—had saved her from the bullet of a murderer, and in the aftermath, something *electric* had passed between them. She felt that confusing jolt now, at a loss to explain why she would be attracted to this good old Southern boy who—between arresting her brother for hacking into the Atlanta courthouse records, resurrecting her father's case and grilling her about her customer's murder—seemed to have made her family's lawlessness his pet project.

"What?" His nose flared and she sensed that he too felt the unwelcome sexual energy bouncing between them.

To break the moment, she narrowed her eyes. "No way are you going to deny me the pleasure of seeing you buttoned into a tux."

Jack frowned. "Sadist."

She smiled and dropped her shoe, trying to compose herself as she pushed her bare foot inside. Her father would call back…of course he would. She wobbled and Jack reached out to steady her.

He gave a little laugh, his gold-colored eyes narrow with sudden concern. "Are you all right? You seem on edge."

Carlotta stared at his big hand on her arm, reminding herself that if Jack Terry appeared concerned for her well-being, it was only because he was trying to get on her good side in the hope that she would lead him to her parents.

She pulled away. "I'm fine, Detective. Follow me."

2

During the ride down the escalator, Carlotta's neck burned with a fiery itch. She was certain Jack Terry could tell she was keeping something from him.

But the brawny detective appeared preoccupied himself. He wore what she was coming to recognize as his off-duty uniform: black T-shirt, worn jeans and black cowboy boots. And, she conceded begrudgingly, he wore it well. His rugged profile, close-cut dark hair and bronze skin made for a compelling view, yet he seemed completely unaware of women's heads turning as they stepped off the escalator and headed toward the men's department.

"So, what's the occasion?" she asked.

"Hmm?"

"The bigwig department dinner."

"Oh. An awards thing."

She lifted an eyebrow as she led him toward the formal wear section. "Are you receiving an award?"

The blush that stained his cheeks spoke for him.

"You are," she said, elbowing him. "What kind of an award?"

He cleared his throat. "Distinguished duty."

"Distinguished, huh? Did you do something in particular to earn this recognition? Like save a kid from a runaway car?"

"Guess the department couldn't think of anyone else to give it to."

"That must be it," Carlotta agreed, humoring his modesty. She angled her head and swept her gaze over the considerable length of him before pulling a jacket from a sleek wooden rack. "Black would be the obvious choice for a tux, but with your eyes and coloring, I'd go with charcoal gray. What are you, about a forty-four long, athletic cut?"

Jack looked surprised, then nodded. "Hey, I saw you this morning at a bank ATM on Piedmont."

She frowned. "My bank is on Piedmont, but I wasn't there this morning."

"Really? Wow, the woman looked just like you, then." He laughed. "No wonder she didn't wave back when I honked. I thought you were ignoring me."

"Apparently it was someone else ignoring you this time." She held out the jacket for him.

He shrugged into it and she sighed in satisfaction as the luscious fabric slid into place, hugging his shoulders perfectly. She adjusted the lapels, dismayed at the little tremors of pleasure she felt when her hands met the brick wall of his chest. Avoiding his gaze, Carlotta steered him toward a mirror. He looked ill at ease…and slightly gorgeous, she realized with no small amount of consternation. Jack Terry was easier to dislike when he was rumpled and wearing one of his infamous ugly ties.

"What do you think?" She made wary eye contact in the mirror.

"It's okay, I guess."

"Just okay? Jack, this is one of the finest suits that money can buy."

"I'm almost afraid to look at the price tag."

"Don't," she agreed. "But a suit like this is an investment—you can wear it to formal dinners, to weddings."

"I'm not much on weddings."

"Funerals, then."

"You're not convincing me."

"Look," she said, smoothing a hand over his shoulder, "sometimes you just have to buy something because it looks so damn good on you."

His eyebrows went up and a smile curled his mouth. "You think it looks damn good on me?"

Her cheeks warmed. "I do."

For a few seconds, that sexy buzzing thing bounced back and forth between them.

"Then I'm convinced," he said finally. "Ring me up."

"You'll need a shirt. And I'll call the tailor to mark your pants."

"I'm in your hands."

Carlotta raised one eyebrow. "Gee, Detective, that almost sounds like trust."

"I trust you—when it comes to clothes."

She recognized the danger of discussing trust while the voice of her fugitive father still resonated in her head, so instead she pulled a smile from thin air. "You should. I promise you'll look so good, no one will recognize you."

He frowned. "Thanks."

"You're welcome."

"How's your brother?" he asked as they walked back to the clothing racks.

"Good," she replied and meant it. "I think Wesley has a crush on his probation officer."

"At least that'll keep him motivated to check in every week."

"That's what I'm hoping."

"Does he plan to keep working for Cooper Craft?"

She nodded, then sighed. "As gruesome as it sounds, this whole body-moving business seems to agree with him." Then she remembered a phone call she'd gotten from her friend Hannah just before her father had called...if it indeed had been her father. "And now my friend Hannah has jumped on the body-moving bandwagon."

"The girl with the pierced tongue and the dog collar?"

"Yeah. She has a thing for Coop, I think."

"Funny, but I gathered that Coop had a thing for *you.*"

It was her turn to blush. "I hadn't noticed."

A dubious light came into his eyes. "Liar. Women know when men have a thing for them."

Buzz, buzz.

"I'm not interested in Coop," she said quickly. Although

the man *had* saved her when Wesley's six-foot python had cornered her in her bedroom. And she recalled the appreciation in his eyes to find her standing on her dresser wearing skimpy lingerie.

"I guess that means you and Ashford are back together," Detective Terry said lightly.

Peter Ashford, her first love, the man who had dumped her when her parents had gone missing and the scandal had burst over the front page of the *Atlanta Journal-Constitution*. Peter had gone on to marry a debutante—the good customer of Carlotta's who recently had been murdered in their palatial home in Buckhead, the wealthiest area in Atlanta. Many, Jack Terry included, had assumed Peter had killed his wife, but in the end, he'd been exonerated. And had expressed interest in picking up where he and Carlotta had left off years ago.

"No, Peter and I aren't together," she murmured, selecting a cream dress shirt and holding it up in front of him. She could feel the heat emanating from his body.

"Really." Jack cleared his throat. "I actually thought about asking you to go to this awards thing…with me."

Startled, she looked up. "You did?"

He suddenly looked as panicked as she felt. "But…considering the investigation into your father's case has been reopened, that might not be such a good idea…right?"

He didn't want to be seen with a fugitive's daughter. That would be a conflict of interest and not good for a distinguished detective's career. The same reason Peter Ashford had dumped her and ripped her heart out years ago when she'd needed him most. Did her father know how much he had damaged her and Wesley's lives? Did he even care?

"Right?" Jack repeated, his expression anxious. He wanted her to let him off the hook.

"Right," she said brightly. "Now let's get the tailor down here and make sure that when your date opens her door, you take her breath away."

He gave an uncomfortable little laugh and Carlotta tamped down her own unease as she called the house tailor. The day was wearing on her—first the mysterious phone call, then Jack Terry dredging up all her troubles, plus this weird physical attraction that had sprung up between them. But the attraction was probably born of the knowledge that nothing could possibly come of it…there were simply too many obstacles.

While she described to the tailor what services they would need, she swung her gaze to Jack and was unnerved to find him blatantly studying her. She squirmed under his gaze and stumbled over her words. The man was too perceptive for his own good—if she spent much time in his company, she wouldn't be able to keep secrets from him.

She hung up and gave him a shaky smile. "He'll be right down."

"Carlotta, is something bothering you?"

Damn those cop's instincts. For one crazy second, she wanted to confess about the phone call, to see if he could trace it and….

And what? Hunt down her father and drag him back to Atlanta to stand trial on the investment-fraud charges, now trumped by charges for being a fugitive? And her mother for aiding and abetting? Would it really be better to have her parents in prison than to have them on the run? Either way, they would be unavailable to her and to Wesley. And if her parents were imprisoned, the stain on the family name would be even more permanently set.

"No, I'm fine. Now…let's get you out of those jeans."

His eyes lit with mischief. "Whatever you say."

She smirked and pointed toward the dressing room. "I meant you need to put on the pants before the tailor gets here."

He frowned and moved toward the dressing room, reluctance in his step.

Carlotta shook her head, but when the dressing room door slid open a bit, she couldn't resist a naughty peek at Jack's reflection as he shucked his boots and jeans, revealing white boxers and long, powerful legs, more tanned than she'd expected. Unexpected heat struck low in her stomach.

Plus ten points, she noted idly, wondering what the Alabama boy did in his free time to acquire that tan. Somehow she doubted it was playing tennis.

"See something you like?"

She glanced up to find him grinning at her as he stepped into the pants. Carlotta straightened. "Don't flatter yourself, Detective."

His rolling chuckle sent vibrations over her warm skin. The arrival of the tailor saved her from more embarrassing banter. Suddenly she wanted to put distance between herself and Jack Terry. The man triggered dangerous urges—the urge to tell the truth being the least hazardous of her impulsive reactions.

She stood back as the tailor, a distinguished older gentleman, took over. To her amusement, Jack seemed uncomfortable to have the man touching him.

"Do you dress right or left, sir?" the man asked as he knelt to mark the hem on the slacks.

Jack frowned. "Excuse me?"

Smothering a laugh, Carlotta silently signaled the detective by pointing to his crotch and flopping her hand right, then left.

When recognition dawned on Jack's face, his neck flushed red. "What difference does *that* make?"

"It affects how your trousers hang, sir," the tailor said crisply.

Carlotta's shoulders were shaking. Jack glared at her and muttered, "Left."

She turned away to enjoy a laugh at the big man's expense, pretending to fold the dress shirt. It was nice to have something to lift her dour mood, if only temporarily…and the episode helped to level the field between her and the man who seemed to hold all the chips in their relationship.

Carlotta looked in his direction to see him holding up his arms while the tailor practically bear-hugged him to mark the waist on the pants. Not that she and Detective Jack Terry had a *relationship*. More of a…an association.

Jack flinched as the tailor made adjustments to the inside seam that had him putting his hands in places where another man's hands obviously had never been. "Is this going to take much longer?" he asked irritably.

"That should do it," the tailor said, standing and smoothing his hand over the back of the trousers—and Jack's ass— which garnered the older man another stern look.

Carlotta pressed her lips together and managed to keep a straight face long enough to thank the tailor. But when the man was out of earshot, she glanced at Jack's perturbed expression and burst out laughing.

"Are you finished humiliating me?"

"Yes, you can take off the pants."

She watched him stride back into the dressing room and craned her neck to see if he would happen to leave the door ajar again. When it clicked shut, she frowned, then was irritated with herself. She had no business looking at Jack Terry *or* liking it—and the man's ego probably didn't need more feeding. Lots of women seemed to go for the base types.

She pursed her mouth as a memory surfaced. Jack had a history with Liz Fischer, her father's former attorney...and lover. The woman had also come to Wesley's aid when he'd been arrested, much to Carlotta's dismay. She didn't trust her, and the fact that Jack had admitted to bedding her was just one more reason to stop looking at him.

Something she had to keep reminding herself when he stepped back out in his snug jeans, the suit draped over his thick arm. Averting her gaze and walking in front of him, she led him to a register.

"I gave you my friends-and-family discount," she said, holding up a little card.

"Thanks."

"You might consider using the difference to buy a decent tie," she suggested. "There's a clearance table over there—two for the price of one."

"Tempting. Maybe next time."

Carlotta swiped his credit card. "You can come back tomorrow to pick up the suit. We can look for shoes then."

"I thought I'd wear my boots."

She made a face.

But Jack was staring at someone over her shoulder, the displeasure on his face clear as he returned his card to his wallet.

Carlotta turned and blinked in surprise to see Peter Ashford standing there, looking polished in dark designer slacks and shirt, his blond hair slicked back, his watch, signet ring and seriously expensive shoes befitting a successful investment broker. "Peter," she breathed.

"Hi, Carly." He eyed Jack Terry warily. "Hello, Detective."

Jack nodded curtly. "Ashford. When did you get out of jail?"

Peter blanched slightly, but stood his ground. "Last night. The charges won't be officially dropped until later this week, but my attorney and the D.A. arranged for an early release."

D.A. Kelvin Lucas, the man who had ordered her father's case be reopened and asked Jack Terry to make it a priority. For such a big city, it was a small world.

"I guess I owe you my thanks for nailing the person responsible for Angela's death," Peter said to Jack.

"Just doing my job," Jack said. "Carlotta was the one who kept insisting you were innocent, even after you confessed. You should be thanking her."

"I intend to," Peter said, gazing at her with affection so palpable, she could feel it settle around her shoulders.

Jack cleared his throat, spearing Carlotta with his sardonic gaze. "See you around."

She nodded absently as he walked away, thinking that the two men were a study in extremes—Jack Terry, rough and aggressive; Peter, cultured and subtle.

Carlotta glanced back at Peter, hoping that he hadn't come to press her about renewing their relationship. She wasn't ready, and neither was he, so soon after his wife's death. "Peter, what are you doing here?"

"I need to talk to you." He looked around as if to ensure they were alone.

She realized that in the wake of Jack's departure, his expression had grown grave and his hands were shaking. "What's wrong?"

He stepped closer and seemed to grapple with what he had to say. "Carlotta, your father—Randolph—"

Her pulse skyrocketed. "What about him?"

"He—he called me."

3

Wesley Wren sat staring at the perspiration beading on the forehead of the real-estate broker sitting opposite him. Admittedly, it was hot as hell in the back of the west-end car repair shop where a game of Texas Hold 'Em had erupted on this stewing Sunday afternoon. But they'd been playing for over two hours and the guy's sweat glands hadn't kicked in until just now, when the last of five cards had been turned up in the community pot.

Wesley hoped that meant the three of clubs worsened the guy's hand rather than giving him a fluky straight that would beat his own full house of three queens and two eights. Because they'd been dealt only two face-down pocket cards and since there were no pairs in the face-up community cards, the only other hand that could beat his full house, four of a kind, was out of the question.

The winner of this hand would walk away with the fifteen grand that was piled on the sticky table between them. Wesley tamped down a spike of excitement. He was in a sweet spot, but he'd been close to the payoff before only to have it snatched away. In fact, he was still smarting from a bad beat in a weekend-long tournament that had left him too broke to make payments to his loan sharks and even deeper in debt to his rich buddy Chance Hollander.

This game had started after he'd dropped off his sister's car for some scratch-and-dent repair. Chance had tagged along and suggested a little gambling to the oily owner. A few phone calls later and a few bored professionals had shown up, ready to part with their easily-earned cash.

He was convinced he needed this money more than Real Estate Man, but two layers of deodorant and a puff of his sister Carlotta's talc on his forehead kept his sweat glands under control at moments like these.

While he waited for his opponent to see the bet, raise or fold, Wesley nursed a pang of regret for once again reneging on his promise to his sister to stay away from gambling. He told himself that the fact that he'd sold the motorcycle that she hated would temper her anger if he wound up losing the five grand he'd gotten for it.

Poor Carlotta. They'd both taken it hard when their parents had been forced to leave town to keep his father out of prison for a crime he didn't commit, but Carlotta had borne the brunt of the fallout, having to raise his smart ass and generally try to keep him out of trouble.

It had worked for the most part. Oh, sure, he'd racked up

some debt and had been caught hacking into the county courthouse records, but no one—not even his buddy Chance or his hot attorney Liz Fischer—knew that his crime wasn't as sloppy as it seemed. The incident had left him with a back door into a database that would hopefully divulge details about his father's case, and an impending community-service job with the city's computer security department that would give him all the access he needed.

The fact that his probation officer had turned out to be a stacked redhead who kept him awake at night was an unexpected bonus.

Carlotta was less convinced that their father was innocent of the charges levied against him, but Wesley chalked it up to her anger. She certainly had a right to her resentment—suddenly saddled with a kid, dumped by her boyfriend and left to scrape by on a retail job. His sister's life hadn't been easy.

Which was why he'd love nothing better than to take home this money and prove that he could contribute more to her life than migraines. And why he was determined to prove his father's innocence so their parents could come out of hiding and they could be a family again.

"Hey," Chance said from a chair where he slouched, watching. "Ain't there some kind of time limit for placing a bet?" Chance had bought into the game too but, as usual, had been eliminated with record speed.

"Yeah, get on with it," the owner of the place said to Wesley's opponent between puffs on a cigarette. The guy stood to get his cut no matter who took home the pot—totally illegal, but no one here was going to call 911.

This money could be the first step toward the kind of life he knew that Carlotta dreamed of: a normal one. If they got their debts paid off, maybe she would even relax enough to start dating. His boss Cooper was nuts for her and he'd seen the way that cop Jack Terry looked at her. Plus her old boyfriend Peter Ashford seemed eager to make amends.

Raise, he urged the guy silently. *Try to bluff me. Put another couple of grand on the table.* Wesley chewed on his fingernail to fake worry over a bad hand. In truth, he had a damned gorgeous hand that he had slow-bid to this point.

Real Estate Man zoned in on Wesley's nail-gnawing, then shifted forward in his chair. "All in," he said, pushing his remaining chips and cash to the center of the table.

Wesley almost wet himself: it was more than he could have hoped for. He wanted to play it cool, but couldn't help grinning as he responded, "Ditto."

Chance lurched to his feet to see the reveal. Real Estate Man groaned and turned over a lousy pair of tens. Wesley threw down his full house with a whoop and the celebrating began. With a rebel yell, Chance picked him up and shook him like a rag doll. Wesley couldn't remember being so happy in all the years since his parents had left. He had finally won a big pot and he couldn't wait to tell Carlotta.

He'd bet it would be the biggest surprise of her week.

4

Carlotta stared at Peter as his words sank in. Her mouth opened, then closed. "My father called *you?*"

He nodded. "Can we go somewhere? You should sit down."

"I…let me clock out."

She went through the motions automatically, refusing to think about what her father's phone calls meant. Was he ready to come home? Turn himself in? Had he heard about Wesley's run-in with the law and wanted to check on them? Then a paralyzing thought seized her—had something happened to her mother?

Panic clogged her throat. She harbored more animosity toward her mother than her father for deserting them. But that wouldn't soften the blow if something had happened to her.

Carlotta allowed Peter to lead the way to a bistro connected to the mall. Walking next to him felt so familiar, it brought moisture to her eyes. He'd been her first love, had proposed to her before leaving for Vanderbilt University. To outsiders the fact that she wore a Cartier engagement ring most of her senior year of high school might have seemed elitist, but Carlotta had been raised with the best things that money could buy—a grand home, exotic vacations, private schools. Marrying into the uber-wealthy Ashford family had seemed the next logical step.

She had loved Peter more than was healthy, she realized in hindsight. When he'd broken their engagement on the heels of her father's scandal, she'd thought she might not recover.

She had, but the experience had callused her emotions. Now Peter was single again and pressing on her heart…along with this bombshell from her father.

By mutual consent, they waited until they were seated at a table and had ordered coffee before tackling the mountain of issues between them. She was desperate to hear about the phone call, but reminded herself that Peter had buried his wife only a couple of weeks ago and had just been released from jail himself.

"How are you?" she asked carefully. Undoubtedly, Angela's death was beginning to settle in and, their bad marriage aside, it had to be a horrific adjustment.

"I take it day to day," he said. He looked haggard, his boyish good looks compromised by the stress he'd suffered.

"Are you planning to go back to work soon?" Peter worked for Mashburn and Tully Investments, the same firm where her father had been a partner and had perpetrated his white-collar crimes.

Alleged crimes, Wesley would say.

Peter nodded. "Walt Tully has been good to me. I went into the office today to catch up. It feels good to be busy and doing something normal. It was quiet. I was the only one around. When my phone rang and your father identified himself, I was floored."

Carlotta fisted the cloth napkin in her lap. "What did he say? Are…are they okay?"

"He said they're fine…healthy, I mean. He said that he'd tried to call you on your cell phone, but that you'd hung up on him."

"I dropped the phone and accidentally disconnected the call."

"Oh. Well, he said he couldn't blame you. But that's why he called me."

"How did he know that you were working at Mashburn and Tully?"

"He said he'd been keeping up with the company."

The company—not his family. That hurt.

"What did he want?"

Peter squirmed. "He wanted me to look for some files."

She frowned. "What kind of files?"

"Having to do with his…case."

"Why?"

"He said that he needed them to prove his innocence."

Anger sparked in her stomach and she pounded her fist on the table. "Innocence? If he was innocent, why didn't he stay and defend himself ten years ago instead of skipping town and leaving his kids high and dry? Why—after all this time—this *ruse* of proving his innocence?"

Peter reached across the table and took her hand in his. "I asked him the same questions, but he said he didn't have time to go into it, only that he needed my help. He said that the paperwork given to the D.A. had been doctored—that the original paperwork would exonerate him."

Carlotta didn't bother to hide her sarcasm. "And where is this original paperwork supposed to be?"

Peter sighed. "He believes one of the partners hid it or destroyed it."

Her father had always insisted that he'd been framed, but the evidence against him had been so damning. And when he'd disappeared, his declaration of innocence had become a moot point. "How convenient. Did he happen to name names?"

"No, just that he didn't trust Ray Mashburn or Walt Tully or the firm's chief legal counsel, Brody Jones."

"Is Jones still with the company?"

"Yes."

"Did my father happen to tell you anything specific or was his entire conversation cryptic and mysterious?"

Peter shifted in his seat. "No specifics. He just asked me to poke around, then he hung up."

She squeezed his hand. "I'm sorry, Peter."

"Sorry? For what?"

"For my outlaw father dragging you into his mess. Have you told the partners that he called?"

"No. Randolph asked me not to tell anyone and I told him that I would help him if I could."

"Peter, you can't do that. You'll jeopardize your job. You should go to the police."

His intense blue eyes bore into her. "I want to help him, Carly. For you...for your family."

The waitress brought their coffee and smiled at their clasped hands. Carlotta pulled her hand from his warm fingers and busied herself pouring sugar into her mug. Her feelings for Peter were so confusing, it made her head—and her heart—hurt to process them. Did anyone ever truly get over their first love? Her suspicions that Peter's parents had pressured him to end their engagement after her father had skipped town had been confirmed, but Peter had accepted the blame for not standing up for their relationship.

And as tempting as it was to slip back into his arms, she and Peter moved in different circles these days. Peter lived in a mega-mansion with a guest house. She lived in a rickety townhouse with Wesley, a giant snake and the world's nosiest next-door neighbor. Peter's acquaintances were members of the inner circle of Buckhead society; her acquaintances were members of Loan Sharks of America.

Over the rim of his cup Peter's expression reflected the turmoil of the past and present that lay between them. He waited until they were alone again before saying, "Did you tell Detective Terry that your father had called you?"

She averted her gaze. "No."

"So maybe you're not really so eager for your father to be apprehended."

Carlotta wet her lips, unwilling to admit that deep down, she was still Daddy's little girl and no matter what he'd done, she didn't want harm to come to him. "I...wasn't sure it was my father. I mean, he said it was, but it's been so long since I heard his voice. And it was so out of the blue." She winced inwardly when she realized she'd forgotten to get her phone back from Lindy.

"So now that you know it was him, are you going to tell the police?"

"I don't know. I don't even know if I should tell Wesley."

Peter cleared his throat. "Detective Terry seems to have gotten awfully buddy-buddy with you."

She looked up. "Jack was just shopping, that's all."

"Jack?" His eyebrows went up. "Since when does *Jack* shop at Neiman's?"

"He needed a suit."

"He was there to see you, Carly."

A flush warmed her neck as she recalled the sexual energy that had vibrated between her and the detective. "If he was there to see me, it's only to stay in touch about Wesley and my father. When the D.A. reopened Dad's case, he assigned it to Detective Terry."

"So are you going to tell him about the calls?"

She shifted in her seat. "I don't know."

"I hate to pressure you, but the sooner you decide, the better. I want to help, but the last thing I need is for the police to descend on my phone records again if you decide later to report it. The partners might not look favorably upon me withholding this kind of information from them."

Carlotta nodded. "I understand. I…maybe we should tell the police and let them handle it."

"Okay. If you want to report the calls, I'll go with you." He reached for her hand again. "We'll do it together."

Her mind raced ahead—telling Detective Terry about the phone calls, enduring phone taps and maybe even surveillance, luring her father into a trap and seeing the triumphant look on the face of that odious district attorney Kelvin Lucas when Randolph "the Bird" Wren was finally apprehended, with cameras rolling and headlines blaring.

Her stomach knotted and she wavered. "Peter, do you think…I mean, is it possible that my father is innocent?"

He shrugged slowly. "I guess anything is possible." His expression turned dark. "I was innocent of hurting Angela, despite the way things looked."

"Of course you were," she said earnestly. "But you didn't run. Rather than face the charges, my father skipped town and let everyone else pick up the pieces."

Peter sighed noisily and the tortured look on his face said he knew that he, too, had let her down. "Carly, I can't imagine all you've been through the past ten years. But no matter how much resentment you have toward your father, you're a kind, forgiving person. I think if there's a chance that your father is innocent, you'd want to give him an opportunity to prove it."

She studied his face. Was Peter flattering her in the hope that her forgiveness would extend to him as well? Or did this man know her well enough to see inside her heart?

Carlotta wet her lips. "Did Daddy say he would call again?"

"Yes, but he didn't say when."

"Did he say where he was?"

"I asked, but he wouldn't tell me. He did seem to be keeping up with local events. He, uh, knew about Angela and offered condolences."

And did her father suspect that Peter wanted to rekindle their flame? Was he betting on Peter's feelings for her to fuel Peter's attempts to help him? A sick feeling settled in her stomach. "Does he know about me and Wesley, about what's going on in our lives?"

Peter hesitated. "He didn't say."

She took a quick drink from her cup to mask the sudden tears.

Peter squeezed her fingers again. "He's alive, Carly. That's something. And I didn't know your father that well, but it's unfair for me to judge him for walking out on you, when I did the same thing." His blue eyes were shadowed with pain. "I know how my actions have haunted me. I can only imagine that your father, too, has deep regrets."

Her heart shifted in her chest. She desperately wished that her failed relationship with Peter wasn't so entwined with her parents' disappearance, because sitting here with him and feeling the hope radiating from him, she could be lulled into thinking that repairing her relationship with Peter *and* her relationship with her parents was possible.

Even desirable.

Did that make her an optimist, or an idiot?

"What do you say?" Peter murmured, and she had the distinct feeling that he was asking her to give him and her father both a chance to prove themselves.

5

Carlotta's mind raced as she stared across the restaurant table at Peter, patiently waiting for her response as to whether she planned to tell the police that her father had called both of them. Unsaid words burned the back of her tongue—a decade's worth of pent-up conversations she hadn't been able to have with her father. Or with Peter.

How could you leave me? Where have you been? Do you think that I'm like a book that you can stop reading, put away for years and then pick up where you left off? There is a hole in my heart in the shape of you.

"Whatever you decide, Carly," Peter said earnestly. "I'll support you any way I can."

Meaning that one word from her and Peter would either help Randolph Wren in his supposed quest for exoneration or nail him to the wall.

As often as she had wished her father safe, Carlotta had fantasized about seeing him squirm, seeing him publicly held accountable, robbed of his freedom—like his disappearance had robbed her of her freedom.

But while running out on his children was reprehensible, it wasn't a crime. He and her mother had left Wesley with her, and legally, she'd been an adult. The sudden responsibility had been staggering, but she'd gotten through each day by telling herself that her parents would return before nightfall. Slowly the days had turned into weeks and months, then years, until one day she'd realized that their parents weren't coming back and that she and Wesley were somehow, astonishingly, surviving. But every time she'd watched Wesley reach a milestone— winning first place in the science fair, struggling with his voice changing, getting his driver's license, being fitted for his prom tux—her resentment toward her parents had magnified.

Sometimes she thought that she hated her parents. But was she willing to see them go to jail?

"I need to think about it," she said finally. "I'm having a hard time trying to absorb everything."

"That's understandable," Peter soothed.

"I'll call you." She folded her napkin and put it on her plate. "Thanks for the coffee, Peter."

"I'll walk you to your car."

"I'm on Marta." Carlotta doubted that Peter had ever ridden the city's public train system—too many germs and no cup holders. "My car's in the shop being painted from when I was side-swiped." By the same person who had murdered Peter's wife.

A similar thought must have gone through his mind because his mouth tightened. "Then let me drive you home."

She hesitated.

"Maybe I'll be able to recall something else from your father's call."

He had to know how irresistible that tidbit would be. "Okay," she conceded.

After leaving several bills on the table, he guided her toward the mall exit nearest the valet stand. His hand hovered at the small of her back, grazing her often enough to dredge up memories of when they had made love as teenagers.

At the time, she'd thought she might combust from the sheer ecstasy of being in his arms. In their circle of friends, they had been the *it* couple: good-looking, rich and head over heels in love. Their future seemed golden. Carlotta hadn't even considered a plan B. When her parents had skipped town and Peter had dumped her and the rest of her supposed friends had fallen away, she had been set emotionally adrift...a scared kid, ill-equipped to finish raising herself, much less a nine-year-old boy. How many days had she longed for Peter's comforting presence next to her, like this?

Within minutes, Peter's navy blue Porsche arrived and he held open the door of the low-slung decadent car for her. Carlotta lowered herself gingerly into the leather seat that wrapped her in a buttery soft cocoon. She reached for her shoulder belt, but Peter's hand was already there, pulling the strap across her body and fastening the belt with a click. He smiled at her as if to say that if she stayed with him, he would make sure she was safe. Closing her door with a soft thunk, he strode around the front of the car, gave the valet a tip that would cover her lunch budget for a week, then swung into his own seat with practiced ease. They pulled away with the smooth growl of a perfectly engineered motor.

In the cozy intimacy of the two-seater, it was impossible not to be affected by Peter's nearness, the way his long body sprawled in the seat, the way his thick blond hair fell onto his forehead, the precise angles of his handsome profile. She knew this man intimately and he knew her body just as well.

The one sobering image was visualizing Angela sitting in this seat only weeks before, unaware that her life would come to such an abrupt and tragic end. Although the woman had indulged some of her darker whims, she hadn't deserved to die. And Carlotta was haunted by the knowledge that Angela had died knowing that her husband carried a picture of Carlotta in his wallet.

Perhaps in deference to the decision she faced, Peter didn't press her for conversation and instead slid in a Jack Johnson CD and turned up the volume. Dusk was descending early on this ominously overcast day, prompting motorists to flip on their lights. A stiff wind ruffled the riotously blooming crape myrtle trees in the median, sending bright pink blossoms across the flared hood of the Porsche. Sunday afternoon traffic around the mall area was as heavy as her mood.

But soon the mellow music began to calm Carlotta's ragged nerves and she laid her head back against the headrest, and closed her eyes.

She didn't want to watch as they left the exclusive area of Buckhead and entered the more shabby section of the city where she and Wesley lived in a town house. She just wanted to listen to the music and imagine that her life had turned out exactly as she'd planned.

In her mind, she and Peter were married and on their way home to their sprawling residence in a gated community where they would relieve their nanny, then tuck in their beautiful children before retiring to the hot tub with a fifty-dollar bottle of wine and making love with a passion that contradicted how long they had been together.

A touch to her hand startled her and her eyes flew wide open. The music had dimmed and the car had stopped.

"We're here," he said quietly.

In the falling dusk, the car headlights illuminated a garage door with peeling paint and a driveway riddled with cracks and stray weeds. Embarrassment welled in her chest. She had let things go around the house. Wesley had repaired and cleaned the small deck in the back, but from the front it looked as if a low-class family inhabited the place.

If the shoe fits, wear it, she thought morosely.

Who was she kidding? If the shoe fit, she'd *buy* it with her employee discount.

Peter adjusted the rearview mirror and stared intently, then checked the side mirrors.

"Is something wrong?" she asked.

"It's probably nothing. I just thought someone was following us."

Her pulse picked up and she turned around in her seat. "You're kidding." Could her father be tailing them? Jack Terry? A loan shark? Good grief, the possibilities were endless.

"Like I said, it's probably nothing. Or just a pesky reporter."

"Have reporters really been following you?"

He shrugged. "A couple were parked outside the subdivision when I left this morning. Guess they wanted to get a shot of the bereaved husband. And I'm sure some of them aren't quite convinced I had nothing to do with Angela's…dying."

"I'm so sorry."

"Why are you sorry? Like Detective Terry said, you're the one who believed in me when no one else did. How can I ever thank you?"

She dipped her chin. "Your discretion in this matter with my father is thanks enough."

"Carly," Peter said, picking up her left hand. "It's really none of my business but what did you do with the engagement ring I gave you?"

"I…had to sell it."

He nodded. "As you should have. I suspect money was tight after your parents left."

"It was. But actually, I didn't sell it until a few weeks ago." In the wake of Peter's wife's murder, the act of pawning the Cartier ring had been as necessary to her emotional security as to her financial security. Keeping it had made her feel as if she were leaving her heart ajar for him to walk back in.

"I see." His voice was thick with disappointment.

"Peter, after running into you again…things were happening too fast between us. I had to do something to slow it down on my end. Pawning the ring helped me to sever ties to the past."

He nodded again. "I understand. And I have no right to ask

you but I hope that severing ties to our past doesn't rule out us having a future."

Her heart pounded furiously. How many nights had she lain awake dreaming of him returning to her like this, asking her to give their love another chance? "I don't know about a future with you, Peter," she said honestly. "As crazy as my life is, I can't say anything for sure."

He squeezed her hand. "Fair enough." Then he nodded toward the dark windows of the town house. "Looks pretty quiet. Is Wesley working?"

"No. He's spending the night with a friend."

"Oh?"

The word vibrated with hope, sending a flush to Carlotta's chest and face.

"I could stay," he offered. "On the couch, of course. I don't like the idea of you being alone tonight."

It was the perfect excuse to be close to Peter, to spend time with him, for them to begin the process of getting to know each other again. He was the only person who could help her sort through this mess with her father. And truth be known, she *didn't* want to be alone tonight. Plus she did have that one good bottle of red wine in the cabinet that she'd been waiting for an occasion to uncork.

She opened her mouth to say yes, but was distracted by the sudden appearance of headlights, then the revving of a diesel engine that brought Hannah Kizer's big graffiti'd refrigerated van up next to them. The Goth-garbed and stripe-haired Hannah hung out the driver's side window, arms waving, pierced tongue flapping.

"Do you know that…person?" Peter asked.

"Kind of," Carlotta said with resignation. She lowered her window, half relieved, half irritated at her friend's timing.

"What the hell happened to you?" Hannah shouted. "I called you back to tell you all about Coop making me a body mover, but your line was busy and then you didn't answer all damn afternoon!"

"Lindy confiscated my phone."

"The whore," Hannah declared, then she narrowed her kohl-lined eyes at Peter. "Hope I interrupted something."

"Peter gave me a ride home," Carlotta said quickly, hoping Peter didn't notice the open hostility rolling off Hannah toward the man who had broken Carlotta's heart. "The Monte Carlo is in the shop."

"I know," Hannah said sourly. "I was going to swing by the mall and give you a ride, but I see Richie Rich beat me to it."

Carlotta gave her friend a stern look. "Hannah, have you ever met Peter Ashford?"

"Only by reputation." Hannah addressed Peter in a suspicious tone, "I attended your wife's memorial service with Carlotta."

"Peter, this is my friend Hannah Kizer."

"Nice to meet you, Hannah."

"Wish I could say the same."

"Hannah!"

"It's okay," Peter broke in, putting his warm hand on Carlotta's knee. "I'll go. Will your friend stay with you tonight?"

Carlotta nodded.

"Call me to let me know what you decide."

She was transfixed by the concern shining in his eyes. "I'll call," she murmured.

He leaned across the console and whispered, "I'm here for you, Carly," then brushed a kiss near her ear.

The sound of Hannah clearing her throat rent the air. Carlotta gathered her purse and climbed out of the car, waving as Peter backed out of the driveway.

Hannah jumped out of the van and slammed the door. "Why the hell did you let him drive you home? His wife is barely dead."

Carlotta frowned. "There's no such thing as barely dead. And you're being awfully judgmental for someone who makes it a practice not to date a man unless he's wearing a wedding ring."

"This is *you* we're talking about. You don't have my natural defenses."

Or as some would say, her natural repellants. "Want to order a pizza?"

"I got an organic veggie lasagna in the back of the van. Will that do?"

"Sounds great."

"Am I spending the night?"

"Would you mind?"

"Can I sleep with Wesley's snake?"

"No."

"Spoilsport. You don't look so good. Did Wesley do something again?"

"Not that I know of. This time it's someone else."

Hannah opened the van door and rummaged through containers in a cardboard box. "You have a lot of disturbed people in your life, Carlotta."

Carlotta spotted a magnetic Body Transport sign leaning against a shelf. Hannah had a wild crush on Wesley's boss, Cooper Craft, and had allegedly convinced him to hire her as a body mover for the morgue. Employing her own brand of twisted logic, Hannah had concluded that her catering van could do double duty, health codes be damned.

Carlotta shook her head behind her friend's back. "You can say that again."

6

"Dude, wake up. I'm starving."

Wesley cracked open an eye and winced at the sunlight streaming into the room. God, his head felt like someone had hit him with a baseball bat. After leaving the card game, he and Chance had really tied one on. He slowly became aware that he was fused to the leather couch in the living room of Chance's condo. He rolled his eyes upward to see his buddy standing over him.

Chance laughed. "Hung over, huh? What a wuss."

Wesley groaned and pushed himself up on one arm. "Do you have to shout?"

"Let's go to the Vortex and get a burger."

The thought of food made his stomach churn, but he sat up and pulled a hand down his gritty face. "What time is it?"

"Almost noon."

Wesley reached for his T-shirt. "I should go."

"Moving stiffs today?"

"I'm on call."

"Man, you were awesome last night. That guy didn't know what hit him. You played that final hand like a pro."

Despite his pounding head, Wesley smiled. "Thanks, but that was a pretty easy crowd."

Chance handed him a few pills and an open can of Mountain Dew. "Here."

Wesley looked at the pills. "What's this?"

"Aspirin, man. Don't you trust me?"

Not entirely, since Chance had his hands in lots of illegal shit. Wesley downed the pills and swished the sugary drink to dispel the god-awful taste in his mouth. Then he pulled his wallet from his pocket and opened it to reveal a thick wad of cash. Relief flooded him that he hadn't lost it or spent it all in his drunken stupor, although he seemed to be down a few bills.

"You sprang for some choice weed last night," Chance said, nodding toward a plastic bag on the coffee table. "I smoked a joint as big as my dick."

Chance's favorite topic was his Johnson.

"Take the leftovers," Chance offered.

"No thanks. If I fail a drug test, I go to jail. Keep it, my compliments." Wesley counted off several bills and handed them to Chance. "And here's the money I owe you."

"Thanks. What are you going to do with the rest of it?"

"Pay off some other debts." Wesley thought of Tick and Mouse, the two thick-necked collectors for the loan sharks he owed, Father Thom and The Carver, who showed up every week. He'd be glad to get those two off his back for a while.

"Oh, come on. Aren't you going to celebrate a little? Buy something for yourself? A new computer? I know how you dig that shit."

"I'm not allowed to have computer equipment under the terms of my probation," Wesley said, jerking his thumb toward Chance's extra bedroom. "That's why I'm storing my good stuff here, remember?"

"What about a car?"

"With a suspended license?"

"You'll get it back sooner or later."

"In like a year, dude. I don't want something sitting in the garage that I can't drive. That's why I sold my motorcycle."

Although a top-of-the-line bicycle would be cool and would give him some mobility.

"How about a kick-ass stereo system?" Chance suggested.

"I'm good with my iPod."

"Some blowout speakers, then. Dude, you gotta buy something fun with the money. You deserve it."

"Yeah, maybe," he said, thinking that he should buy something for Carlotta for all the crap he'd put her through. Maybe something for the house, something they both could enjoy.

"Come and hang out while I eat." Chance laid his meaty arm across Wesley's shoulders. "I've been thinking about a partnership."

Wesley was immediately wary. "What kind of partnership?"

"You always said you wanted to make it to the World Series of Poker."

"Yeah, so?"

"So I'm thinking that with my trust fund and your card smarts, maybe we can make it happen."

Wesley's pulse jumped: Chance definitely had the cash to bankroll his dream. Sure, with the body-moving gig, the community-service job that was supposed to start soon and delving into his dad's case, he had a lot on his plate. But after a bumpy couple of months, his luck seemed to be changing. And while he'd promised Carlotta that he'd give up gambling, with Chance behind him, last night's take was trivial to the money he could potentially win.

Besides—if he were careful—Carlotta wouldn't have to know.

He looked at Chance. "I'm listening."

7

"I appreciate the ride to work," Carlotta said to Hannah. She took a drag on a cigarette, then handed it back with a shaking hand.

"No problem." Hannah inhaled on the shared smoke. "Sorry you're having such a crummy time. Have you decided whether to tell the police about your father calling?"

"Not yet. And you can't tell anyone, Hannah. I haven't even decided whether or not to tell Wesley." And she hadn't mentioned that her father had called Peter because she wanted to keep him out of it.

"I'm as silent as the grave." Hannah clicked the barbell in her tongue against her teeth for emphasis, then squinted. "Are you sure you're okay? You look like hell."

"I didn't get much sleep," Carlotta admitted. None, actually. Not even after pleading exhaustion to Hannah and turning in early, leaving her friend to sit on the couch watching cable on the small television with the distorted picture. She'd been on edge all night, hoping the phone would ring, praying it wouldn't. And on top of everything else, there was Peter burnt into her brain, into her heart. And the disconcerting image of Jack Terry's face, looking as if he actually cared.

"Give yourself a break. You've been through a lot lately, with Wesley's arrest, then Angela Ashford's murder and now all this."

Carlotta tried to smile. "Guess it's all hitting me. Post-traumatic stress disorder, maybe. I feel a little out of it."

"Yeah, when I saw you jogging yesterday morning a couple of blocks from your house I yelled, but you were in a freaking trance."

Carlotta frowned. "That was someone else. Have you ever known me to jog?"

"No, but I've never seen you gaga over a guy before either, like the way you are with Peter Asshole."

"Be nice. And I'm not *gaga* over him. We have…history."

"He dumped you when you needed him most and now—after you've made it on your own—he expects you to take him back?"

Carlotta retrieved the cigarette and drew on it hard. "Made it on my own? That's a laugh. My life is a *disaster*."

"What? And his is something to brag about?"

"He's successful."

"And conspicuously rich. Yeah, I noticed. He was also in a dysfunctional marriage which ended when his wife was murdered. The man has issues, Carlotta."

"Don't we all?" she murmured, finishing the cigarette, then grimacing as she snubbed it out. Peter would hate her smoking, even sporadically. Then she glanced at Hannah in her black-leather getup and acknowledged there were other elements of her life that Peter would have a hard time accepting—her friendship with this good-hearted oddball being one of them.

Yet he seemed eager to try....

"You know there are drugs for what you're going through."

"Excuse me?"

"Antidepressants. They'll take the edge off."

"I don't need drugs, I need normalcy."

"Like that's going to happen. You need to get laid. And not by Peter, that's way too messy. Don't you know someone who's good for a night of hot sex with no strings attached?"

Why did Jack Terry's face emerge in her head? "No one comes to mind," Carlotta said sourly.

"Too bad. Sex is great for working out the mental kinks."

"If that's the case why are you so messed up?"

"Very funny. Quantity doesn't necessarily equate to quality. Seriously, Carlotta, you should at least consider seeing a shrink."

Carlotta sighed and rubbed her temples. She was going to have to do a better job of checking her emotions if she were going to keep her father's call a secret from Wesley and Jack Terry. She could really use Wesley's poker face right about now—especially since with his promise to her, he wouldn't be needing it anymore. She tried not to think about what mischief he might have gotten into with Chance last night.

Hopefully it was something harmless, like beer and girls. Wesley was an adult and she had to stop obsessing over his whereabouts, but old habits died hard.

Hannah glanced at her quiet cell-phone screen and slammed her palm against the steering wheel. "Why hasn't he called?"

Carlotta lifted an eyebrow. "Which of your married lovers are we talking about?"

Hannah smirked. "I'm referring to Coop. I thought he would've called by now to have me help him move a body."

Since Hannah had a huge crush on Wesley's boss, Carlotta chose her words carefully. "Maybe he had a funeral today. Or maybe Wesley is out with him. I'm sure he'll call you soon."

"I hope so. I can't wait for my first assignment."

"Hannah, I'm not so sure that body moving is the kind of job that one should feel so *enthusiastic* about."

Hannah waved off her concern. "Death fascinates me. I guess that's why I'm so intrigued by Cooper—you have to be a special person to work around bodies all the time. Do you think he has a casket at home?"

"I certainly hope not." Even though his job of running his uncle's funeral home and moving bodies for the morgue was creepy, Cooper Craft was a surprisingly normal-looking guy. Attractive, even. He'd hinted, as Jack Terry had said, that he was interested in Carlotta, but Cooper was so intellectual, he intimidated her.

Of course, nothing earthbound intimidated Hannah.

"I've always wanted to lie down in a coffin, you know, just to see what it's like."

Carlotta grimaced. "We'll all know soon enough, Hannah. You can let me out here," she said, pointing to a mall entrance.

"Okay. Do you need a ride home after work?"

"No, thanks. I hope my car will be ready by this evening. But if not, I can take the train."

"Okay. Are you sure you're okay to work today?"

Carlotta managed a smile. "With a mortgage and loan sharks to pay, I don't exactly have a choice." Sudden tears welled in her eyes. Mortified, she tried to blink them away. "Sorry," she mumbled.

"Hey, don't apologize," Hannah said, looking concerned—and panicked—at the sight of tears. "Promise me you'll call later."

"I promise," she said, then jumped out before she completely broke down.

Maybe Hannah was right, she thought as she dabbed at her eyes. Maybe she needed to talk to someone with professional objectivity, someone who could give her advice on coping with disillusionment, on how to let go of the past.

But that would have to wait. For now she needed to decide whether to tell Jack Terry about her father's phone calls.

She was hanging her clothes in a locker in the employee break room when a familiar male voice said, "I heard Lindy nailed you yesterday."

Carlotta closed her locker door and smirked at Michael Lane, friend, coworker, and self-proclaimed queen of the shoe department. "She confiscated my phone. I have to go to her office and ask for it back like a good girl."

"Yikes, good luck with that."

"Thanks a lot."

"I was kidding. You're one of her top salespersons. Lindy's not going to fire you."

"*Was* one of her top salespersons," Carlotta corrected, feeling dangerously close to tears again. "I've been toppled by Buckhead Barbie."

"Oh, you've met Patricia."

"She was following Lindy around yesterday like a shih tzu."

"Funny you should say that. You know Patricia's only doing so well because of the new line of doggie wear in accessories. Those little inflatable bathing suits are flying off the freaking shelves."

"No, I could be doing more. I've lost my touch."

"You're just in a slump." Michael gave a dismissive wave and glanced over a memo he was holding. "Hey, you're in luck. Lindy's off until Wednesday."

Carlotta blinked rapidly. She wouldn't be able to get her phone back, wouldn't know if her father had called again. There was a way to check messages from another phone, but she had never set up a PIN to access the system remotely. She'd told herself she'd decide whether to tell Jack about the calls after retrieving her phone, but another forty-eight hours of torture loomed before her.

"There, there, it's just a phone," Michael soothed.

"It's not just the phone," she murmured. "It's…personal."

"With all this business of Angela Ashford's murder behind you, I figured you'd be skipping and singing."

"No skipping and—lucky for you—no singing."

He angled his head. "Is your brother in trouble again?"

Poor Wesley. Everyone automatically assumed he was the root of all of her problems, even now when there were so many more potential culprits. "No, it isn't Wesley."

"Having financial problems?"

She gave him a flat smile. "Yeah, but what else is new?"

"Good grief, why don't you file bankruptcy and get it over with?"

His advice rankled her. She didn't like people knowing so much about her perpetual indebtedness. "I told you, I'm not that desperate…yet."

"So if it's not Wesley and it's not money, what is it?"

"It's…personal."

Michael's eyes gleamed with interest. "Want to talk about it?"

Carlotta hesitated. As chief grinder of the store's gossip mill, Michael was always looking for grist. "Actually, I was wondering if you could recommend someone…professional… who I could talk to about…everything."

"Oh. My therapist, Dr. Delray, is fabulous and he accepts our company insurance. He's taking new patients only on referral but I'd be happy to put in a phone call."

"That would be super. And if you don't mind, Michael, I'd like to keep this quiet."

He made a zipping motion across his lips and Carlotta hoped that she could trust him.

On the other hand, anyone who'd been privy to her recent goings-on might be relieved to know that she was seeking help.

She took her place on the sales floor and tried to push aside thoughts of her father. But as the day unfolded and customers blended together, her imagination began to spin wild scenarios.

If her father was aware of some of the details of her and Wesley's lives, was he spying on them? The notion had her distracted, looking around, constantly scanning for someone hiding behind clothes racks. Would she even recognize her father? He was bound to have aged in ten years and no doubt had altered his appearance to avoid detection. Same for her mother.

She glanced around, suddenly claustrophobic as shoppers zigzagged by her. Either one of her parents could be within easy reach and she wouldn't know it.

"Hello, Carlotta."

Carlotta turned to see one of her best customers, Dixie Neilson, walking up wearing a cheery smile. The flamboyant, trim older woman with a dramatic shock of silver in her dark hair—and her impressive purchases—never failed to lift Carlotta's spirits. "Hi, Dixie. What can I do for you today?"

"I need a new dress, darling, for a dinner party. I was thinking something red and slinky and ridiculously expensive."

Carlotta laughed. "I think I have just the thing." But while she was helping Dixie select a dress, she continued to scan the throng of shoppers. Later, while she rang up Dixie's sale, a tall man by a rack of women's cruise wear caught her eye. He seemed out of place as he flipped through the hangers of bright clothing. Who wore a long coat in the dead of summer? And he kept looking in her direction....

She handed Dixie the dress in a garment bag and said goodbye. The long-coated man was still there, still looking her way.

Carlotta wet her mouth and tasted perspiration on her upper lip. She could spot a disguise a mile away; she'd donned enough of them in her party-crashing days.

A touch to her arm startled her so badly, she cried out.

"Easy, girl," Jack Terry said. To the people who had turned to stare, he sent an easy smile, dissolving their idle interest.

Carlotta's heart leapt to her throat as she perused his dark suit and tacky red, white and blue striped tie. He was on duty. "What are you doing here?"

"Trying to get your attention. You're awfully jumpy."

She told herself to relax or else she'd only raise his suspicion. "Sorry. I guess I'm more tired than I realized."

"Ashford keep you up late?" he asked dryly.

She hesitated, trying to decipher the expression on his face. Jealousy? Impossible. More likely, he was still smarting over the fact that he'd been wrong about Peter's guilt in Angela's murder. "That's none of your business, Detective."

One eyebrow arched. "Back to 'Detective' are we?"

"Looks like you're on duty."

"I am, which is why I need to make this quick."

Her stomach flipped. Did he know about her father's phone call? "Need to make what quick?"

"I got a call that my suit is ready."

"Oh." She exhaled in relief. "Right."

He squinted at her. "Are you okay?"

"Yeah." But she glanced again at the suspicious-looking man, who nervously averted his gaze.

"Someone you know?" Jack murmured.

She had horrible thoughts of her father being apprehended in the middle of Neiman's. Wouldn't her boss Lindy love that? "Uh, no."

Too late—Jack zeroed in on the guy. She tried to distract

him by stepping into his line of sight, but since he towered over her, that was practically impossible. He stepped around her and strode toward the man, who turned and began to walk away quickly. Jack broke into a jog and Carlotta raced after him, her heart thudding. "Jack, wait!"

But he ignored her, reaching one long arm forward to capture the man by the back of his collar, bringing him up short with a choking sound. "The jig's up, buddy."

Carlotta skidded to a stop beside them, her mind racing to reconcile the man's features with those of her father.

"This is harassment," the man stammered.

Jack shook the man's shoulder hard enough to make his head loll. "Open your coat. Now."

The man complied reluctantly with long, bony fingers—fingers that proved he wasn't Randolph Wren in disguise. Until this moment, she had forgotten how large and capable her father's hands had been…hands that had once pulled her close for hugs or to tweak her nose in a moment of teasing good humor.

When the man's coat hung open, Carlotta gasped. The garment was lined with clear pockets, each one stuffed full of jewelry or small clothing items.

"Getting your Christmas shopping done early?" Jack asked the man.

"I'm not the criminal here."

"Right, buddy. Do yourself a favor and keep your mouth shut." Then Jack looked at Carlotta. "Maybe your security department should take it from here."

Carlotta located the nearest phone and called security, feeling like an idiot for not pegging the man for a shoplifter. This thing with her father was driving her mad.

After the man had been handed off, she accompanied Jack downstairs to pick up his suit, keenly aware of his big body near hers. His size was comforting but this new cordiality had her off-balance. Of course, he was probably playing her, hoping she'd cooperate with the investigation into her father's disappearance.

Guilt stabbed her because she knew she held the one piece of information that he'd been hoping for. Communication from Randolph Wren. And possibly a way to lure him in.

"Thanks for catching that guy," she murmured.

"It's my job to catch the bad guys," he said easily.

She swallowed hard, acknowledging that everyone considered her father one of the bad guys. If she confessed to Jack Terry about the phone calls, she could end this ten-year ache, but would it only lead to something worse—an irrevocable break in her relationship with her parents and maybe with Wesley? And would it destroy this tentative friendship with Jack Terry that seemed to be developing?

No, Carlotta decided on the spot, she wouldn't tell Jack about the phone calls. She'd handle it with Peter's help. And who knew, it might come to nothing anyway.

She located the garment bag with Jack's name on it and unzipped it to double-check that it was the suit he'd selected and that it was indeed ready.

"Want to try it on?" she asked, flashing back to her glimpses of him half-naked during the initial fitting. Hannah's suggestion of a night of meaningless sex came to Carlotta as visions of her and Jack tangled together in the dressing room flitted through her head.

"That's okay," he said. "I trust you."

At his offhand comment, she pasted on a smile and assuaged her guilt by letting the threat of making him shop for new shoes slide. Passing a table of ties, she scooped up a gorgeous black and deep purple tie that would complement Jack's dark coloring.

"My treat," she said, stuffing it into a jacket pocket. "You'll look stunning when you accept your award. When is the ceremony?"

"Two weeks from today," he said, then shifted from foot to foot. "Listen, Carlotta…about this awards dinner…"

She looked up. "Uh-huh?"

The detective pulled his finger around his collar, further loosening his hideous tie. "I know I mentioned before that I'd thought about asking you if you wanted to go with me."

She froze. He was on the verge of asking her—something he'd never do if he knew what she was keeping from him. Her stomach churned with the sudden realization that despite everything looming over her and Jack Terry, she wanted very much to go on his arm and see him accept his award.

The color rose in his cheeks. "Well—"

"Carlotta Wren?"

She turned to find a man standing in front of her, holding a clipboard in one hand and a vase of at least two dozen red long-stem roses in the other hand. "I was told I could find you here. These are for you, ma'am."

Her eyes widened. "For me?"

"Yep. Sign here."

She signed her name, still perplexed when the man handed her the hulking bouquet. "I wonder who they're from."

"I can guess," Jack offered wryly.

Carlotta realized he was referring to Peter. Although it was just the kind of grand gesture he would make, she was surprised and a little disappointed that he was pushing her so soon after their conversation about taking it slow.

"Thanks for helping me pick out the suit." Jack swung the garment bag over his shoulder as if it contained a sixty-dollar rental instead of a thousand-dollar tux. "I'll see you around."

"Okay," she said to his rapidly retreating back, craning to watch him leave. She wondered why she felt so let down when spending an evening with Jack Terry was just a bad idea all the way around.

With a sigh, she ferreted out the card in the roses.

Carlotta, thanks for a great time. Mason

Carlotta glanced over the brimming arrangement that had easily cost a couple of hundred dollars, then bit her lip.

Who the heck was Mason?

8

"**I**'m sorry, ma'am, but we don't reveal the names of our customers," declared a hurried-sounding man on the other end of the phone.

"But I think the flower delivery might have been a mistake," Carlotta protested. "I don't know anyone by the name of the person on the card."

"Nice try. Look, sweetie, if you want to find out if your boyfriend is sending flowers to someone else, you're going to have to ask him."

Carlotta blinked. "But I—" She stopped because the man had hung up.

"Omigod," Michael exclaimed as he walked into the break room. "Who sent you the to-die-for roses?"

Carlotta hung up the phone and studied the bewildering bouquet she'd set on the corner of the stained lunch table. "I have no idea." She showed him the card. "I don't know any-one named Mason. Does it ring a bell for you?"

Michael shook his head. "Some guy you met in a bar maybe?"

"No, I'm sure of it." Her nerves were unraveling. Had her father sent the flowers? Was it some kind of message? Or was it simply a misdelivery?

"Then you must have a secret admirer. Someone dropped a mint on these American beauties."

Her expression must have reflected her dour mood, because he shook his head with a sigh, then produced a business card. "Here. Dr. Delray said he could squeeze you in Wednesday afternoon at six, but only for thirty minutes, so you'll have to talk fast."

"Thank you." She folded the card into her pocket.

Michael fingered a perfect bloodred rose and sighed. "Meanwhile, if you don't want this guy, send him my way, okay? Buh-bye."

"Bye." She carefully removed one long-stem rose and stroked the velvety petals. Had her mother liked roses? Her father? She couldn't recall. And Mason wasn't a family name that she knew of, nor a place they'd been, nor a pet they'd owned. If the roses were from her father, the message was lost on her. She tightened her grip on the stem in frustration and was rewarded with a zing of pain as a thorn pierced her palm, drawing blood.

"Dammit!" Carlotta put her mouth to the tiny wound, feeling the return of tears that were too common lately. She wondered if Michael's shrink would be able to help her, or would her life scare even a trained professional?

Pushing aside the troubling thoughts, she picked up the pay phone and dialed the number to the auto body shop. Carlotta hated the blue muscle car that she'd gotten stuck with after taking it on a twenty-four hour test drive that had gone wrong, but since she owed more for the car than it was worth, she was resigned to driving it until it was paid for or until the wheels fell off.

She had hoped the wheels would have fallen off by now, but no such luck.

The repair shop was recommended by Wesley via his odious friend Chance, so even though it had taken in her car immediately and promised a quick turnaround, she was leery. After several rings, a man answered with a half-grunt, told her to hold, then told her that the Monte Carlo wasn't ready yet. "Wednesday," he promised.

She pinched the bridge of her nose. "What time Wednesday?"

"After noon?"

"Okay," she said wearily, then hung up.

Carlotta turned and eyed the enormous bouquet, weighing the hassle of getting the flowers home on Marta versus the cost of a cab in rush hour. With a sigh, she slung the strap of her bag over her shoulder and scooped up the vase. During the trip through the mall and the half-block walk to the train station, she garnered lots of enviable stares. On the packed train however, the stares became murderous as she inadvertently poked an eye here, snagged someone's clothing there.

"Sorry," she mumbled to no one and to everyone standing near her in the shoulder to shoulder crowd. To save space, she brought the bouquet closer to her face but the sickeningly sweet scent of the roses reminded her of death—of the scent that permeated the funeral home that Cooper Craft ran.

She wondered if he'd called Hannah yet for a "body run" or if he and Wesley were working together today. Body moving wasn't the sort of job she'd hoped Wesley would get, but with his recent arrest record and probation, she couldn't complain. At least he was bringing in money legitimately, making his weekly payments to the thugs he owed and staying away from the card tables. And Coop seemed to be a good influence on Wesley, which was a relief. After raising Wesley, she had enormous respect for single mothers; the pressure was relentless. So was the guilt.

Things should have been so different for Wesley. For her. The thought only fueled her frustration and confusion over her father's cryptic phone calls. What should she do? Report it? Wait? Report it, then wait?

"Lindbergh," the conductor announced. "Lindbergh is your next station."

The train slowed to a swaying halt and the doors lurched opened. Carlotta pushed her way to the platform and rode the escalator to the street level. A whipping wind had descended with the promise of rain before she could walk the few blocks home.

She picked up the pace, cursing the questionable repair shop and thinking that if she'd known her car wouldn't be ready, she wouldn't have worn her Stuart Weitzman mules to work. They were good for standing still or for sashaying around the sales floor, not so good for eating up uneven sidewalks while

wrestling an enormous vase of roses. By the time it started to
rain, she had the beginning of a serious blister or three. She
muttered a string of curses as she tried to shield her Nancy
Gonzalez clutch. It was last year's style, but didn't deserve
water spots.

She glanced around at the slightly shabby homes in her
neighborhood, Lindbergh or as locals liked to say, *east* Buckhead. When they'd moved here after her parents had lost their
lavish home, Wesley had called it Limberg, like the cheese,
and her mother had said it was fitting. The cramped, nondescript town house had been a jolt to them all after living
large. Even the weather in this part of town seemed to re-
flect the plight of the people who lived here—not quite as
good as anywhere else. She'd bet that a few miles away in
Buckhead, skies were blue.

She was hobbling in pain by the time she reached the stoop
of their home. The rain had stopped, but she was thoroughly
drenched as she fumbled with the flowers and her key ring.

"Well, aren't you special?"

Carlotta turned her head to see their neighbor Mrs. Winningham standing on the other side of the fence she'd erected.
The tall, skinny woman sported a bright red helmet of teased
hair, elastic-waist polyester pants and a shiny button-up shirt.
In her arms she held an umbrella and her dog, Toofers, the
ugliest, meanest canine imaginable. Over the years, the bi-
zarrely black-tufted dog had sunk its razor teeth into Wesley
more times that she could count. And always when they could
least afford a trip to the emergency room for stitches.

"Hello, Mrs. Winningham. Hello, Toofers."

Toofers growled at her, and the woman gave him a reassuring pat. "Nice flowers, Carlotta. Do you have a man friend?"

"Uh…no."

"There've been a lot of men coming around lately. The man who drives the dark sedan, for instance, and the man with the fancy little sports car and the man who drives the white van."

She'd bet the woman had copied down all the license plates, too. "Those are just friends of ours, Mrs. Winningham."

"What about the woman with the striped hair and the chains?"

"Uh…that's another friend."

Her neighbor frowned. "Are your parents ever going to come back for you?"

Carlotta almost dropped the vase of flowers, then considered throwing it at the biddy and her bite-happy pooch. Instead she gritted her teeth. "I wouldn't count on it, Mrs. Winningham."

"Your townhouse is in terrible disrepair. It makes the entire street look bad."

She so didn't need this.

"I wasn't happy when the two homosexuals moved into the house next to yours, but they have at least updated the place and keep it looking nice. Although that solarium sticking out in the backyard does block the view to the houses on the other side."

Carlotta gave the woman a flat smile. The two men who had moved in next door about five years ago kept to themselves and had never talked to her or Wesley. Then she bit into her lip. Maybe she should make an effort to get to know them. They probably thought everyone in the neighborhood was as homophobic as this woman.

On the other hand, if they were witness to some of the goings-on at the Wren house, they were probably keeping their distance for a reason.

"You must have noticed that Wesley spruced up our back deck. We'll get to some of the other things as soon as our budget allows."

The woman sniffed. "From the looks of what was carried in there today, you got money for other things."

It was Carlotta's turn to frown. "What do you mean?"

The woman lifted her shoulders in a dramatic shrug. "It's not my place to say." She turned and walked away, leaving Carlotta to stand there soggy and miserable.

The door opened suddenly and Wesley stood there smiling. "Hey, sis!"

Instantly, she was suspicious. "What's wrong?" she asked as she limped into the living room.

"Nothing's wrong. Need a hand? Wow, where did you get the flowers?"

"Never mind," she said absently, dripping on the carpet and staring at something past Wesley, something that even upstaged the little aluminum Christmas tree that had stood in the corner ever since their parents had taken off. "What is that?"

Wesley grinned. "It's a big-screen TV."

"I can see that." The sixty-inch screen was hard to miss since it took up most of the real estate in the room. "What is it doing in our living room?"

"Surprise! I bought it for you."

"For *me?*"

"For us. Isn't it great? The old one was about to go out any-way." He looked so pleased with himself, just like when he was little and had brought her frogs.

She touched her stinging, injured palm to her forehead. "Wesley, this had to cost a fortune. Where did you get the money?"

"I sold my motorcycle."

She conceded a spurt of relief and a tug of affection that he would sacrifice something he loved, but her generosity was short-lived. "I'm glad that you sold the death machine but Wesley, we could have spent that money on a hundred other things!"

"You don't like it?"

He looked so wounded that she bit her tongue and counted to three. "Of course I like it, but..." She gestured to the bas-ket of overflowing statements that she hadn't bothered to open in too long to admit. "But we need to pay *bills!* Catch up on the mortgage! And what about those thugs you owe?"

"I made my payments this morning—a day early."

"What about next week?"

His shoulder sagged as he gestured toward the massive tele-vision. "I just thought it would make you happy. You've been so morose lately."

Here came those damned tears again. Oh, God, and hic-cups too. The wide-eyed panic in Wesley's eyes at the water-works made her turn away. Carlotta wiped her cheeks and said over her shoulder, "We'll talk about this later."

"Okay," he muttered. "Oh, sis, there's a phone message."

She came up short. Had their father called? She turned on her heel, inhaling sharply into a hiccup. "Did you listen to it? Who was it?" The shrillness of her voice vibrated in her ears, but she couldn't help it.

He frowned. "It was Peter. He wants you to call him back. He sounded weird."

She swallowed and forced her muscles to relax. "Okay. Thanks." She turned back to the hallway and walked toward her bedroom.

"Are you going to call him?" Wesley called behind her.

"No," she said blandly. "I'm off work tomorrow. Don't wake me up until Wednesday." She was putting off the inevitable, but she didn't care. She just wanted everyone—fugitive father, body-moving brother, interfering cop, schizoid friend and repentant ex-fiancé—to leave her the hell alone.

Was that too much to ask?

9

"Wren," barked the woman behind the desk, leveling a stare on Wesley as he slouched in a chair waiting to see his probation officer for their regular Wednesday meeting. "You're up."

He sprang to his feet, then remembered to play it cool and slowed his stride as he approached the office of E. Jones. He'd asked, but she'd refused to tell him what the E stood for. She said that he didn't need to know that much about her.

He knocked on the door with two sharp raps of his knuckles and waited for her sexy voice to call out. The glass of a nondescript framed print on the wall was a passable mirror. He glanced at his reflection, nodding in approval over the two-day old beard; he'd heard that women liked the scruffy look. Then he ran his fingers through his light brown hair to give it a tousle and pulled on the lapels of a sport coat that Carlotta had bought for him.

"Let me know when you're finished primping," that sexy voice said right behind him.

Wesley started, then turned to see E. Jones laying those big green eyes of hers on him, her pink mouth curled into a wry smile. Heat flooded his neck. "I wasn't primping."

"Right." She reached past him and opened her door, then preceded him inside. "Close the door and have a seat."

Still smarting, Wesley did as he was told.

"How did you get here?" she asked as she settled into a chair behind a neat desk and opened a file folder that had his name on it.

"Bicycle."

Her eyebrows went up. "You didn't ride your motorcycle?"

She'd busted him previously by following him when he'd left his appointment. Not only had he been driving his motorcycle with a suspended license, but he'd gone on a drug drop for Chance to make some money. E. had caught him red-handed and had let him off with a warning as long as he took the delivery back where it had come from.

"I sold my motorcycle and bought a bike."

"Ah. Does that mean you can pay your five-thousand-dollar fine to the court?"

For reparations to the city for the little hacking job he'd done into the courthouse records. "Uh, no."

"You didn't make a profit?"

"I did, but I bought a new TV. The one we had was shot." E. had also seen their place, thanks to a surprise drop-in visit. The woman now knew pretty much everything about him— his family history, where he slept and who he hung out with.

And that the dusty box of Trojans in his bathroom medicine cabinet had never been opened.

"That's nice, but in your situation do you think a TV should have been your top priority?"

He shifted in his seat. "I wanted to do something nice for my sister. Don't worry, I'll still be able to make my weekly court payment."

"Good." E. sat back and scrutinized him. "Are you staying out of trouble?"

He swallowed involuntarily. Could she possibly know about the gambling? "Yeah, I'm clean."

"Are you still hanging around with that friend of yours?"

"What friend?"

"The one who is such a good friend that he would ask you to do something that could ruin your life."

Wesley cracked his knuckles. "I'm not giving you his name."

"I don't want his name. I don't care if he flushes his life down the drain. I only care about you."

He stopped, wondering if she meant it, and on what level. Was she saying that she cared only because she was responsible for getting him through probation and out of the system with as little fuss as possible? A great-looking woman in her mid-twenties could never be into him. Could she?

"How's your sister?" E. asked, breaking the tension. "I read about her involvement in the Buckhead murders. Sounds like she was lucky to escape with her own life."

Wesley nodded, unwilling to think about how close he'd come to losing his sister. "Carlotta is tough." Then he grinned. "She has to be to have put up with me all these years."

"Do you stop to consider the impact your actions have on her life?"

"Not enough," he admitted.

"Is that fair?"

"No one in my family has gotten a fair shake."

"Oh, right. You believe that your father is innocent of the crimes he's charged with."

He sat up straighter. "Yes."

She angled her head. "If he's innocent, why do you think he would skip town? Leave his family?"

Wesley shrugged to cover the anger accumulating in his chest. "I don't know, and it's really—" He wiped his hand over his mouth.

"None of my business?" she finished for him.

He glanced around her office. "Don't you have a cup for me to pee in or something?"

She gave him a flat smile, then rifled through the papers in his file. "I have good news. I've spoken with Richard McCormick at the central IT department. He said he could meet with you later this week to set up a time when you could begin your community-service work."

Excitement skittered along his skin, but he tamped down his reaction. "When?"

She handed him a piece of paper. "You need to call him."

"Okay. Thanks."

E. removed a plastic cup from a drawer. "And you do need to give a urine sample before you go."

"Okay." He stood to leave. "Are we through? I need to get to work."

"Still moving bodies?"

"Yeah."

She seemed amused. "And do you still like it?"

"Like it?" He scratched the scruff on his chin. "I don't know. It's something that has to be done, and I'm better at it than most, my boss says."

E. nodded and studied him in a way that made him uncomfortable, like she was wondering when—with his dysfunctional family, friends and part-time job—he was going to blow.

"See you next week," she finally said, then looked down at another folder—another misfit case. "And you might think about shaving before you meet with Mr. McCormick about that job."

He frowned at her bent head, then left, wondering what it would take to impress the unflappable E. Jones and if he would ever have a chance with a woman like her.

After whizzing in the cup and leaving it with the dough-faced uniformed attendant, Wesley walked out into the summer heat, removed his jacket and shoved it in his backpack along with the papers E. had given him, then unlocked the new bicycle and headed for home.

On the way, he thought about the postcard that his parents had recently sent, postmarked Miami. The message had been simple, *Thinking of you* or something like that. He'd hidden it because Carlotta had threatened to burn any more postcards they received. But she'd found it in the tennis-ball can in the garage where he'd hidden it along with his emergency stash of cash. Instead of asking him about it, she'd put it in her purse and somehow Detective Jack Terry had gotten his hands on it. Now the jerk cop was probably stepping up his efforts to find their father, which meant that Wesley needed to get his hands on his father's secure case files as soon as possible.

The sooner he started his community-service job "to improve the security of the city's legal records," the better.

Cooper Craft was waiting for him when Wesley wheeled into the driveway. He stored the bike in the garage, shrugged back into the sport coat, then swung up into the passenger seat of the plain white van that Coop typically used when retrieving bodies for the morgue; he saved the hearse for more ceremonial pickups. "Hey man, been waiting long?"

"Just a few minutes. How was your probation meeting?"

"Fine." Coop seemed to know a lot about the probation system. Wesley wondered if the man would ever give him details about how he'd gone from being the coroner to retrieving bodies for the morgue and running his uncle's funeral home. "What's on the schedule today?"

Cooper gave him a wry look. "For you, a shave." He gestured to the glove box. "There's an electric razor in there. Use it. And where's your tie?"

Wesley pulled a tie out of the pocket of his jacket, then rummaged for the razor. "Where are we going?"

"Grady Memorial Hospital first, then Crawford Long, then St. Joe. Then a couple of nursing homes and a delivery back to the funeral home. A full day."

Wesley nodded, flipping on the razor. He noticed that Coop looked more pensive than normal, that a muscle ticked in his jaw beneath his neat sideburns. "You okay? Sorry I kept you waiting."

"No, you're good." Coop looked a little sheepish. "Actually, I've been thinking about what you said."

"What was that?"

"That if I wanted to get your sister's attention, I needed to do something bold."

Wesley grinned. "What did you have in mind?"

"I don't know. Does she like flowers?"

"No offense, dude, but getting flowers from a funeral director seems a little morbid, don't you think?"

"I wasn't going to send her a damn wreath."

"Whatever. Besides, some guy sent her, like, two dozen red roses Monday."

"Oh. Who was that?"

"Peter Ashford, I guess. She didn't want to talk about it. She's been acting strange the last couple of days, moping around. I'm kind of worried about her."

"She's been through a lot lately."

"Yeah, I guess." But Wesley remembered the glazed look on Carlotta's face the night before last when she had walked away from him. She looked as if she were ready to unplug herself from the world. And the only evidence that she'd left her bedroom yesterday was the empty cookie jar.

"So do you think I should ask her to dinner?"

Wesley shrugged. "Dude, you're asking the wrong person. I bought a new TV for the living room and instead of being happy about it, she yelled at me."

One corner of Coop's mouth went up. "How big?"

"Sixty inch, high-def ready, plasma monitor."

"Sweet. That must have set you back a load of cash."

Wesley shifted in his seat. "I sold my motorcycle."

"Still."

He decided to keep quiet.

"You playing cards again?"

Anger sparked in his belly. "What if I am?"

"Then you're being stupid," Coop said casually. "Probation is another word for second chance. Don't give your sister something else to worry about, *capisce?*"

"Yeah," Wesley mumbled. "Hey, Carlotta said that you hired Hannah to help you move bodies?"

Coop snorted. "Hired? More like surrendered. The woman is a steamroller. I told her I would call her *if* I needed her, but I warned her that wasn't likely to happen."

"According to Carlotta, Hannah didn't hear the last part and is pissed that you haven't called."

"Christ, is she going to cast a spell on me?"

"Don't push it, man—with Hannah you never know. Besides, I'm supposed to start my community service soon, so unless you have someone else to fill in, you might have to bite the bullet and call her."

"Maybe she can give me some insight into your sister."

Wesley shook his head. "Good luck with that. I've lived with Carlotta for nineteen years and haven't figured her out."

Coop laughed. "That's the fun part about being with a woman, when she keeps you on your toes."

Wesley glanced sideways at his boss who seemed downright…giddy. He knew because it was the way he felt when he thought about E. Jones.

A couple of under-employed body movers lusting after

beautiful, independent women. They were both way out of their league.

"Something *bold*." Cooper thought out loud.

"And fast," Wesley said, thinking of Peter Ashford, Detective Jack Terry, and Carlotta's current state of mind. "Before she does something that we'll both regret."

10

Wednesday afternoon on her break, Carlotta headed toward the general manager's office with a stone of dread in her stomach. The sight of Patricia Alexander coming out of Lindy's office further soured her mood.

"Hello, Carlotta," the blonde said primly.

"Hi, Patricia."

The woman reached forward and patted Carlotta's arm. "I hope you know that we're all pulling for you in your time of crisis."

"Excuse me?"

Patricia lowered her voice. "I know your family history— my mother was in the Junior League with your mother. And then you were caught up in all that scandal with the Angela Ashford murder." She shuddered. "All that stress was bound to catch up with you sooner or later. I'm sure that's why your sales have fallen off a cliff." Her waxy lips drew back in a false self-deprecating smile. "I was just lucky enough to be working here when it happened."

Carlotta returned an equally disingenuous smile. Her hands practically shook from wanting to slug the obnoxious woman, but instead of saying all the vile things that burned her tongue, she simply sidestepped Patricia as if she were a piece of furniture in her path and proceeded to Lindy's office. After a few calming breaths, she knocked on the door.

Lindy looked up from a paper-strewn desk and removed her glasses. "Come in, Carlotta. Sit down."

Carlotta took a seat opposite her boss, her gaze riveted to her cell phone lying on the desk. Her fingers itched to snatch it up to see if her father had called again.

Lindy scrutinized her for a few seconds, then sighed. "I don't quite know what to do with you, Carlotta. In the space of a few weeks you've gone from being the associate with the highest sales to being the associate with the highest maintenance."

"I've been dealing with some things in my personal life," Carlotta murmured, feeling moist around her hairline.

"I know," Lindy said, nodding. "Angela Ashford's death was a terrible tragedy. I'm sorry you were implicated and I'm relieved that the murderer was apprehended. I feel bad for you, Carlotta, but it's caused a lot of upheaval around here too. And it doesn't give you license to break the rules. You know that having a cell phone on the sales floor is strictly prohibited— and one of my pet peeves."

"Yes, I'm sorry. It won't happen again."

Lindy's mouth flattened into a line. "I'm afraid I also have to mention the overdue balance on your store account. This isn't something that I normally concern myself with, but the amount is excessive."

A flush started at her collarbone and worked its way up. "I'm a little behind on my bills."

"Unfortunately, your company credit card has been suspended until you can reduce the outstanding balance."

Carlotta could only nod in mortification. She hadn't bought anything on her employee discount in a long time—okay, a week or so—but she'd really been cutting back. She hadn't bought those new Chip & Pepper jeans that she'd wanted so badly, nor the Diane von Furstenberg satin wrap dress that would be the singularly perfect dress for an awards dinner and ceremony—if she ever needed it. But apparently the finance charges on her account were compounding faster than the speed of light.

Lindy clasped her hands together. "And I understand that a detective has been coming to see you here? The detective who apprehended the shoplifter?"

"Yes, but he wasn't here on business. He was shopping for a suit."

"So you don't have any outstanding issues with the police department?"

"Um…well…there are a couple of things—"

Lindy's mouth tightened and she lifted her hand. "I don't need or want to know any particulars. But I've decided to suspend you for two weeks so you can get these personal issues worked out."

Carlotta blinked. "Suspend?"

"Without pay."

She felt faint. "Without pay?"

"I thought you would prefer it to being fired."

Panic blipped in Carlotta's chest, and she back pedaled. "Yes...a suspension would give me time to...regroup. But won't it leave the department short-handed?" she asked, hoping to appeal to the woman's business sense.

"Patricia Alexander is going to fill in for you while you're gone."

Carlotta's intestines cramped.

"And when you return, I expect you to be back to one-hundred percent."

"A-absolutely."

Lindy pushed the cell phone forward. "You can go ahead and clock out."

Carlotta nodded like a bobble-head doll, telling herself that she should be grateful that Lindy hadn't fired her outright. But missing a paycheck was likely to send her already precarious mountain of bills toppling. She curled her fingers around the phone, glad to hold on to something solid, then turned and left the office before Lindy could change her mind.

She waited until she was in the break room to examine her phone. As she feared, the display was shot and even with a fully juiced battery, none of the functions worked. She groaned. On top of everything else, she'd have to spring for a new phone. Fighting back tears of frustration, she gathered her things and walked to her service provider's kiosk in the mall.

"Can I help you?" asked a sulky-faced young woman.

Carlotta held up her phone. "It's broken. I need a new one."

The girl grunted. "We're having a special on our camera phone." She handed a display model to Carlotta.

Her first instinct was to say she didn't need the camera feature, but what if her father showed up? A picture might come in handy to prove he'd been there. "How much?"

"Three hundred fifty-nine, plus a deposit. You want the same service plan as before?"

"Sure, that's fine."

"And the same number?"

"Yes."

"I need your name and cell phone number."

Carlotta gave it to her and tapped her foot, impatient to hear any messages that might have accumulated for her. Had her father called back? Left a number where she could reach them? Told her their whereabouts?

"Uh, there's a problem," the girl said, squinting at the computer screen.

"What kind of problem?"

"Your account is, like, way overdue."

Carlotta straightened. "Maybe a little—"

"And your balance is like huge."

"It can't be *that* big."

"Try sixteen-hundred dollars, lady."

Carlotta's eyes widened. "That's impossible."

"Says here you got another phone just last week—our top of the line model. And you've been using it to make international calls?"

She shook her head. "I didn't buy a new phone and I don't make international calls."

"Maybe you forgot."

Carlotta pushed her tongue into her cheek. "No, I didn't forget."

The girl shrugged. "Sorry, I have to go by what it says on the screen and it says you can't buy any more equipment until you've paid off your balance."

"But I don't have sixteen-hundred dollars!"

"Wow, it sucks being you." The girl reached forward and plucked the camera phone from Carlotta's hand.

Carlotta wanted to scream, but in the back of her mind, she thought of the stack of unopened bills at home—how long had it been since she'd looked at her statement? She just sent in a check for fifty bucks every once in a while and as long as the phone kept working, it seemed like an adequate payment strategy. But maybe the company charged late fees, interest.

"I at least need to access my voice-mail messages," she said weakly.

"No can do. You have to go through customer service, but they'll expect a payment first."

She bit her tongue, trying not to think about the crippled phone that might contain a message from her father. Steeped in a frustrated fog, she headed for the mall entrance nearest the Lenox Marta station. At least she'd be able to pick up her car and not have to depend on the train during her involuntary vacation.

She boarded to ride south, giving in to the sway of the train as her unoccupied mind raced in circles. The events of the last several days descended on her and she could feel a prick of panic on the periphery of her consciousness, threatening to unravel the tightly woven facade she tried to maintain.

Scenes replayed in Carlotta's mind—Wesley's arrest, the re-opening of her father's case, Angela Ashford's murder, Peter's arrest, the subsequent attempt on her own life, her father's phone call, Wesley's irresponsible antics, her suspension. And ever-present was the guilt over just wanting her life back, fighting the temptation to run away like her parents had. To wipe the slate clean and simply start over someplace new, maybe in a tropical setting. She could sell souvenirs on a beach somewhere, meet a guy who'd never heard of Randolph Wren, who had a regular job that had nothing to do with her father's old firm or law enforcement or moving bodies—

When the train lurched to a halt, her head snapped up and she realized she'd missed the east-west connection station of Little Five Points by three stops. Then a rogue memory slid into her mind and she gasped. She'd completely forgotten her appointment with Michael's therapist, Dr. Delray.

A frantic glance at her watch told her she had been expected forty-five minutes north five minutes ago. She lumbered off the train and sat in a miserable lump on a bench waiting for another train to take her back in the opposite direction. This was shaping up to be one of the worst days ever.

Over an hour later, Carlotta alighted from the westbound train to walk the two blocks to the service station. She felt herself zone out to the point that she seemed disembodied. She could see herself walking, shoulders hunched, moving at a snail's pace. When she finally reached the grubby, deserted lobby of the repair shop, she couldn't remember exactly how she'd gotten there and had the bizarre feeling that she'd blacked out, that she'd lost a block of time.

She shook herself and glanced around the smelly shop with trepidation. Since Chance Hollander had recommended this place, chances were good that something shady was going on in the back room. She just hoped that Wesley wasn't somehow involved. She rang a bell on the counter, ready to do battle if her car wasn't ready.

An ass-scratching guy appeared. His shirt patch read Ted and he wore a slightly bewildered expression.

"Hi," Carlotta said cheerfully. "I'm Carlotta Wren and I'm here to pick up the Monte Carlo."

"Very funny."

"Excuse me?"

Ted gave a little laugh, then crossed his arms. "That's a good one, you almost got me."

She squinted. "Is my car ready?"

He scratched his jowly cheek. "It ain't here."

"Where is it?"

He lifted his hands. "You already picked it up, lady."

Her eyes went wide. "Uh, apparently not, since I'm standing right here."

He leaned into the counter and spoke to her as if she were addled. "I saw you with my own eyes." He shoved a piece of paper in her direction. "There you go."

At the top of the paper was the imprint of her credit card and at the bottom was her signature, dated an hour earlier.

Carlotta's vision blurred and she pressed her hand against her throbbing temple. Was she losing her mind? Had she picked up her car and simply forgotten?

She was suddenly overcome with the most pervasive sense of utter exhaustion. Minor aches and pains—her pinched feet, her pressurized temples, her strained shoulders—seemed to converge and amplify, sending waves of stinging awareness cascading over her body. She leaned against the counter for support, breathing deeply. Her job, her parents, Wesley, their debt, Peter. The mountain of stress had depleted her energy and was messing with her mind. In that desperate moment, Carlotta understood why people turned to drugs and booze for temporary relief. Right now she'd give anything for a reprieve from reality.

After all that she'd been through, she had fooled herself into thinking that she could deal with anything on her own. But it had become too overwhelming…she had obviously reached her emotional limit, she thought as she gazed wildly at the hairy man behind the counter. This wasn't the life she was supposed to have.

"Lady, are you okay?"

She crumpled the paper in her hand and murmured, "Yes. Thank you." Then she stumbled out into the deserted parking lot and turned in a full circle, fighting the panic that clawed at her. Bright spots of light flashed behind her eyelids and her hands began to shake. Her mother, Valerie, had once been checked into a hospital for exhaustion, the elitist code for a nervous breakdown. Along with the gap between her front teeth, had she inherited her mother's "crazy" gene?

Carlotta bit down on her lip until she tasted blood. Great. On top of everything else, she was going insane. Minus ten points.

11

"**P**opular day to die," Wesley remarked wryly, closing the van door on their last scheduled pickup.

"Some days are more preferred than others," Coop agreed as they wheeled the gurney toward the morgue delivery entrance.

"Do you ever get used to the smell?" Wesley asked with a grimace.

"I'm a mouth breather. And yeah, you get used to it."

Coop stopped at an intercom to identify himself and their cargo, and they were buzzed in. Coop moved through the cold, harshly lit hallways of the morgue with ease and familiarity, even whistling under his breath.

His old stomping grounds, Wesley had learned, although he didn't know the full details of why Coop no longer worked at the morgue. And although almost everyone treated Coop with respect, the chief medical examiner had made his presence known more than once, and it had always resulted in words between the two men. But just as they had several times that day, they handed off the body to a crypt orderly and retraced their steps to the exit with no incident. Coop continued to whistle, but his shoulders seemed tense, as if he expected a confrontation.

"Craft," Wesley heard behind them.

They turned to see Dr. Abrams, the coroner, moving toward them. He wore stained scrubs, but unlike previous encounters, the man's body language seemed conciliatory.

"Yeah, Bruce. What's up?" Coop asked.

Abrams looked grim. "Got a jumper on the Seventeenth Street bridge—a woman and it's bad. I sent a couple of M.E.s to the scene, but I need someone experienced to help recover the body."

Wesley swallowed hard, remembering how he'd tossed his cookies after helping Coop peel a teenager off Interstate 75.

"I can do it," Coop said.

"I'd appreciate it," Abrams said with a curt nod, then walked away.

"You up for this?" Coop asked him as they returned to the van.

"Sure," Wesley said, hoping he sounded braver than he felt. At least he hadn't scarfed down a burrito beforehand like last time.

Dusk was falling and traffic was thick. With the aid of a magnetic flashing light that Coop put on top of the van, they made the drive in about ten minutes. The scene was impossible to miss with flashing lights both on the bridge and below on the interstate. Traffic was backed up to the horizon. Wesley's chest swelled with importance when Coop flashed ID that allowed them to proceed through the emergency vehicles. But as they approached the corded-off area, Wesley braced himself for the sight of the body. Considering that he could see at least three sheeted locations, this was shaping up to be a bad scene.

Suddenly a man appeared in front of the van and held up his arm. Wesley recognized Detective Jack Terry. Coop stopped and waited as Terry strode to the driver side window and looked in.

"Wesley," he said, "I need for you to get out and stay with me."

Wesley frowned. "What? Why? I can handle this."

"Just do it," the detective said, his voice strangely gentle. The detective exchanged a glance with Coop and gave him an almost imperceptible shake of his head, as if to say not to question him.

The hair on the back of Wesley's neck stood up. Something was very wrong. "I'm not going anywhere until you tell me why."

The detective's jaw hardened and Wesley realized suddenly that the big man was fighting emotion. "It's Carlotta."

"What about Carlotta?" Wesley asked, his voice spiking in a squeak. Then he realized the detective was holding a driver's license—a familiar driver's license. Disbelief stabbed him

even as he glanced up to the bridge to see the jumper's abandoned car sitting amidst flashing squad cars.

A dark blue Monte Carlo. Carlotta's car.

12

June Moody handed Carlotta a second Blue Moon martini to go with the cigar she'd managed to smoke to half its original size. "So you have no idea what happened to your car?"

Carlotta sipped the martini, grateful she'd had the presence of mind to seek out June at Moody's Cigar Bar. The sixtyish woman was a brick wall disguised as a lacy curtain. "I simply don't remember picking it up, but I must have. I probably parked it somewhere in the mall's parking garage."

"It'll turn up," June said. "You wouldn't be the first person to forget having done something. And with the stress you've been through, it's understandable."

"Thanks." Carlotta took a drag on the cigar. She could get used to these. They delivered a bigger punch than her ultra lights. And she hadn't felt something this substantial in her hand in…a long damn time.

"So what else is bothering you?" June asked, inhaling on her own stogie with the practiced ease of a woman who ran a cigar establishment.

Carlotta barked a laugh. "The latest? I heard from my long-lost father."

June's expression turned serious. "I thought he was—"

"A fugitive? Yep. He called me on my cell phone this week, can you believe it? I was so stunned, I dropped my phone and hung up on him."

"Did you inform the police?"

Carlotta shook her head, enjoying the way the alcohol made everything swimmy. "I should, shouldn't I?"

"That's your decision, honey."

Carlotta took another drink. "I'm tired of making decisions. I'm tired of being responsible."

June nodded thoughtfully. "So you're just going to let everything ride?"

"Maybe."

"Are you going to tell your brother?"

"I don't know. Wesley doesn't need another reason to misbehave."

"There you go, being responsible again."

Carlotta frowned. "Let's change the subject, shall we?"

"Okay." June leisurely stirred her own martini. "So…you and Cooper Craft."

Carlotta frowned harder. "There is no 'me and Cooper Craft.'"

"That's not what I observed the other day when you ran into him in here."

"He's my brother's boss. Do you know that the man moves bodies for a living?"

"Someone has to. And Coop's a good guy." She winked. "Cute, too."

Carlotta blushed, remembering Cooper's confession a couple of weeks ago that he was "crushing" on her. They had been in front of the town house, Coop waiting for Wesley. Caught off guard, Carlotta had protested that they didn't have anything in common, that he was an intellectual. And Coop had insisted that she was smarter than she wanted people to believe. "Do you know him well?" she asked June.

"I guess so. I knew him in the bad days."

"The bad days?"

"His drinking days. When he was the chief medical examiner."

She squinted to recall what Jack Terry had told her about Coop's past. "I heard he was fired."

"He was, and it got nasty. But he's gotten his life back on track, and he seems happier now."

"He was a big help in solving Angela Ashford's murder."

"Doesn't surprise me. I heard he was the best at what he did. So you're not interested in Coop, huh? Is there someone else?"

Carlotta squirmed as the images of two other men dodged in and out of her mind. "It's complicated."

June laughed. "Honey, *life* is complicated." She gestured to the slumped, bleary-eyed patrons around them in the upstairs smoking lounge. "And it's a good thing, too, because otherwise we wouldn't need vices and I'd be out of business."

Carlotta nodded, then drained the rest of her drink and stubbed out her cigar with an unfocused hand. "I'd better get home." Then she gave a dry laugh. "Not that anyone is missing me."

"I'll call you a cab," June said. "And don't worry—I'm sure you'll find your car soon."

Carlotta tried to smile, but it took too much effort as she slid off the stool. Being vertical sent the alcohol zooming to her head, but June offered her arm gracefully, as if nothing was wrong.

As they walked down the worn wooden steps, Carlotta caught a whiff of the woman's exotic perfume and again marveled at the dichotomy of June Moody's elegant pencil skirts and perfectly starched blouses over a pinup figure, the woman's beautifully manicured hands holding a pungent stogie. She wondered what it would have been like to have the rock-solid woman for a mother instead of the weak-willed Valerie Wren.

"Do you have any children, June?"

June's step faltered for a split second. "A son."

"Oh? Where does he live?"

"As far away from me as he can get," June said with a laugh. "He's a career army man."

"Grandkids?"

"None that I'm aware of. Here you go," she said, holding the front door and ushering Carlotta toward the cab. "Cheer up, things will look better in the morning."

Carlotta hiccupped. "Promise?"

"I promise," June said, patting her hand.

Carlotta dropped into the seat, gave the cab driver her address, and laid her head back, closing her eyes against the psychedelic blur of passing lights. She knew she would feel like hell in the morning, but for now she was grateful for the rosy blur the vodka had put on the day's events. Despite June's assurance, Carlotta didn't want to think about tomorrow, about her physical and emotional to-do lists that kept growing like some kind of giant fungus. Or about the melancholy feeling that pulled at her, the nagging sense that her life wasn't really her own—

"Is this it?" the cab driver said over his shoulder. "Looks like a party."

Carlotta turned her head and squinted at the lights blazing from the town house. In the driveway sat Coop's white van and a dark sedan that she recognized as Jack Terry's. Her heart fluttered in her chest. Was Wesley in trouble again? Had her father called again or—she gulped—had he shown up?

She handed the driver the last cash in her wallet and scrambled out of the cab in slow motion. She was still nursing a buzz, but adrenaline had a way of sobering a person quickly. After a few stumbles, Carlotta kicked off her shoes and carried them. With the help of the handrail, she made it up the steps to the front door and turned the handle. She practically fell into the small living room where Wesley sat with his head in his hands and Coop's hand on his shoulder. Jack Terry stood a few feet away, in front of the big-ass television, his shoulders drooping.

At her unladylike entrance, they all turned to look at her.

"What happened?" Carlotta asked. "Is something wrong?"

It took her a few seconds to realize the three men were staring at her as if they were seeing a ghost.

13

Carlotta looked from Wesley to Coop to Jack, from one stunned expression to another. "Would someone please tell me what's going on?"

Before anyone could speak, the door opened behind her. Carlotta turned and couldn't contain her surprise to see Peter standing there. But strangely, he looked equally surprised to see her.

"Carlotta," he breathed, then took her in his arms for a forceful embrace. "You're okay."

While her blood surged at the fervent body-to-body contact, she was still confused. And from the looks that Jack, Wesley and Coop gave her as Peter continued to cling to her, so were they.

She pulled back and gave Peter a bemused smile. "Of course I'm okay." She gave a little laugh. "Can't a girl go out for a drink without everyone freaking out?"

Wesley stood and the realization that he'd been crying sobered her further. "Wesley?"

He strode forward, then past her and out the front door, letting it slam behind him, his footsteps pounding down the sidewalk. She turned back to Jack and Coop, who now stood next to each other. "One of you explain what just happened. *Now.*"

They exchanged bewildered glances, then Jack ran a hand over his haggard face. "We all thought you were…dead."

She couldn't help the laugh that bubbled out. "Dead? And here I thought *I* was the one going crazy."

Coop lifted his hands. "A woman jumped off the Seventeenth Street bridge. She had your driver's license in her wallet and was driving your car."

Carlotta's eyes bulged. "Driving my car?"

"I was sent to the scene and Wesley was with me…"

She blanched. "Wesley was called to the scene to move a body and was told the body was mine?"

Jack nodded. "We all thought it was you."

Peter clasped her hand feverishly. "When Wesley called me, I almost went out of my mind."

"We were *all* concerned," Coop said, eyeing Peter as if he were an interloper.

Carlotta pulled her hand from Peter's and touched her head, her sluggish mind churning. "But couldn't you tell it wasn't me?"

Coop cleared his throat. "No. The woman was…in pretty bad shape."

Carlotta's stomach lurched, sending the taste of vodka and

acid to the back of her throat. She covered her mouth, and felt Peter's hand at the small of her back, steering her toward the couch. She sat heavily, dropping her shoes and purse to the floor.

"Do you know how this woman could have gotten your car?" Jack asked.

She swallowed hard to regain her composure. "When I went to pick up my car today from the repair shop, the guy looked at me as if I'd lost my mind. He told me that I'd already picked it up. He showed me my credit card imprint and my signature."

Jack frowned. "Why didn't you report the car stolen?"

She shook her head. "Because I've been a little out of it lately and honestly, I wasn't sure if…that is, I couldn't remember…"

They were all looking at her as if she did need to be committed.

Jack stepped forward. "At any rate, it looks like someone was masquerading as you. Was your purse stolen recently?"

She shook her head again.

"There've been a rash of identity-theft cases in Buckhead," he said. "Most of the victims are frequent shoppers or people working retail. Are you having credit problems?"

Carlotta bit into her lip. She was, but what else was new?

Then she snapped her fingers, or attempted to—her fingers didn't quite connect. "I tried to replace my cell phone today and the woman told me an ungodly amount had accumulated on my account and that I had bought equipment that I'd never heard of."

Jack nodded. "Maybe someone *has* stolen your identity."

Coop made a thoughtful noise. "Someone suicidal."

She looked at Coop. "But you'll be able to identify the body, won't you?"

Coop shifted from foot to foot. "A medical examiner will, yes. But meanwhile, I need to go and unwind a few things."

"Unwind?"

Coop checked his watch, then looked as if he were weighing his words. "Chances are good that your demise was reported on the eleven o'clock news. I need to call the morgue and let the M.E. know we have a Jane Doe." He walked toward the door, but stopped in front of Carlotta. "Are you going to be okay?"

She nodded. "But Wesley…"

"I doubt if Wesley got very far. I'll see if I can find him and have a word. He was pretty shaken up." He gave her a wry smile. "I guess we all were."

She was struck by the concern in his gentle eyes, glad that he'd been with Wesley during the ordeal. "Thank you, Coop. Whatever I can do to help you find out who the woman is, just let me know."

"I will."

He left and Jack Terry stepped forward. "I need to ask you a few questions."

"Can't it wait?" Peter asked, still hovering.

"No. And if you don't mind, I'd like to talk to Carlotta in private."

Peter's mouth tightened. "As a matter of fact, I do mind."

Jack took one step closer to Carlotta, but leveled his gaze

on Peter. "That might have sounded like a request, Ashford, but it wasn't. This is a criminal investigation now."

Carlotta looked back and forth, feeling the testosterone boomeranging between the two men.

"Uh, guys, I'm still in the room."

They both looked down at her, challenging her to choose one and send the other one walking. Jack's black eyes flashed with authority, Peter's blue ones were filled with possessiveness.

"Peter," she said, standing and turning toward him. "I'll call you tomorrow, okay?"

He clasped her hands. "Promise? We have a lot to talk about."

Carlotta knew what he was referring to, but from the noise that Jack made in his throat, it was clear he thought Peter was referring to something more personal.

"Yes," she murmured. "Thank you for coming over."

He leaned forward and planted a kiss near her ear. "I love you," he whispered, then pulled back, threw Jack Terry a parting glare and left.

Carlotta turned around to face Jack Terry who looked at her intently in the expanding silence. "You gave everyone quite a scare."

"I didn't mean to, Detective."

He lifted his hand and almost touched her arm before stopping and gesturing to the couch. "Why don't you sit?"

She rubbed her scratchy eyes and sighed. "Do you mind if I get something to drink?"

"No offense, but it looks like you've already had plenty to drink." He sniffed. "And to smoke. Do I smell a cigar?"

She lifted her chin. "Yes. And I was talking about *coffee*."

"Wouldn't mind a cup myself," he said, jamming his hand into his hair. "It's been one hell of a night."

She pointed. "The kitchen is that way. I'm sure your coffee is better than mine, and I need to find my brother."

Jack relented with a nod. "Don't disappear again, okay?"

The tone of his voice stopped her. Embedded in the sarcastic remark was a seed of concern that sounded almost personal. Before she could respond, he disappeared into the kitchen. Carlotta frowned after him, then pushed open the front door and stepped out into the circle of light shining on the stoop, in search of yet another man in her life who confounded her.

Coop's van was gone and for a moment she wondered if perhaps Wesley had gone with him, then she noticed a movement under the weeping willow tree near the sidewalk. Wesley's thinking place. When he and the tree were small, he would hide beneath its drooping limbs that had reached to the ground. Later, when their parents had disappeared and the tree had lifted its canopy, he had taken to climbing its sturdy branches and staying there with a book for hours at a time. Once he'd climbed so high, she'd had to call the fire department to bring a cherry picker to get him down. When she'd chastised him, he'd said he'd thought if only he could get high enough, he would eventually see their parents coming back.

Now he sat with his back against the tree, absently stripping the long narrow leaves from a bit of branch. His profile was barely discernible in the darkness. Carlotta walked barefoot through the dew-laden grass and sat down next to him.

Neither of them said anything for a while, allowing her to soak up the night noises of insects and slow-moving cars. This time of night, this time of year, their neighborhood was almost pretty.

Finally she inhaled deeply and puffed out her cheeks in an exhale. "I'm sorry about the scare, Wesley. If the tables were turned and I thought something had happened to you, I don't know what I would've done."

He gave a hoarse laugh. "Celebrated, probably."

"How can you say that?"

Wesley sniffed. "Easy. Because I've been a big pain in the ass to you."

Her heart tugged sideways. "I wouldn't say a *big* pain in the ass."

He laughed, then turned to look at her and his eyes clouded. "I thought you were gone. I thought I'd driven you to…" His voice broke off on a sob.

She put her arm around his neck and rocked him toward her, her throat clogged with emotion. "I'm right here. And yes, you've caused me a few sleepless nights, but I can't believe you'd think I would just leave you like—" She bit her tongue.

"Like Mom and Dad?"

She hesitated, then gave his shoulders another hug. "I'm not going anywhere, got it?"

He nodded and she felt him exhale. No matter how many times she'd told him, he had no idea how much she loved him, how impossible it would be for her to abandon him. She felt sorry for her parents sometimes, that they hadn't felt that kind of love for Wesley. Or for her.

"Why don't you come inside?" she asked softly. "Detective Terry is making coffee."

"Mighty friendly of him," Wesley said, his voice drenched with suspicion.

"He has to question me. He thinks someone might have stolen my identity."

Wesley laughed. "Why would anyone want your identity?"

"Thanks a lot." She punched his shoulder, but was glad to see him returning to his smart-ass self. "Are you coming in or not?"

"Not. At least not yet. I'll hang out here until he leaves."

"Suit yourself," she said, then pushed to her feet and brushed the grass off her skirt.

When Carlotta climbed the steps again to the front door, fatigue pulled at her, but the aroma of strong coffee carried her to the kitchen. Jack had rolled up the sleeves of his shirt and his dreadful tie lay on the counter. He stood next to the coffeemaker, pouring brew into two mismatched mugs.

"I see you found everything," she said, glancing around the dated decor of the kitchen, feeling a twinge of shame, then anger that she cared what this man thought of her or her family home. Then she gave a dry laugh. "But I forget that you saw everything when you searched our house during Wesley's arrest, didn't you?"

He handed her a mug of coffee and skimmed her, head to grass-stained toes, with his dark gaze. "Well, I didn't see *everything*."

Her skin hummed with awareness, but Carlotta blamed it on the dwindling buzz. She averted her eyes and took a seat at the table stacked with mail and other clutter where a note-book, pen, and police radio lay. "Will this take long?" she mur-mured, then took a sip of the surprisingly good coffee.

"I hope not," he said. "I was really hoping to get some sleep tonight."

"Me, too."

"Then let's get to it." Jack picked up the pen and took a deep drink. "Now then...tell me about this business with your cell phone."

She relayed the details, excluding the part about why she had dropped her cell phone in the first place.

"I'll need your account number," he said.

She balked, wondering how closely he might examine her phone records. "I...don't have it handy."

"That's all right. I have your cell number so I'll go from there. When did you first notice unusual activity on your bill?"

"Uh, I didn't." Carlotta glanced at the pile of mail and her cheeks warmed. "I'm a little behind on my payments."

A corner of his mouth twitched, as if to say he wasn't sur-prised. "Tell me about the incident at the body shop."

She told him the name and address of the place and what the man had said to her, and described again the evidence that someone else had picked up her car.

"And he thought it was you?"

"Yes, he seemed certain that I had been in the shop ear-lier."

"So maybe this woman looked like you."

"Or maybe she was wearing a disguise. Wigs are easy to come by, you know."

"Oh? Are you speaking from experience?"

Her cheeks warmed. "Just general knowledge." She took a quick drink from her mug to divert attention from the subject—no use divulging her own party-crashing techniques. That was all in her past anyway. Although her wigs and a few getups were still in the garage, in the trunk of the white Miata that had simply died on her, which had led to test-driving and getting stuck with the Monte Carlo.

"You should contact all three credit bureaus tomorrow," he said. "Get a current credit report to see if any other suspicious activity shows up."

"Okay." Although she'd promised herself that she would get her finances in order, at the moment, it seemed like a daunting task.

"Can you think of anything else unusual that's happened lately?"

Carlotta angled her head at Jack. "You mean other than being implicated in Angela Ashford's death, being stalked by a murderer and the little shootout in the mall parking deck?"

"Yeah. Other than all that."

She stopped as the thought of her father calling came back to her with ringing clarity. Could the two incidents possibly be connected?

"What?" Jack asked tersely. "You're hiding something from me, I can tell."

Her mind raced for a plausible lie, then seized upon something perfectly legitimate and pointed to the vase of fading roses sitting on the breakfast bar. "Actually, I was thinking about the flowers I received yesterday."

"From Peter?" he asked dryly.

"They weren't from Peter. The card was signed 'Thanks for a great time, Mason,' but I don't know anyone by that name."

"Did you call the florist?"

"Yeah. I tried to tell them the delivery must have been a mistake, but I didn't get very far."

Jack nodded. "So maybe our ID thief had a date as you, and the guy sent you roses meant for her."

"Maybe." She frowned. "*I* haven't had a date as me in ages...how could someone *posing* as me have a date?"

"Maybe you shouldn't be so prickly."

"Excuse me?"

"Sorry—didn't mean to say that out loud." He coughed lightly. "Do you still have the card that came with the flowers?"

Carlotta nodded and parted the roses to retrieve the card. "I don't see it. I had it in the break room at work, but I must have dropped it on the way home. Ow!" She grimaced at the drop of blood on her finger.

Jack reached for her hand and removed a handkerchief from his pocket to wrap around her finger.

"I need you to write down the name of the florist."

"If I can remember it." Then she remembered the postcard from her parents that he'd confiscated from her days earlier. "I don't guess anything came of the last piece of correspondence you took from me?"

He frowned. "One case at a time, okay? Although with you, I'm starting to lose track."

She crossed her arms, all too aware of her over-bandaged finger. "Are we finished here?"

"I guess so—for now."

"Where's my car?"

"Impound lot. And now that we have a different crime on our hands, it'll probably be a while before you get it back."

"Oh, that's perfect."

"Can't be helped, but I'll keep you posted."

Carlotta bit into her lip. "You can reach me here. I, uh, decided to take a few days off from Neiman's."

Jack seemed preoccupied with putting away his pen, then he gave her a sympathetic look. "It's okay, Carlotta. I contacted your boss after the accident, hoping that you were still at work. I know that you're on suspension."

"Oh." Her cheeks flamed with embarrassment. "Does Lindy think I'm dead, too?"

"I didn't tell her why I was calling."

"So you thought that being suspended had driven me to suicide?"

He looked uncomfortable. "Well, there were other things. Wesley said you'd been in a funk the past couple of days. And you have been through a lot."

"Since you put it that way, I guess I do have every reason to throw myself off a bridge."

He reached forward and cupped her chin, running his thumb along her jawbone. "Don't even joke about something like that."

His intensity and tenderness surprised her. Carlotta blinked as the moment went from teasing to passionate. Her lips parted and she was struck with the feeling that Jack Terry could be her strongest ally. Or her most dangerous adversary.

He wet his lips.

She wet hers.

Then he dropped his hand and stood up. "Get some rest, okay? Not everyone gets a second chance at living."

She followed him through the living room to the door and stood there as he backed out of the driveway, the headlights of his car sweeping over her. Suddenly the incongruity of what had transpired began to sink in, along with the scene she had confronted when she arrived. All of them—Wesley, Jack, Cooper and Peter—had thought she was dead. Her words to June that no one would miss her came back to her. The men in her life had appeared to be affected by her alleged suicide.

And, Carlotta realized when she saw her hand shaking on the door handle, so had she. The tremor encompassed her arm, then her shoulders, then her entire body. She'd been plagued by the feeling that her life wasn't entirely hers. And she'd been right. Someone had taken her identity, then taken their own life.

Resolve swelled in her chest. She had to find out who the desperate woman was—and prove to herself that the two of them had absolutely nothing in common.

14

Carlotta roused slowly from the thick haze of sleep to the insistent ringing of the telephone. She pulled the covers over her head, hoping Wesley would get it. When the noise persisted, she dragged herself out of bed and searched for the extension buried under a pile of clothes on her dresser. Her head pounded from last night's excursion to the cigar bar. She might have narrowly escaped death, but right now she felt somewhat less than alive.

Pushing the hair out of her eyes, she yanked up the receiver and croaked, "Hello."

The silence of an open line sounded in her ear.

"Hello," she repeated.

A click sounded, disconnecting the call. With a frown, Carlotta glanced at the caller ID to see that it had been made from a one-call Internet dialing service, like those used by political campaigns around election days. She groaned and returned the receiver to the clothes' pile, only to hear the doorbell ring three times in succession.

"The one morning I could sleep in because I don't have a job," she mumbled, "and people won't leave me the hell alone."

"Wesley!" She opened her bedroom door and yelled again. "Wesley, are you here?"

From behind his door sounded the drone of a fan which he sometimes used to soundproof his room. He didn't answer and the chiming continued.

Carlotta sighed and walked to the front window, guessing the time to be about six o'clock. She shoved aside the curtain to see Jack Terry's sedan sitting in the driveway and him standing on the stoop in the semi-darkness, his finger on her bell.

How fitting.

She groaned, unlocked the door and swung it open, leaning heavily on the doorknob. "Detective, why didn't you just spend the night?"

"Maybe some other time," he said, pushing past her and grabbing her arm. He pulled her out of the doorway, then closed the door.

"Ow! What's with the manhandling?"

"Sorry," he said gruffly, then yanked the curtain closed. "We need to talk...again."

She smothered a yawn. "Can I at least get a robe—and an aspirin?"

He skimmed the bare limbs exposed by her sleep shorts and

jersey camisole and the barest hint of teasing humor sparked in his dark eyes. "If you insist."

She frowned and jerked her thumb toward the kitchen. "You know where the coffeemaker is." Carlotta retraced her steps to her bedroom. As she tied the belt of her favorite yellow chenille robe around her waist, she caught a glimpse of her bed-head hair and the dark circles under her eyes. Oh, well, when the man showed up unexpectedly at the crack of dawn, what did he expect?

But her nonchalance fought with the rising panic in her chest as she made her way back to the kitchen. Now fully awake, she knew that Jack Terry's appearance couldn't be good news. Her one comfort was that Wesley was safe in his room.

She padded into the kitchen and took in the view of Jack standing with his back to her, looking out the window over the sink as the coffeemaker sputtered and sent the aroma of strong coffee floating on the air. He was dressed in slacks, shirt and tie; his hair was still wet from the shower. A shiver of awareness ran over her at the sight of a man in her kitchen at this hour.

She cleared her throat to announce her presence.

Jack pulled the curtain closed and turned to face her, his expression tense. It was some consolation that whatever he was about to tell her, he wasn't happy about being the messenger.

"Are you going to make me ask?"

He gestured to the table, still strewn with the mugs and paper napkins from last night. "Have a seat."

"We could take our coffee out on the deck," she suggested, nodding toward the back door.

"Not a good idea. I came to ask you to lie low for a while."

She took a seat at the table and pushed her hair over one ear. "What do you mean?"

Jack poured their coffee, then joined her at the table. From his pocket he removed a packet of aspirin and slid them across the table to her. "Kelvin Lucas was my alarm clock this morning. He read the report about the jumper—identified as you—in the newspaper this morning. I told him it was a case of mistaken identity."

"Bet that ruined his day," Carlotta said dryly, thinking of how the D.A. had threatened her in the courtroom after Wesley had been released on probation. She tossed back the tablets and chased them with coffee so strong it made her gasp.

"Lucas doesn't have anything against you. It's your father he wants."

"And?"

"And he suggested that instead of correcting the news report, we…let it ride for a few days."

Her eyebrows shot up. "Let it ride? You mean, let people believe that I killed myself?"

He shifted uncomfortably, then gave her a curt nod.

She opened her mouth to ask why, then realization dawned. "He thinks the news will bring my parents out of hiding."

Jack nodded again.

"And what do you think about the idea?" she asked, feeling sick to her stomach.

He took his time answering. "I can't say I agree with the methodology, but he's probably right."

She swallowed hard. "You think my parents will show up at my funeral?"

He looked up, his eyes suddenly sympathetic. "You don't?"

The clump of emotion in her chest was expelled in a harsh laugh. "I have no idea." Then Carlotta chose her words carefully. "What makes you think they would even hear about it?"

He stood to gather the newspaper from the counter. *Her* suicide had made page two of the *Atlanta Journal-Constitution*. The nighttime photo showed her Monte Carlo on the overpass surrounded by emergency vehicles, looking down at another scene of chaos below. The headline read "Buckhead Woman With Troubled Past Takes Own Life."

Her breath caught at the photo, knowing that pieces of a body lay under the sheets on the street. "Christ, what does a person have to do to make the *front* page in this city?"

"From the last postcard your parents sent," Jack said, "they're aware that you and Wesley still live at this address, so I'm assuming that they're keeping tabs on you to some degree." He coughed lightly. "And Lucas said he'd make sure that the story hit the wires today."

So everyone in the country would think she was dead. "My boss...my friends." Hannah, God, she couldn't let Hannah think she was dead.

"We can let your employer in the loop, but the fewer people who know, the better. Wesley and Coop will have to go along too. And Ashford, since he knows. *If* you agree to this," he added.

She put a hand to her forehead. "I can't think right now. What would I have to do?"

"Stay here, away from the windows. Don't leave the house and don't answer the door or the phone. We'll have the house under surveillance and put a tap on the phone."

"But what about the truth? What about the woman who died?"

"I already talked to Dr. Abrams. He and I will quietly conduct the investigation into her identity."

Her mind spun with the ramifications—Jack Terry didn't know it, but her father *was* keeping tabs on them. And as terrible as it would be to lure her parents out under such a horrible pretense, how much worse would it be if they didn't bother to show? She wasn't sure if she could withstand that kind of blow.

Carlotta shook her head. "I can't do it."

Jack pressed his lips in a thin line. "Lucas thought you might have reservations, so he told me that he could arrange for Wesley's five-thousand dollar fine from the arrest to be rescinded and perhaps his probation time reduced."

"If I agree to this…hoax?"

"Right. And then there's the reward money."

Carlotta squinted. "*What* reward money?"

"Ten years ago the firm that your father worked for put up a one-hundred-thousand dollar reward for information leading to the capture of your father. It's still in effect."

She blinked in surprise. "Mashburn and Tully? I had no idea." Did Peter know?

"Lucas said if this pans out, he'll arrange for you to have the reward money."

"For turning in my father?"

Jack put down his cup and reached forward to touch her arm. "I know this is hard for you, but think of it as a way for you and your brother to…make up for lost time. Wesley could go to college. And you could start over too—do things that you've always dreamed of."

She bit into her lip in confusion. The ramifications were simply too far-reaching for her to comprehend.

"Carlotta, your father *will* be caught eventually, especially now that Lucas is back on his trail."

"And you," she said, pulling her arm away from his touch.

"And me," he agreed. "Luring your father in like this is the safest way to take him into custody. If we have to hunt him down, someone could get hurt."

One or both of her parents or even Jack. Her mind raced; there had to be another way. She could tell Jack about her father calling her and Peter and let him follow those leads to Randolph Wren. But if she did it this way, Lucas would fix Wesley's fine. And the reward money…Wesley could go to Emory with that kind of money…become a scientist…cure something.

To stall for time, she took another drink but the coffee left a metallic taste in her mouth.

Jack's phone rang. He glanced at the screen. "That's Lucas. I need your answer."

"What's going on?"

Carlotta turned to look at Wesley, who walked into the kitchen, dressed for his job as a body mover.

Her brother with the genius IQ was moving bodies for a living.

"Tell Lucas I'll do it," she said to Jack.

Jack stared at her for the space of two heartbeats, then stood and walked to the far end of the kitchen to take the call.

"Lucas?" Wesley asked. "Kelvin Lucas, the asshole D.A.? What's going on?"

"Sit down and I'll tell you," Carlotta said, feeling resolute, but ill. "Don't interrupt. And—for once—you're going to do exactly what I say, young man. No arguments."

15

Wesley stared at Carlotta, unable to believe what she was proposing. Incredulous, he pushed up from the table and snorted with anger. "Pretend you're dead to draw out Mom and Dad? *No way.*"

Carlotta sighed. "I know it sounds drastic, but it also makes sense."

"For the lousy reward money?" he screeched. "We'd be selling out to the cops!" He glared at Detective Terry who was returning his phone to his belt.

"It's a good deal for you, Wesley," the man said. "If everything goes as planned, Kelvin Lucas is willing to reduce your probation and your fine."

Wesley set his jaw. How dare the man stand in his kitchen and patronize him. Fury pumped through his body, propelling him closer to Jack. He lifted his finger to within inches of the man's nose. "You, get out of my house."

"Wesley—" Carlotta began.

"You're just Lucas's errand boy," Wesley sneered. "You can tell that fat bastard that we're not going along with it, we're not going to betray our parents."

"Wesley, your parents betrayed *you,*" the detective said quietly.

Wesley didn't think, only reacted. His fist shot out, but Jack Terry dodged it and grabbed his arm.

"Wesley!" Carlotta shouted behind him. A chair clattered to the floor.

The brawny cop held on to his arm with a steely grip, his expression menacing. "I'm going to overlook that because you've been through a shock over your sister."

"I don't need your sympathy." Wesley wrenched his arm away.

"That's enough," Carlotta said, stepping between them. "It's already done, and you're going to go along with this, whether you like it or not." Her face softened. "Wesley, this is for the best for us...for me."

At the anguished look in her deep brown eyes, Wesley bit down on the inside of his cheek. He wanted her to be happy, not to be so burdened. But was this the answer? He felt as if he were in a vise, being squeezed on all sides, caught between his parents and his sister, all of whom he loved.

"You can't stop it, Wesley," Detective Terry said. "And we need your cooperation."

"Please," Carlotta added.

Wesley closed his eyes. "What would I have to do?"

"Just be alert," the detective said. "Answer the door and the phone and if it's a neighbor or a friend, you have to pretend that Carlotta's...gone." He shot an apologetic look at her. "If one of your parents calls, we'll trace it, but you'll need to keep them on the line as long as possible and try to get them to come here to the house."

"What if they call on my cell phone?"

"Tell them that you need to call them back, then get their number and call me. If that doesn't work, then say your battery is dying and to call you at home."

Wesley gave a curt nod, registering the fact that adrenaline was flowing through his veins at the thought of talking to his dad soon—possibly within hours. What would he say? And if his father was taken into custody, could he really get a fair trial?

"Also, when you're coming and going from the house, you might be approached."

"By one of my parents?"

"It's what we're counting on."

"And then what am I supposed to do?"

"Try to get them to come into the house. I'll be here."

Wesley noticed the confusion that passed over Carlotta's face. "You'll be here?" she asked.

The cop nodded. "Didn't I mention that I'll be staying here until this is over?"

16

At Jack Terry's casual pronouncement, Carlotta felt her jaw go slack. "You're staying here?"

"I told you that I'd have the house under surveillance."

"I thought that meant you'd be sitting in your car across the street!"

"In this heat? Besides, this is the best place for me to be if your father calls or shows up in person."

"Day and—" she gulped "—night?"

"That's right."

"But there's no place for you to sleep." Her voice had risen a couple of octaves.

"You're not sleeping in our parents' bedroom," Wesley said through gritted teeth.

"I wouldn't think of it," Jack replied evenly. "The couch

will be fine. And look on the bright side—if your father shows up today, it won't be necessary for me to stay the night."

Carlotta swallowed hard. *The bright side?* Her father could be in custody by nightfall. She and Wesley could start over. Jack Terry would be out of her life. Why didn't those thoughts cheer her more?

The sound of a vehicle pulling into the driveway broke into her thoughts. Her pulse spiked. Was it possible that her parents had heard the news already? That they'd been within driving distance of the house? Wesley walked into the living room and called, "It's Coop. I'm outta here."

"Tell him what's going on," Jack said. "Let him know that Kelvin Lucas is going to speak to the coroner to make sure that they're on board with our—"

"Lie?" Wesley cut in.

"Plan," Jack finished. "And be alert to anyone who might be following you."

Wesley looked at Carlotta. "What about Hannah? What am I going to tell her when she calls?"

She glanced at Jack. "We can tell Hannah, can't we?"

"No. Too many people already know." He looked at Wesley. "If anyone asks, you have to pretend. Remember, it won't be for long."

"How long?" Wesley asked.

"A few days. We'll play it by ear, but Lucas said that if they don't show within a day or two, we should plan a memorial service." The detective seemed to hesitate, his gaze darting to her, then away. "And if for some reason we haven't heard from them by the end of the service, then we'll call off the surveillance."

For some reason—like they just didn't give a damn.

Wesley didn't respond, but his mottled face was proof of what he thought of the entire idea. He left the house with a bang of the door that resonated in the silence.

She and Jack were alone.

He shifted from foot to foot. "Wesley's question reminded me that you need to call your boyfriend and tell him to keep quiet."

She pursed her mouth. "Peter isn't my boyfriend."

"The sooner, the better—before he tells a neighbor or goes into the office."

"Okay, okay." She picked up the handset and used the call history to bring up Peter's phone number, then hit the dial button. The phone rang four times, plucking on her nerves, then Peter's sleep-soaked voice came on the line. "Hello."

"Peter, hi, it's me, Carlotta."

"Carlotta, hi. Are you okay?"

She could picture him lying in bed among decadent designer sheets, pushing his blond hair out of his eyes and swinging his long legs to the floor. Her midsection tightened, as well as her grip on the phone. "Yes, everything is fine."

Jack was walking around making sure the curtains were closed, but she knew he was listening to every word. The awkwardness of standing in her robe talking to Peter while he was in bed and while Jack stood only a few feet away toyed with her concentration. She turned her back to Jack so she could focus on her conversation. "But I have a favor to ask."

"Anything," Peter said.

"For now, we're not going to correct the news reports that it was, um, me who jumped off the bridge."

A confused, disbelieving noise sounded over the line. "Are you saying that the police are going to let everyone believe that you're *dead?*"

"Uh, yes."

"Why?"

"I believe the prevailing reason is the hope that my parents will reveal themselves."

"What? That's sick!" Peter exclaimed, sputtering. "They can't make you go along with it."

"I agreed to it, Peter. I have my reasons."

"Did you tell them—"

"My phone is being tapped," she cut in before he could mention her father's phone calls. "And Detective Terry is here conducting surveillance."

"Surely he's not staying in the house with you."

She glanced over her shoulder to see Jack smirking at her, as if he could guess the direction of the conversation. "As a matter of fact, he is."

"Then I'm coming over there too."

"No," she said quickly. "That's not necessary and it might cause problems. I need for you to go along."

"I'm supposed to *pretend that you're dead?*"

In the split-second of silence that followed, the ugly thought darted through her head that until only a few weeks ago, she *had* been dead to him. It was a stark reminder that she still harbored resentment for the way their relationship had ended. Carlotta struggled to keep her tone light. "It's only temporary."

"I'm sorry, I can't go along with this."

"But Peter, you have to——" She was interrupted by Jack relieving her of the phone, his expression sour.

"Ashford, this is Detective Terry. You'll keep your mouth shut unless you want to take it up with the D.A., got it?" He disconnected the call unceremoniously and set the phone on the table with a bang.

She crossed her arms. "Nice bedside manner you got there."

Jack raked his gaze over her yellow chenille robe. "It's true that no one ever accused me of being gentlemanly in bed."

She angled her head and gave him a flat smile. "How *is* Liz Fischer?"

He pierced her with a defiant, sexy stare. "Fine, last time I looked."

"Is she under surveillance too?"

"Liz is an officer of the court and your father is a fugitive. If he contacts his former attorney, by law she has to report it."

"So, you're expecting her to rat out her former lover to her current lover?"

Jack shifted uncomfortably. "Why don't you go put some clothes on?"

She gave a dry laugh. "So I can keep you company? I've got news for you, Detective—since I'm supposed to be dead, I'm going back to sleep. You can...surveil."

"Fine. I'm going to put my car in your garage."

Carlotta frowned, uncomfortable with the implied intimacy—and the sensual image his offhand comment had put into her head. She flounced back to her bedroom and slammed the door, then fell on her bed, knowing she was way too keyed up to go back to sleep. She heard him leave the house, then return. She felt Jack Terry's presence in the house as if he were some supernatural entity, everywhere at once.

As she lay there, she tried to get her mind around the idea that soon everyone would think she was dead—her coworkers, her friends, her neighbors and her parents. Instantly her stomach balled up in fear. How would people react to the news? Would anyone really break stride or would they simply shrug and nurse a "sure glad it wasn't me" sensation while they honked the horn at the too-slow car in front of them.

When her thoughts turned to her parents, Carlotta brought a pillow to her stomach to counter the sudden sharp pain. Deep down, she was terrified her parents wouldn't show. They had proved their extreme selfishness when they'd abandoned her and Wesley and nothing over the past ten years gave her reason to believe they had changed. They might conclude that Wesley was an adult now—older than she was when they had skipped town—and could take care of himself. They might decide that nothing would be accomplished if they came forward.

Miserable, she dragged herself out of bed and headed to the shower, trying to focus on the positive things that could result from this little charade. If their father did show up and was taken into custody, Lucas would help to wipe Wesley's record clean. And the reward money would be enough to send Wesley to college and away from Atlanta while the trial played out in the court system and in the media.

When she stepped under the showerhead, however, and allowed the water to cascade over her naked body, her thoughts stubbornly turned to Jack Terry, who had planted himself in her living room—and her life—as if he belonged there. If her life had been allowed to run its natural course, she would have been happily married to Peter Ashford for several years now and her and Jack Terry's paths never would have crossed.

But her life had been derailed, so instead of being a Buckhead wife with few worries, she was in debt up to her eyeballs, unexpectedly unemployed and temporarily dead.

And sharing close quarters with a watchdog possessing a thickly muscled body that made her think wayward thoughts. Just how ungentlemanly was he in bed? Did he ever let his guard down? And were she and he destined to communicate solely in cagey sound bites and flirtatious banter?

She slid a lathered sponge over her body, allowing her mind to run rampant. The sight of Jack half-dressed in the changing room came back to her and she imagined what it would be like to have him holding the sponge, running his big, soapy hands all over her body, doing ungentlemanly things to her—

Suddenly the water pressure dropped, then blasted out icy cold; he was running hot water elsewhere in the house. Carlotta shrieked, jumping around to escape the frigid water. She turned off the shower and dove into a towel, her teeth chattering, more so when the cool air from the overhead vent hit her.

A knock sounded on the bathroom door, eliciting another gasp.

"Are you all right in there?" Jack asked. "I heard you screaming…hope I didn't interrupt something."

Irritated, she yanked on her robe, then opened the door. "You made me take a cold shower."

He managed to take in the length of her—from wet hair to damp toes—before he grinned. "I didn't realize I had that effect on you."

She narrowed her eyes at him even as her cheeks warmed. "Get out of my bedroom."

"Ah, there's the Carlotta I know—prickly." He gestured to her bedroom, the unmade bed, clothes strewn everywhere. "And are you always this messy?"

"Are you still here?"

"No," he said, backing away. "By the way, I made breakfast."

Dammit, how did he know she was starving? She frowned. "Enough for two?"

"If you hurry."

She hurried. A quick blast of hot air to her long hair dried it enough to pull back into a ponytail. A swipe of powder and some lip gloss sufficed as makeup. She pulled an ancient pair of Levi's and a red John Butler Trio T-shirt from her closet, and pushed her feet into a pair of whisper-thin flip flops. She considered making her bed, but didn't, just to spite Jack.

On the way through the living room, she stepped over a bulky black duffel bag and stopped to listen to "CNN Headline News" playing on the big-screen TV that dominated the cramped living room.

"Investigators are still looking into what may have caused Atlanta resident Carlotta Wren to jump to her death last night from the Seventeenth Street bridge."

She gasped when her high school senior picture flashed on the screen. My God, how young she looked. And how naive.

"Wren was eighteen when her father, investment broker Randolph Wren, and his wife, Valerie, disappeared, allegedly to evade the fraud and embezzlement charges levied against Mr. Wren when he was a partner at the Atlanta firm of what was then Mashburn, Tully and Wren. No one has heard from the Wrens since. Atlanta police say that Ms. Wren may have been despondent over her brother's recent arrest and being suspended from her job."

"Nice photo," Jack said next to her. "I'll bet you were a cheerleader."

She turned to glare at him. "Did you have to tell them that I'd been suspended from my job?"

"Sorry. It goes to motivation."

She ran her hands up and down her arms. "This is creeping me out. The report sounds so believable."

"It's supposed to. And it's on all the wire services."

Carlotta imagined her parents having breakfast—her father drinking raw eggs, her mother drinking vodka—and hearing that she'd taken her life in such a hideous, public way. Would her father think it had something to do with him calling her? Would they, as the police believed, come running to console Wesley and mourn their only daughter or would they, as she believed, convince themselves that what was done was done.

Jack's hand settled on her shoulder, his eyes reflecting that pseudo-caring look that so confused her. "Why don't we eat before the food gets cold?"

She followed him slowly, watching numbly as he dished up

a mountain of eggs and pan-fried chicken breasts. He licked the end of his thumb as he studied her. "By the way, you look pretty good for someone who's supposed to be dead."

"Very funny."

"I hope it was okay to raid the refrigerator."

"Okay by me. That's Wesley's domain."

His mouth crooked into a half-smile. "Why doesn't that surprise me?"

She sighed as she poured them each a glass of orange juice. "You've got me all figured out, don't you, Detective?"

He set two piled-high plates on the table and waited until they'd both sat down before giving her an intense look. "No, I don't have you figured out...yet. I wouldn't have figured you for a Levi's kind of gal, for instance."

His scrutiny unnerved Carlotta. She dipped her fork into the eggs and took a flavorful bite, making an appreciative noise before asking, "What else would you like to know?"

Jack put away an enormous mouthful of food before replying. "I guess the first thing that comes to mind is why someone who looks like you isn't married with a couple of kids."

She concentrated on cutting a bite-size piece of chicken. "I guess I've been busy raising Wesley."

"He's a grown man. You can't use that excuse anymore."

She gave a little laugh. "What makes you think I want to be married and have kids? I kind of got my fill of the whole domestic scene."

"Or maybe you were just waiting for Ashford to come to his senses."

She bristled. "If that were so, it would make me rather pathetic, don't you think?"

"But now that his wife is gone," he pressed, "he's hoping to pick up where the two of you left off."

Carlotta looked down at her plate. "I think so, yes."

"Because he still cares about you or because he feels like a bastard for leaving you when your parents skipped town?"

She didn't respond—hadn't she been asking herself the same question? Instead she decided to turn the tables on him. "What about you, Jack? Ever been married?"

He laughed, a big, booming sound. "Nope. My line of work doesn't exactly lend itself to a white picket fence."

"No kids?"

"Nope."

"Really? You seem like the kind of guy who would want to replicate himself," she said dryly.

"I think one of me in the world is enough."

She lifted her glass of orange juice. "Well, we agree on one thing at least."

He smiled and lifted his own glass. "It's a start."

Jack turned his attention back to his food and Carlotta puzzled over his comment. The start of what?

The phone pealed, sending her pulse into orbit. Was it her father? Her mother? A bill collector?

"Will the machine kick on?" he asked.

She nodded, almost nauseous by the fourth ring when her own voice sounded. "Leave a message for Carlotta or Wesley after the tone." Then the sound of wailing filled the room.

"Wesley," cried Hannah, "I just heard…tell me it's not true. That sister of yours cannot be dead!"

Carlotta's heart pinched at her friend's mournful sobs. "Jack," she pleaded.

But he only shook his head.

"I'll try you on your cell," Hannah sputtered. "If you get this message, call me and tell me what I'm going to do without her. How dare she kill herself, the bitch." Then she disconnected the call.

At Hannah's angry tone, Carlotta had to smile. Her friend did not emote well. Still, she felt miserable and teary for putting her through so much anguish.

"It's only temporary," Jack said. "The sooner your father shows, the sooner—"

The ringing of the doorbell cut him off. Carlotta gripped the edge of the table as Jack wiped his mouth with a napkin and pushed to his feet. "Stay out of sight," he ordered.

17

Wesley blinked as Coop snapped his fingers in front of his nose. "Earth to Wesley. We're here."

He looked around to see that they'd arrived at the address of their residential pickup. "Sorry, dude, I'm a little distracted."

"Understandable. Are you sure you shouldn't be at home today?"

"I'm sure."

"Won't people think it's weird that you're working if your sister is supposed to be dead?"

"Dude, if she's dead, then it makes sense I'd be with you, right?"

"I guess so. But you need to take your anger down a notch or two."

Wesley alighted and walked with Coop toward the front of the modest ranch home. A police car and one from the medical examiner's office sat in the driveway. "It's just, what gives them the right to do this to my family?"

"Your father broke the law, Wesley."

"My father is innocent," he said through gritted teeth.

"I meant when he skipped bail. He's a fugitive, and the D.A. wants him brought to justice. Don't you want to see him again?"

"Not like this. Not lured in like some kind of animal."

Coop didn't respond and Wesley had the feeling that his boss believed the lies about his father. His chest ached with frustration, and he was still smarting over the fact that both Detective Terry and Coop had been witness to his emotional meltdown when he'd thought that Carlotta was gone. But he knew one button to push to get Coop on his side.

"And it burns me up thinking about Detective Terry staying in the house with Carlotta."

Just as he suspected, a muscle ticked in Coop's jaw. "But she agreed to it."

"I saw her face when he told her he was moving in. She wasn't happy about it."

Coop's jaw relaxed. "She'll be safe with Jack Terry."

"That depends on your definition of safe," Wesley muttered.

Coop rang the doorbell, waited a few seconds, then entered the house. It was unusually cold and instantly, the stench of death and decay filled Wesley's nose. He fought the urge to gag. A police officer stepped into the hallway, holding a hand-kerchief over his nose and mouth.

"We're here to take the body to the morgue," Coop said, flashing identification.

"She's in here."

Wesley followed Coop into a small bedroom, swallowing past the dreaded anticipation of seeing yet another dead person—they were all so different, their manner of death as individual as they had been in life. Even the old geezers who stroked out at the nursing homes all had a different look about them, meeting death with unique expressions and positions.

Inside the small bedroom, his gaze immediately went to the ceiling fan, where the body of a young woman hung, one end of a colorful scarf wound around the base of the fan and the other end knotted around her neck. Other than the scarf, she was nude. Her head lolled to the side, her face swollen and almost purple. Her arms and legs hung limply—her body swaying oh, so slowly. Wesley covered his nose with his sleeve.

"Looks like a cut-and-dried suicide," the masked M.E. said, filling out forms. His camera sat nearby. "I figure she's been here maybe two days."

"More like four." Coop handed Wesley a mask to put on.

The M.E. frowned. "Did Abrams send you to check up on me, Coop?"

"No, he wouldn't do that."

The man sighed. "Okay, I give. Why do you say four days instead of two? What did I miss? Color of her fingernails, libidity?"

"The four days' worth of newspapers on the stoop," Coop said, jerking his thumb over his shoulder. "And with the air conditioner running so high, the decomp was slowed." He turned to the cop. "Who found the body?"

"I did. She hasn't been to work, so her boss called the police."

"Was there a suicide note?"

The M.E. stood, his expression dry. "Do you want to take this one, Coop? Oh, no wait—you're not an M.E. anymore, only a body mover."

Wesley looked at Coop to see how he'd take the slight.

But if the man's remark had affected Coop, he didn't let on. "It's all yours, Wells. Let us know when you're ready to bring her down." He looked at Wesley and nodded toward the hallway.

Wesley followed him out and pulled down his mask. "You don't think it's a suicide?"

"No, Wells is right—it looks like a cut-and-dried suicide." Coop shoved his hands in his pockets.

"But?" Wesley probed.

"But it's always nice to have a suicide note."

"Do most people leave them?"

"No, but most women do."

Wesley nodded, tucking away the tidbit of information. "What about last night's jumper?"

Coop shook his head. "No note."

"You still don't know who it was?"

"That's the coroner's job."

But Wesley could tell from the man's body language that he was itching to look into the case himself. "So when are you going to tell me what happened?"

"What do you mean?"

"Why did you lose your job as coroner?"

Coop looked away for several long seconds. "Because I was a drunk and I betrayed the trust of the people who believed in me." He leveled his gaze on Wesley. "Once that happens, your life is never the same."

Wesley blinked hard at Coop's sincerity. "Did you get fired?"

"Oh, yeah. And rightfully so."

"But you're brilliant. I've seen the way that Abrams and the other M.E.s treat you—they respect your opinion."

Coop laughed. "Far from it. I overstep my bounds way too often, but old habits are hard to break."

"Hey, Coop," the M.E. called from the doorway, his expression contrite. "Can you give me a hand?"

"Sure," Coop said amiably.

Wesley put his mask back in place and followed Coop back down the hall to the woman's bedroom. He helped bear the weight of the woman's body so the cop could loosen the knot around the base of the fan. Shouldering the left side of her body, he had a sudden appreciation for the term *dead weight*. Even with the mask, the odor was overwhelming. He wondered if people who were suicidal would go through with it if they could only visualize the state in which they'd be found.

Or maybe it was her way of getting back at a world that had ignored her.

Despite the swollen state of her face, it had pleasant-enough features. Her house was ordinary, her surroundings adequate. What could have happened in this woman's life that could make her so desperate she would tie a red-and-yellow striped scarf around the ceiling fan and her neck and then jump off the bed?

Worse, what could drive someone to jump off the Seventeenth Street bridge to certain death on the congested highway below? Last night he hadn't had room for any emotions other than the rollercoaster of believing it was his sister, then finding out it wasn't. But now he felt a tug of compassion for the woman who obviously had felt as if she had no choice except to end her life in such a violent way.

After lowering the woman to the bed, he and Coop went to retrieve the gurney. Wesley's cell phone vibrated and he pulled it out, wincing when he saw the display. "It's Hannah, I'd better get this over with."

"Make it quick," Coop said.

He pushed the connect button, and held his mouth away from the mike so he would sound distant. "Hello?"

"Wesley," Hannah wailed. "It's me. What the fuck happened?"

No one could accuse Hannah of beating around the bush. "I guess you heard."

"Yes, but I don't believe it. I have to hear it from you. Is it true, Wesley? Is she really dead?" Her voice broke on a sob, reminding him of his own grief when he had thought his sister was dead.

"Hannah, I can't—"

"Wesley, just *tell* me. Is Carlotta dead?"

He wanted to tell her the truth, but Coop was watching him out of the corner of his eye and he knew his boss's sense of integrity would drive him to tell Jack Terry or the D.A. if Wesley reneged on Carlotta's promise. Plus telling Hannah would be like shouting the truth from the top of the Bank of America building with a megaphone.

"She's…gone," was all he could manage to say.

"Omigod, omigod, omigod!" Hannah screamed, then burst into new tears.

Wesley held the phone away from his ear and winced.

"I knew she was depressed but I didn't think she'd kill herself! Oh, fuck! Wesley, you must be out of your mind."

For going along with this ruse. "Yeah," he murmured. "But I really don't want to talk right now."

"I understand," she said through her sobs. "But call if you need help with the…arrangements. God, I can't believe we're talking about Carlotta's funeral."

"I know—it's surreal."

She heaved a long, shuddering sigh. "I guess this means you'll be taking some time off work. Tell Coop that I'll be glad to fill in."

Wesley bit back a smile. "I will."

"And Wesley, there's one thing you should know…your father called Carlotta Sunday."

He nearly dropped the phone. *"What?"*

"At least she thought it was him. She wasn't sure. Before she could say anything, she dropped her cell phone and broke it. Do you think that had something to do with her suicide?"

Wesley's mind reeled. How could Carlotta keep something like that from him? "I can say for a certainty, Hannah, that it didn't. I have to go. Bye." He shoved his phone back in his pocket, feeling as if he might explode. Was that why Carlotta had gone along with this scam, because she thought their father was nearby?

"I'm sure Hannah's all broken up," Coop said.

"Yeah," he managed, trying to act as if nothing were wrong, when everything was. "And she said she'd be glad to fill in for me if you need help."

Coop grimaced. "Christ, I'm going to have to call her, aren't I?"

"Sooner or later." His lips moved, but his mind raced with the thought that his father had called Carlotta and he immediately wondered why *he* hadn't heard from him. After a couple of minutes of near-panic, he realized he had to get a grip. He tried to calm himself with Hannah's words that Carlotta hadn't been sure it *was* their father.

His thoughts moved to how quickly Hannah had been willing to believe that Carlotta had killed herself simply because she'd been moping around lately. Indeed, the number of suicides he'd attended since starting this job only a few weeks ago was shocking—and here they were handling another one.

"Why do you think people kill themselves?" he asked Coop.

Coop shrugged. "It's easier than facing their demons. Death can be very...*alluring* to someone who's disenchanted with life."

"Have you ever thought about it?" Wesley asked, then held his breath.

"No," Coop said earnestly. "I've indulged in self-destructive behavior, but being surrounded by death has given me an appreciation for life. It's taken me a while to realize it, but dammit, I want to be happy." He gave Wesley a little smile. "After this run, what do you say we stop in and check on your sister?"

Wesley wondered briefly if Coop would make Carlotta happy. "I say that's a good idea."

After all, he had a bone to pick with his dear, departed sister.

18

Carlotta peeked out the slit in the curtain and exhaled. "It's just our neighbor, Mrs. Winningham, the nosiest woman on the face of the earth."

"Are you two close?" Jack asked.

"Hardly. She thinks that Wesley and I are dragging down the neighborhood."

"What's she holding?"

"Looks like a casserole. She probably came to get the scoop on my demise in exchange for potato salad."

"Did your parents know her?"

"She was here when we moved here, yeah."

"I guess I'm asking if there's a chance that they know her well enough to approach her about delivering a message to you."

Like her father had with Peter. "I don't think so," she said dryly. "My mother refused to talk to the neighbors because she was convinced that moving here was an illusion and we'd be back in our big house soon."

Jack backed away from the window, apparently willing to let Mrs. Winningham believe that no one was home. "Tell me about your parents."

She shrugged as she made her way back to the kitchen. Her appetite had vanished, but she was craving a cigarette and hoped a cup of coffee would quiet the urge. "You have the files on them."

He settled back into his place at the table and resumed eating. "Tell me something that isn't in the files."

"Coffee?"

"Sure."

As she poured them each a cup, she mentally sifted through all the stored memories about her parents, conceding that the more recent bad memories had written over some previous good ones like a computer hard drive. She set his mug down next to his plate, then leaned against the counter. Her hands suddenly seemed very cold and cradling the hot coffee felt good. "They were a beautiful couple," she said finally.

"I've seen pictures. You look like your mother."

"She was much prettier."

"That's debatable."

She let the compliment pass, uncomfortable with this sense of intimacy that had settled around them. "And Wesley looks like my father."

"Were they good parents?"

She scoffed. "You mean before they abandoned us? I guess so. They weren't mean to us and we were well provided for."

"But?" he probed, his dark eyes searching.

"But my father worked all the time and my mother drank all the time."

"Oh."

Carlotta sipped from her cup. "I'll bet your parents were the salt of the earth, weren't they?"

He nodded. "Still are."

"That's nice."

"I'm lucky."

It was her turn to nod. "But I have Wesley, so that makes me lucky."

"Despite the trouble he's been in?"

"Yeah."

"You love him like a mother."

"I don't know. I suppose. All I know is that he's the only person in this world I truly care about."

His mouth lifted in a smile. "Then he's the lucky one."

She smiled back. "He's good to me too. He cooks for me. And he bought me that monstrosity of a television in there."

"That must have set him back a pretty penny."

"He sold his motorcycle."

"Is he still making payments to his loan sharks?"

She frowned and gave him a pointed look. "I'm going to stop talking. You know way too much about my family."

"Fair enough," Jack said, picking up their plates and setting them in the sink. "I need to get to work anyway."

"Doing what?"

"Surveilling," he said, mimicking her. "I'm going to set up

some cameras so I can keep an eye on things outside. Mind if I look around?"

"As if I could stop you." She pushed away from the counter to follow him.

He walked into the living room and checked the view from both windows without moving the curtains. To her consternation Carlotta found herself checking out the view of him from behind, how the expanse of his shoulders tapered to a narrow waist. She couldn't remember when she'd been so physically aware of a man…but then again, when had she been in such close quarters with a man other than Wesley?

"What's the story behind the Christmas tree?" he asked mildly.

She glanced over to the corner at the small aluminum tree that had lost much of its luster over the past ten years and had suffered much abuse. "My mother put it up before she…left."

"And you didn't want to take it down?"

"Wesley wouldn't let me."

"And the gifts underneath?"

"We never opened them."

His eyes widened. "Never? Didn't it cross your mind that they might have left a clue inside as to where they'd gone?"

"Yes, but I promised Wesley I wouldn't open them. It meant a lot to him that we wait until our parents came home."

"I'm surprised the police didn't go through them when your parents first disappeared."

"We hid them."

Jack went over and picked up the small gifts, shaking them.

"You could open them now, Carlotta, and this might all be over. Wesley wouldn't have to know."

She walked over and took a gift from him, this one wrapped in "Ho, Ho, Ho" red and green paper, the cellophane tape now yellowed and brittle. "Yes, he would. I'm not going back on my word to him."

He circled his hand around her wrist and suddenly the air was sexually charged. "Carlotta Wren," he murmured. "I can't figure you out. You keep throwing me curve balls."

Her throat closed as his gold-colored eyes locked with her gaze and his touch seemed to seep into her skin. "Jack, I don't understand sports analogies. And I don't know if I can trust you."

"That's wise of you," he murmured, lowering his mouth to within an inch of hers. "Around you, I don't trust me either."

His breath brushed her lips and she felt herself sinking into him. He was giving her the chance to pull away, to run, to slap him. Instead she flicked out her tongue and coaxed his mouth to hers. He descended with a groan, searing his lips against hers in a scorching kiss that sent desire coursing through her body. His tongue delved deeper into her mouth as the kiss grew in intensity, both of them fighting for breath. At the sound of something hitting the floor, she realized distantly that she'd dropped the wrapped gift, but the thought was quickly overridden with wonder that her body was alive—and on fire.

She fisted her hands in his shirt as he slid his hands down her back and over her rear, molding her body to his. Shock waves vibrated through her breasts and thighs, and longing erupted in her midsection.

"I've wanted you," he said against her lips, "since the first time I laid eyes on you."

She sighed into his mouth, reveling in the wall of warm, muscled body all but enveloping her. The scent of strong soap and minty aftershave filled her lungs, strumming her senses higher. Through their clothing, she could feel the ridge of his erection pressing into her stomach. She rocked her hips against his—closer, tighter, harder—

"What the hell's going on here?"

Jack released her and she jerked toward the noise and the breeze. Wesley and Coop stood at the front door staring at them. Wesley looked appalled and Coop looked—disappointed?

19

Carlotta's stomach bottomed out as Wesley turned his fury upon Jack. He strode forward and shouted, "Is this why you concocted this whole charade, *Detective?* So you could get into this house and into my sister's pants?"

"No," Jack bit out, hands jammed on hips. A muscle worked in his jaw.

Her full-body flush of desire morphed into mortification. "Wesley—"

"How could you?" he said to her, his face twisted in disgust. "This guy arrested me and is trying to trap Dad, and you're....*fooling* around with him? Whose side are you on?"

Her heart squeezed. "Wesley—"

"This is none of your business, son," Jack said, stepping forward. "This is between your sister and me."

Wesley's mouth tightened and his face turned scarlet.

"I'm not your son. And the deal's off. I'm not pretending anymore."

"Nothing has changed," Jack said quietly, "including the deal." He looked at Coop, who had averted his gaze. "Close the door, Coop."

Coop looked at her, then Jack, his expression unreadable. "I think I'd better go."

"Take Wesley with you," Jack said.

"Yeah, we were just…checking in. Come on, Wes. We need to get back to work."

Wesley set his jaw, beseeching her with his eyes to fix things—to call off the deal with the D.A. and send Jack Terry on his way.

"Go, Wesley," she said evenly. "You don't have to worry about anything here."

His shoulders fell and he fairly shook with anger, but with a parting glare at Jack, he shoved past Coop and disappeared through the door.

Coop exchanged a wordless glance with Jack that excluded her completely, then he turned and walked out, pulling the door closed behind him.

For several long seconds she and Jack stood in the silence that sucked at the room. Carlotta closed her eyes and berated herself for her lapse. If she could've done only one thing to complicate the already messy situation, it would be to body-kiss Jack Terry.

Minus ten points.

As proof, her body was still tingling in the aftermath. A reminder of how long it had been since she'd had sex—so long that a man she *disliked* could get her engine revving. As of now, she officially had no pride. Not sure what to expect, she turned toward him.

"Jack—"

"Carlotta—"

They stopped and looked at each other. Regret and remorse filled every line on his rugged face and she was certain hers was equally telltale.

"Me first," he said, pulling a hand down his face. "I like you—more than I should. But—"

"But we can't do this," she finished. "It would be completely inappropriate."

"Right. I could lose my job."

"And I'm not looking for complications."

He nodded. "So, for now I guess we should just agree to resist."

"Right," she said, crossing her arms. "We're adults. We don't have to act on every…urge."

"It wouldn't have happened if not for the close quarters," he agreed.

"As long as we try to avoid each other—"

"And stay busy—"

"This should work out—"

"Just fine."

She inhaled, then exhaled slowly. "So…I suppose you want to see the rest of the house."

He nodded, but clearly was still preoccupied.

Tamping down the vestiges of lust that still pulsed through

her body, she ushered him down the hall to Wesley's room on the left. Its bedroom window faced the front yard.

"I remember the snake from before," Jack said, eyeing the aquarium with Wesley's six-foot python curled inside.

"That's Einstein," she supplied from the doorway. "The bane of my existence, but Wesley adores the thing."

He fingered aside the blind that covered the window. "Same view as the living room."

He came back out into the hallway and she closed the door behind him. "And you've seen my room," she said lightly, opening the door a few inches. "No windows."

"Uh-huh." He gave her a teasing grin. "The day we searched the house and arrested Wesley, I thought your room belonged to a teenager."

Heat flooded her cheeks as she surveyed the childish white bed and matching dresser, chest of drawers and vanity.

"It's still the same as when your parents left, isn't it?"

She nodded as she closed the door. "We haven't exactly had the money to redecorate."

"I think you've left things the same on purpose."

"That's ridiculous." Irritated at how quickly the man could trigger a 180-degree mood swing, she led him farther down the hall to her parents' bedroom and opened the door onto the dated decor that was perfectly frozen in time.

Jack gave her a pointed look. "You were saying?"

She heard him distantly, but like every time she opened this door—which wasn't often—Carlotta was swept up in the past.

The room was basically the way her parents had left it.

When it had become clear that they were missing, the police had searched the room—the entire house—removing calendars, letters, photographs and financial records. She remembered righting overturned bottles on her mother's vanity, picking up her father's ties and returning them to his cherrywood valet stand. A layer of dust coated most things, making them fuzzy and indistinct.

"Wesley cleans in here sometimes," she murmured, touching an empty picture frame that had once held her parent's wedding photo. "In the weeks after they first left, I had to drag him out of here. He was convinced our parents were hiding somewhere, and would check under the bed and the closet compulsively." She shook her head at the memory.

"I've gone through the boxes of items that were removed from the house," Jack said, walking around, opening and closing random drawers.

Carlotta crossed her arms and hugged herself. "And did you find anything helpful?"

"No." He walked over to the closet door and opened it. Her parents' clothes were wedged inside and dozens of shoe boxes were stacked on the floor. "Looks like they didn't take much with them when they left."

"That's right. A few clothes and my mother's good jewelry." Apparently they'd wanted to cut ties with everything from their previous life—keepsakes, friendships, their children.

"The car they were driving was found abandoned in Alabama, but there were no signs of foul play."

"Wesley was sure they'd been kidnapped."

"What happened to the car?"

"Impounded, like mine," she said with false cheer.

He frowned. "It was never returned to you?"

"It went back to the bank."

"Oh. When did you receive the first postcard?"

Carlotta sighed. "We've been over this."

"Remind me."

"About six months after they first disappeared. It was post-marked Michigan."

"But you didn't turn the postcard over to the police?"

"No. I didn't trust anyone."

"Not even Liz, your father's attorney?"

She smirked. "Especially Liz."

Jack must have picked up on her desire to change the subject because he strode to the window and opened the mini-blinds a sliver. "What about the neighbors on the other side? Did they know your parents?"

"No. It's a gay couple. They moved in about five years ago, so they never met my parents."

"I'll set up a camera here, one in the living room and one in the kitchen. I can set up a monitor—to oversee everything—on the bar in the kitchen."

"Fine," she said, feeling stiff and disconnected from the situation. Eager to leave the room that still smelled faintly of her parents, she turned to go.

Jack clasped her arm, stopped her. "Hey."

His golden eyes pinned her to the spot like a butterfly being trapped for a bug collection. "What?"

"Aren't you a little excited at the possibility of seeing your parents again after all these years, of at least knowing that they're alive?"

Her chest felt constricted under an avalanche of emotion, compounded by Jack Terry's confusing touch. Once again she considered telling him that her father had called her and Peter, but at this stage, it seemed pointless. In fact, lately everything seemed pointless. She exhaled slowly to steady her voice. "I just want all of this to be over, Detective. And just maybe my brother and I can get our lives back on track. Back to the way they were supposed to be."

His fingers tightened around her arm. "Do you really think you'd be happier if your life had continued on the path your parents had you on?"

The sound of a car pulling into the driveway caught their attention. Carlotta's heart beat wildly. Jack released her arm to discreetly lift one of the slats, then his mouth dove in a frown. "Speaking of history, your boyfriend is here."

20

"I could kill him!" Wesley seethed, pounding his fist on the dashboard of the van. The image of his sister welded to Detective Jack Terry was burned into his brain.

"Settle down," Coop said, staring straight ahead to the road. "Breaking your hand won't accomplish anything."

"And Carlotta—"

"Is human, Wesley. And I've got a news bulletin for you— she's also a woman. A damn good-looking woman who, by your own admission, has spent the better part of her life taking care of you."

Wesley ground his teeth. Nothing made him more angry than the truth.

"Has it ever occurred to you that your sister might be lonely?"

"Dude, I try not to think about my sister in that way."

Coop smiled. "I know. I have a sister. But like it or not, Carlotta has the right to have a life of her own. One that includes a man—"

"Okay, enough already. I'm not a prude, I'm just questioning her taste. Here I was worried that she was going to go back to that asshole Peter Ashford, only to find her playing tongue-tennis with that cop."

Coop's hands tightened on the steering wheel. "I don't like it any more than you do, but she's a full-grown woman and she has the right to make her own decisions."

"Even bad ones?"

"Yeah, even bad ones."

"What if he…coerced her?"

"Carlotta looks like she can take care of herself in that department and from where I was standing, she wasn't exactly fighting him off."

"I just don't get what she sees in someone like him."

"He did save her life in the Angela Ashford murder case."

"But he's a jerk!"

Coop shrugged. "Some women like guys with a hard edge—the gun, the badge, the bravado. They think it's exciting, I guess."

"Where does that leave guys like us?"

Coop looked over. "With lots of hobbies."

Wesley didn't add that most of his anger toward his sister was rooted in the fact that she hadn't told him that their father had called. Christ, even if she wasn't sure it was Dad, she should have told him about it.

Wesley's phone vibrated in his pocket. He pulled it out to

glance at the caller-ID screen and an involuntary smile curled his mouth.

Coop slowed the van. "Is it one of your parents?"

"No, my probation officer."

"Oh." Amusement played on Coop's face. "You'd better get it then."

Wesley connected the call, remembering to sound casual. "Yeah."

E.'s voice came over the line. "Is this Wesley?"

"Yeah."

"Wesley, this is Eldora Jones. How are you?"

His eyebrows climbed. So the "E" stood for Eldora—nice. "I'm fine," he said, fumbling. "Great, actually."

"Great?" She sounded puzzled. "I heard on the news that your sister died."

"Oh." His stomach dropped with a thud when he remembered the lie he was supposed to be upholding. And if he divulged the truth to E., it might get back to the D.A. "Um…" He stalled for time to inject a believable note of sadness into his voice. "I mean great considering…what happened."

At his pitiful-sounding voice, Coop gave him a sideways glance.

She made a mournful noise. "I'm so sorry, Wesley. I know that you and your sister were very close. I can't believe how brave you're being."

Brave? He sniffed. "That's because I know that my sister is in a better place."

Coop's eyebrow shot up.

"Your entire family, gone," she said tearfully.

"Yeah," he responded with a heavy sigh, "I'm all alone now."

Coop rolled his eyes.

"Wesley, my heart is broken for you. Is there anything I can do?"

He pursed his mouth—he hadn't counted on the sympathy that would be coming his way once the news of Carlotta's "suicide" got out.

"I don't know," he began, wondering how much he could push his luck. All kinds of carnal images of E. comforting him cartwheeled through his mind.

"I already arranged for your community service to be pushed back," she said. "I called Mr. McCormick to let him know what happened."

Wesley frowned. If his community service was postponed, it would be that much longer until he could start delving into his father's case records. In fact, Kelvin Lucas might cancel his community service altogether as part of the deal his sister had struck.

Damn.

"And I'd like to attend the service if you're going to have one."

"Uh…I haven't decided yet."

"I understand," she said softly. "Will you let me know?"

"Sure."

"And let me know if there's anything I can do."

A tiny pang of guilt stabbed his chest, then dissipated. "I will. Thanks for calling." He disconnected the call, then flushed when he realized Coop was looking at him, shaking his head.

"What?" Wesley demanded.

"How hot is she?"

Wesley considered lying, but changed his mind. "Very."

"Milking the situation a little, aren't you?"

"Might as well get something out of it."

"Seems to me you're the one benefiting the most all the way around."

The words cut deep. Wesley bit down on his tongue until the blast of pain matched the level of his anger. "I didn't make the deal."

Coop narrowed his eyes. "What are you going to do if your father contacts you directly?"

Wesley turned his head away from Coop.

"Wesley, answer me."

He looked back. "I'm not going to give him up." Then he glared at Coop. "Are you going to tell the detective?"

Coop didn't say anything for a few seconds, then murmured, "No. It's your family's business."

"Thanks."

"Besides, maybe you'll get lucky," Coop said mildly. "Maybe he won't make his presence known at all."

Wesley chewed on his sore tongue. "Are you saying that my parents won't care that Carlotta's dead?"

"No—"

"Because they care," he cut in, hating the defensive squeak in his voice.

Coop looked sympathetic. "I'm saying that maybe your dad will sense it's a trap."

Wesley chewed on the skin around his thumbnail. That

would definitely explain why his parents would stay away, be-cause they did care, dammit.

His phone vibrated again. He glanced at the screen and saw it was Chance calling. "It's a friend. Do I have time to take this?"

"Yeah, we're still about five minutes away from our pickup. In fact, after this one I can take you back home if you want."

Wesley made a face. "No way I'm going back as long as that cop is there." He connected the call. "Hey buddy, what's up?"

"Man, I just heard about your sister. Fuck, I'm sorry as hell."

"Oh. It's okay, man."

"Did she really take a dive off the Seventeenth Street bridge?"

"Uh…yeah."

"Christ, did you have to view the body?"

"Uh…no."

"Oh." Chance sounded disappointed. "The news said she was depressed or something."

"Uh-huh."

"Damn, did she have to do a base jump without a rope? Why couldn't she just slit her wrists and bleed out in the bath-tub like most chicks? Or take a handful of sleeping pills? I could've gotten her all the Valium she wanted."

"Er…thanks, man."

"Are you having a funeral?"

"I don't know."

"If you are, I can get you a casket cheap. Display model."

"Er…thanks." Chance meant well. "There is one thing you can do for me."

"Name it, man."

"Can I crash in your spare room for a while?"

"Sure. I don't blame you for not wanting to be in the house alone."

Wesley smirked. It had more to do with the fact that if his dad *did* show up at the house, he didn't want to be there when the net was lowered. "Okay, I'll be there in a couple of hours."

"Cool. This dying shit calls for an expensive bottle of Kentucky bourbon. We'll tie one on to make you feel better, dude."

Wesley shook his head, suspecting that Chance would get a head start on the planned drinking binge. "Okay, later." He disconnected the call.

Coop cleared his throat. "I couldn't help overhearing. You're going to leave Carlotta alone in the house tonight?"

"She won't be alone, remember?"

"Yeah, I remember." Coop shifted in his seat. "Do you think it's wise to leave her—them—alone?"

Wesley shrugged, enjoying his boss's discomfiture. "You were the one who said she was a full-grown woman who had the right to make her own decisions."

Coop frowned. "Even bad ones?"

Wesley reached over to clap his hand on the shoulder of his lovesick boss. "Yeah dude, even bad ones."

21

"I'll answer the door," Carlotta said, pushing past Jack.

Jack snagged her arm. "You're not supposed to be seen, re-member? And for that matter, neither am I."

"But Peter won't leave," she said, wondering suddenly if her father had been in touch with him again.

Jack gave her a wry look. "Yeah, I kind of noticed that he's hard to get rid of."

The doorbell rang and Jack cursed under his breath as he strode toward it. He unlocked the door, then quickly stood to the side and yelled, "Get in here, Ashford!"

The door opened and Peter walked in, pinning a glare on Jack. Then his gaze landed on her and his face softened.

"Close the door," Jack ordered. "What the hell are you doing here?"

Peter scowled. "I came to see Carly."

"You shouldn't be here. This is an active investigation."

Carlotta stepped forward, irritated with Jack. One kiss and the man was starting to act possessive. "Detective, don't you have cameras to install?"

Jack frowned in her direction, then picked up the huge black duffel bag and moved into the kitchen.

She waited until he was out of earshot before asking, "Is something wrong?"

Peter reached for her hand. "Only that I'm scared all over again every time I hear something on the news about you taking your own life. I had to see you."

"I'm fine," she murmured.

"Holed up in this house with that Neanderthal?"

"I heard that," Jack called from the kitchen.

She sighed and pulled Peter farther away, toward the hallway. "Peter, he's just doing his job. Besides, Wesley will be here with me." She glanced toward the kitchen to make sure Jack wasn't still listening and whispered, "Have you heard from my father?"

He shook his head. "No, but the thought crossed my mind that he might call again. I don't suppose that you or Wesley have heard from him?"

"No."

"What should I do if he does call me?"

Carlotta worried her lower lip. "Play along, try to get him to come to the house or to my memorial service."

He grimaced. "They're having a funeral for you?"

"If it comes to that."

"So you've decided to turn him in."

She nodded. "It'll be the best thing for me and Wesley, I think. To put this mess behind us."

"And start over?" Peter asked hopefully.

After an uncomfortable few seconds, she nodded again.

"Then why don't you just tell the police that your father called us and let them trace the calls?"

"Because the D.A. is offering incentive if I go along with his plan. If I told him, he'd probably remove his offer from the table."

"Does this have something to do with the reward money?"

She blinked. "You know about that?"

He lifted his hands. "It's folklore within the company—that the partners were so furious when your father left town that they offered a reward for information that would lead to his capture."

"I had no idea," she murmured. "Jack told me about it only this morning." Then Carlotta flushed with embarrassment. "Yes, the D.A. said if we went along and my father came forward, he would make sure we got the reward money." She wet her lips. "I know it sounds…callous, but it would be enough to send Wesley to a good college."

"You don't owe me an explanation," he said gently.

"Peter, you could have simply told someone about the phone call and maybe collected that reward money for yourself."

His eyes clouded. "I could never do that."

She smiled up at him, her heart expanding with affection.

"Excuse me," Jack said, making a noisy entrance into the living room with a camera and yards of wiring.

Peter frowned in his direction. "Have you found out yet who was impersonating Carly?"

"Not yet, Ashford. There's only one of me."

"And for that we are eternally thankful," Peter muttered. Then he looked at Carlotta. "I should go."

"Yes, you should," Jack said. "And don't come back until this is over, got it?"

Peter's mouth tightened, but he nodded curtly.

Carlotta touched his arm. "I'll see you soon."

He leaned down, brushed a kiss on her cheek and whispered, "Call me if you need me. Keep your bedroom door locked." He inclined his head. "Detective."

"Ashford."

When Jack had closed the door behind the man, he arched his eyebrow at her. "A kiss on the cheek?"

She crossed her arms, rankled that he had her comparing their two kisses. "He's being sweet. You've never kissed a girl on the cheek?"

"Yeah, my mother." He carefully situated the camera on the window ledge and checked a small handheld monitor. "And what was all that whispering about?"

"Nothing," she said casually. "Peter just wanted to make sure I was okay."

"You certainly have your share of watchdogs."

Her cheeks flamed at the reference to them having been caught in the act by Wesley and Coop. To change the subject, she went to look over his shoulder. "How does this work?"

"Simple—the cameras send images to this monitor. I can

watch all three camera views from the kitchen, if you don't mind me setting up shop in there. That'll give me the chance to make some phone calls."

As if on cue, the phone rang and her heart hammered until the voice of a credit card employee came over the phone, telling her in a menacing voice that if she didn't make the minimum payment on her balance, her account would be turned over to a collection agency.

When the message ended, she sighed, too tired to be embarrassed.

"I take it you get lots of those types of calls," he said.

"Yes, Detective, I do."

He kept working. "You know that makes you a good target for identity theft."

She frowned. "Why?"

"Because you said yourself that you don't check your statements, and that you're always behind on your bills. Someone could've been using your credit cards and driver's license for months and you wouldn't have known it.'

"I don't need a lecture, Jack."

"I didn't mean to lecture. I'm just pointing out how things like this happen."

She snapped her fingers. "You thought you saw me at the ATM at my bank on Piedmont?"

"Right."

"Maybe it was the woman who stole my identity."

He pursed his mouth. "It's a good place to start."

"And Hannah said she thought she saw me jogging around here."

"I take it, it wasn't you?"

"No, I don't like breaking a sweat."

His eyebrows arched, causing her to squirm.

"But maybe it's the same woman. If so, maybe she lives nearby."

"Okay," Jack nodded. "All possibilities."

"The driver's license, was it a fake?"

"No, it was a copy of your actual license, easy enough to obtain by mail with the right information. I have a call into the DMV to fax me a copy of the request."

He picked up more equipment and carried it down the hall to her parents' bedroom. Carlotta took the opportunity to slip into her bedroom and ferret out a pack of ultra-light cigarettes from her underwear drawer. She turned on her stereo and went into the bathroom and sat down on the lid of the commode to light up.

Her lighter was on the fritz, but she finally got a flame going. The first drag on the cigarette was like nirvana. She felt like a junkie pulling the smoke into her lungs and reveling in the first tickle as the nicotine rushed into her bloodstream. Instantly, her life seemed better—more tolerable, less complicated. All she had to focus on at the moment was inhaling and exhaling. That was doable.

A screaming siren rent the air, sending her heart to her throat. It took her a few seconds to realize that the fire alarm above her was going off. "Dammit," she muttered, standing on the commode to wave the air beneath the alarm frantically. The siren was deafening and relentless. She put the cigarette in her mouth so she could wave with both hands.

"It might help if you put out the cigarette," Jack said dryly.

She looked down to see him standing in the open doorway. He calmly reached forward and plucked the cigarette from her mouth and extinguished it in a pool of water sitting in the sink. Then he used the door to fan the room clear of smoke, silencing the siren.

"What is this, high school?" he asked, extending his hand to help her down.

"No," she said primly, accepting his hand to lower herself to the ground. "I don't want Wesley to know that I smoke— occasionally. I don't want to be a bad influence on him."

Jack rolled his eyes. "Admirable, but I'm sure if Wesley wanted to smoke, he'd smoke."

She frowned. "Are you finished with the cameras?"

"Are you finished trying to set the house on fire?"

"Do you have to criticize everything I do? I'm doing the best I can." To Carlotta's mortification, tears welled in her eyes.

"Hey," he said gently, reaching out to tug on her arm. "I was teasing you. Don't cry. It's the only situation that the academy doesn't prepare us for."

She laughed and wiped at her eyes. "Sorry, I'm having a bad decade. The cigarettes, they give me something to do with my hands."

He grinned. "Well, if that's all you want, I could think of some alternatives."

She pursed her mouth. "Jack, we can't."

He lifted his hands. "What? I just meant that I have my laptop and you can help me with the investigation into your twin."

"That would be my *dead* twin."

"Right."

She sighed. "Give me a few minutes to clean up in here, then I'll join you."

"Okay." Then he smiled a smile that made her breath catch and she had a crystal clear image of a dedicated man just doing his job, caught in the turbulence of Randolph Wren's destructive wake, just like her. And she had information that could possibly bring an end to the turmoil more swiftly than this agonizing waiting game.

"Jack?" she said, struck with the urge to confess.

He turned back. "What?"

Then she remembered their earlier conversation. Being adults meant they didn't have to act on every urge.

"Never mind."

22

The rest of the day passed in relative quiet, considering the prior few weeks of Carlotta's life. The best thing about being dead, she realized, was that for the most part no one expected much from you.

Except your creditors.

Four more collection agencies called, with ominous warnings that she would regret not making arrangements to get her account up-to-date. With those words ringing in her head, Carlotta dove into the basket of unopened bills and began to try to decipher just how bad things were.

Using a service available to law enforcement, Jack ordered credit reports on her social security number from all three reporting bureaus. "Might as well get your cell-phone records, too."

"Is that necessary?" she asked, wondering if the call from her father would somehow stand out.

"Since we know that someone bought an unauthorized phone on your account, it's one of our best leads."

If someone else was using her phone number or account, it would be the perfect way to explain away a strange phone number. Or she could always say that she answered the call, but no one responded.

If the Wrens had one talent, it was telling a good lie.

Plus ten points.

"What was the name of the florist who delivered the roses?"

"I don't remember," she said.

"Would you know it if you saw it again?"

"Maybe."

He handed her the four-inch thick A to K volume of the Atlanta yellow pages and she begrudgingly turned to florists.

An hour later, to take a break from the yellow pages, she decided to clean the house. Armed with a vacuum and a can of Pledge, she gave the place a once-over to remove the worst of the accumulated dust and grime. From multiple surfaces in her bedroom, she gathered enough clothing for two loads of laundry—including Jack's handkerchief that he'd wrapped around her thorn-bitten finger—and found a missing shoe.

All the while, Jack sat at the kitchen counter like an automaton and monitored the surveillance cameras, but only a kid selling magazines stopped by, and later Hannah to put a black wreath on the door.

Carlotta wanted to go to her, but Jack was adamant. So with a heavy heart she watched her Goth-garbed friend trudge back to her refrigerated van, grimacing at making her cry off her black eyeliner and blow her pierced nose.

"If you don't mind me asking," Jack said, wincing at the monitor, "how on earth did the two of you become friends?"

"Uh…I don't think I want to tell you."

He lifted a dark eyebrow. "At the risk of incriminating yourself?"

"It's not like we did anything illegal…really."

"You talking about the party-crashing?"

"Yeah. She was catering a big party and let me in through the kitchen. We've been friends ever since."

"Charming."

"I knew I shouldn't have said anything."

"I'm just not into parties and fancy events. I look for excuses to get out of those kinds of things."

"Like your awards dinner?" she asked, wondering if he'd go alone.

He pursed his lips, then nodded.

"So you never did tell me what the award is for."

Jack shrugged. "It's not for anything in particular I did."

"Does this have something to do with the comment the D.A. made when he reopened my father's case that you always get your man?"

The color rose in his cheeks. "I guess I have a pretty good success rate in the department."

And bringing in Randolph Wren would be another feather in his cap. Pushing aside the disturbing thought, she asked, "So Jack, what's your idea of a fun night out?"

"You mean on a date?"

"It's hard to imagine you on a date. I'm being hypothetical."

"Well, anything centered around a steak dinner generally makes me pretty happy."

"Figures," she said. "I don't like red meat."

"See," he said mildly, never looking up from the monitor, "it would never work out between us."

"I didn't say I've never eaten it," she muttered. "It's just not my favorite. I mean, sometimes even *I* get a craving for a big steak."

He glanced up from the monitor. "Can we change the subject please?"

"Okay, what exactly do you plan to do if my parents show up?"

"Take them into custody."

"And haul them off to jail?"

"I'd probably get a uniform here to do the transport."

"And then what?"

"And then I'll help the D.A. make his case."

"Has it ever occurred to you that my father might be innocent?"

To her surprise, Jack nodded. "Sure. But you have to admit that his actions are more indicative of someone who's guilty."

"Or someone who's been framed?"

He squinted. "Is that what you think?"

She shrugged. "I'm just asking if my father shows up, do you think he'll get a fair shake? Kelvin Lucas seems to be gunning for him."

"Lucas has been known to bear a grudge, but I have confidence in the legal system. Unfortunately, your father has compounded the initial investment fraud charges by choosing to become a fugitive. Those charges will be harder to dispute." He leveled his gaze on Carlotta. "And in my book, those are the more serious charges because he abandoned his family."

Peter was willing to forgive her father, but Jack looked as if he wouldn't mind taking a swing at Randolph Wren. And at the moment, she appreciated his anger on her behalf. Jack was the kind of man who respected physical and personal strength, the kind of man who would never walk away from a family obligation.

Did that explain why he shied away from having a family of his own? Because he knew it would take an emotional toll on him?

And was that why she too, avoided relationships that became too personal? Because she wasn't willing to be so tied down, so obligated?

They both seemed to turn inward as the afternoon wore on. Occasionally, Jack asked her for a piece of personal information to gather more background on her financial records. By the time this investigation was over, she thought ruefully, she would have no secrets from him.

And hadn't that been her original perception of him—that if she spent a lot of time in his company, she would feel compelled to share more about her life than was healthy?

She waited all day for her friend Michael Lane to call and at least ask about a memorial service in her honor; she was closer to him than anyone else at work. Instead, Patricia Alexander called and left a high-pitched message that "all of Carlotta's coworkers at Neiman Marcus were just devastated by the news of her death" and would like to be informed if the family was planning a memorial service. Carlotta snorted. She was sure that Patricia was torn up about her competition being out of the picture. The stick woman was probably doing cartwheels now that she thought Carlotta's job would be hers permanently. Lindy probably wouldn't say anything to Patricia about the ruse, but her boss might have let Michael in on the secret, which would explain why he hadn't called.

She bit into her lip. But then again, maybe people just really didn't care that she was gone. It wasn't as if she'd made a difference in anyone's life. Other than Hannah, she didn't have many truly close friends. Jolie Goodman had been a good friend to her, despite the fact that she and Hannah had pulled Jolie into party-crashing and had gotten all of them in trouble way over their heads. But Jolie had met the man of her dreams and moved to Costa Rica. Her parting gift to Carlotta had been a new autograph book—since her original had been ruined in one of their escapades—and enough cash to get the loan sharks off her back, sparing the life of Carlotta's precious little white Miata which remained crippled in the garage, but intact. She would always be grateful to Jolie.

Most of her former friends—girls who had once been her social peers—would probably find her death more interesting than her life. Over an expensive lunch at the club, they would shake their heads and say it was such a shame that Carlotta Wren's situation had degraded to the point that she had taken her own life…no doubt, Peter Ashford had rejected her again…and just like Carlotta to go out on a headline…she always had been so greedy for attention….

Just as dusk was descending, the phone rang again and Carlotta braced for another bill collector to tell her what a bad person she was. Instead, Wesley's voice came on the line. "Hey, it's me. Just wanted to let you know that I'm staying at Chance's until this is over. Later."

Carlotta froze in the ensuing silence, afraid to make eye contact with Jack, wondering if he, too, had been jolted by the news that the two of them would be spending the night in the house alone.

"Since it's going to be just the two of us," Jack said, removing his suit jacket and loosening his bad tie, "why don't we order a pizza?"

"Fine with me," she managed.

"Fellini's is the best," they said in unison, then laughed.

"At least we agree on pizza." He reached for the phone. "How do you feel about the Braves?"

"Baseball is okay," she said. "I have a lot of the players' autographs."

"Good girl."

His intended compliment unnerved her, as well as the thought that this was shaping up to be a rather cozy night in. Especially since they were keeping the lights low to minimize the chance that someone would see her silhouette.

"Do you want a beer?" Carlotta offered.

"I'd love one," Jack said, "but I can't drink on the job. Soda or water is fine."

By the time the pizza had arrived, Jack had moved the surveillance equipment to the living room where he kept one eye on the monitor and one eye on the Braves game. "This is some television," he said with a certain amount of awe in his voice as he set the pizza box on the coffee table in front of the couch.

"The players' heads are bigger than mine," Carlotta observed. "A television is too big when you have to move your head to see the entire screen."

He laughed. "It's a guy thing."

"So I gathered. Jack…what do you think a TV like this would cost?"

"Around ten thousand."

She nearly choked on her soda.

"Let me guess. Wesley's motorcycle wasn't worth that?"

"No."

"So where do you think he got the money?"

"I'd rather not say." The last thing she needed was for Jack to report something that might extend Wesley's probation. And while there were flashes of moments where she trusted Jack, this wasn't one of those moments.

"I understand," Jack said. "But if he's doing something shady, Carlotta, you know that in the long run, it's going to catch up to him."

Instead of responding, she bit into a slice of pizza.

Over the course of nine innings, they devoured the pizza and a two-liter bottle of soda. The game was close and had them shouting on more than one occasion, but she noticed that Jack often checked the camera monitor. Near the end of the game, something on the monitor caught his attention.

Carlotta's pulse blipped. "Do you see something?"

"Someone in the back yard," he murmured.

Carlotta leaned in to look closer at the image moving in the dark and when she saw the watering can, she relaxed. "It's just one of my neighbors watering their flowers."

"The nosy one?"

"No, one of the gay guys."

"What do they do for a living?"

"I don't know. We've never really had a conversation. I think they must run some kind of Internet business because they're always having packages delivered and picked up."

He nodded, then watched until the guy reentered his house via the solarium that Mrs. Winningham so resented because it blocked her view of the rest of the neighbors in their back-yards.

When they turned back to the game and sank into the cushions on the couch, she realized that somehow the distance between them on the couch had closed and their bodies sprawled toward each other. The evening had taken on the feel of a comfortable, friendly get-together, as if she and Jack had been dating for a while.

Except for this intense physical attraction, there was nothing comfortable or friendly about it, at least not on her end. His long, muscular arms extended from rolled-up sleeves and the hint of his undershirt showed through the unbuttoned vee in his dress shirt.

An undershirt—that was classic. Carlotta knew he must be uncomfortable in his slacks and dress shoes, but she didn't dare suggest that he do anything to lose more clothing.

He was aware of her too, she could tell. The way his peripheral vision took her in while he sipped from his glass, the way his movements had slowed, as if he were restraining himself. Suddenly he sat forward. "I need to make some phone calls, check in with the precinct."

"Of course," she said. "And I'm getting tired, so I think I'll go ahead and turn in. I'll get you some linens for the couch."

"Thanks."

They both stood and walked quickly away from each other. From a hall closet she retrieved sheets, a lightweight throw and a pillow, which she left on the couch. She looked toward the kitchen and heard Jack's voice as he responded to phone messages and handled various problems that had popped up in his absence. It would be like that for anyone involved with Jack, Carlotta realized. He would be on the job 24/7. The only reason he'd spent so much time with her lately was because she was a case.

She had to keep reminding herself of that.

And she had so many other things to be concerned about right now—like the possibility that her father or mother could walk up to the door at any moment.

Or that they wouldn't.

And who was the woman who had masqueraded as her? And why had she ended her life?

Yet even with her head full of seemingly unfixable problems, when she lay down on her bed, one more thought wormed its way inside: the kiss she'd shared with Jack Terry. What would've happened if Wesley and Coop hadn't interrupted them? Would they have had sex? And just how good would it have been?

She hadn't had sex in a long while. She and Peter had come close a couple of times after his wife had died, but the timing had been wrong and in the end either she or he had stopped before things had gone too far. She assumed that his lovemaking would be as gentle as it had been when they were teenagers.

Conversely, she kept thinking about Jack's teasing comment that he was no gentleman in bed. She had visions of slick skin and tangled limbs and utter exhaustion. Her body felt moist just thinking about being with him.

Carlotta put a pillow over her face and moaned into it. She hoped her long-lost parents showed up soon. She wasn't sure how much longer she could be alone with Jack Terry and not do something stupid.

23

Jack was already dressed in a dark suit and tacky green tie and watching the monitor at the breakfast bar when Carlotta emerged from her bedroom the next morning. The sight of him was a sensual jolt to her system and she realized that some time between first meeting him at the police precinct and this morning, Jack Terry had grown on her.

He was a damned good-looking man.

"Hope you don't mind," he said. "I showered in Wesley's bathroom."

"I don't mind." She poured cup of coffee. "Hope the couch wasn't too lumpy."

"It was fine. I'm used to sleeping wherever."

She raised an eyebrow and he cleared his throat. "On the job, I mean."

Liz Fischer probably had grown-up bedroom furniture,

Carlotta mused. And a maid. From the fridge, Carlotta grabbed a bagel and a jar of strawberry preserves. "Any news?"

He picked up a sheaf of papers sitting near his laptop and portable printer. "I have your credit report. It isn't pretty. I need you to take a look at it and tell me if anything looks suspicious."

In the midst of swallowing a bite of bagel, she suddenly lost her appetite. She took the report, her stomach churning. After a quick scan of the pages, she started over, feeling more and more sick. She should've filed for bankruptcy long ago, like Michael Lane had urged her to do. "There are at least five credit cards here I've never heard of. And two overdrawn accounts at a bank that I've never done business with." She put her hand to her forehead. "How will I fix this? I can't lose this house—it's all we have."

"Relax," Jack said. "You're not going to lose your house. It'll take a while to straighten out, but I'll help you."

Her chest expanded with appreciation. The man had his faults, but he had a way of making a person feel safe. "What should I do?"

"You'll need to sit down with Wesley and go through your statements and the credit reports carefully and compare them to your purchases. Once you've identified the transactions and cards you didn't approve, then we'll send an affidavit of identity theft to those creditors."

"But Wesley's name isn't on any of my credit cards."

Jack took a sip from his coffee mug and seemed to weigh his words. "Can you be sure that he or one of his friends hasn't used your cards or opened an account using your information?"

She opened her mouth to deny that Wesley would do something like that, then snapped it shut. Her brother wasn't exactly the poster boy for honesty. Only a few days ago he'd lied to her about the money for the television, and she wouldn't put anything past that friend of his, Chance Hollander. "I'll let you know."

"Meanwhile, I checked with your bank, and there was an ATM cash withdrawal against your bank credit card Sunday morning around ten. I'm thinking that's when I saw the person I thought was you. Are you sure you didn't make a withdrawal Sunday?"

"I told you I didn't," she said, and it came out sounding just as she felt—testy.

He pursed his lips. "Look, I'm just double-checking because when I saw you Sunday at the mall you seemed a little…out of it."

Because her father had just called.

"And when you came in the other night, you admitted you thought it was possible that you had picked up your car and forgotten about it."

Carlotta stuffed another bite of bagel in her mouth and nodded.

"I'm just giving you a chance to change your story before I ask the bank to go through their video to get a picture of the person who made the withdrawal."

"I'm not changing my story," she mumbled.

"Good. Then I need for you to take another look at the florists to see if you can remember who sent those flowers. I'm going to try to track down the mysterious Mr. Mason."

"Jack, the woman stole my car—can't you get her prints from the steering wheel or something?"

"The car was dusted, but the shop had cleaned it inside and out and the woman was wearing thin gloves."

"In the middle of summer?"

"She obviously didn't want to leave behind traceable prints."

"So that must mean she's in the system. Hasn't the coroner been able to take her prints and run them?"

"No. Apparently, she put her hands out to break her fall and…there are no prints."

She winced. "When do you think I'll get my car back?"

"In a few days. But it's a little banged up."

"Huh? I just had it fixed!"

"Apparently the lady drove into the side of the bridge before getting out to jump."

"Oh, that's just great. Now I have to get it fixed again. I *hate* that car!"

"Look on the bright side. With the reward money, you'll be able to buy a new ride."

Carlotta blinked. Was he judging her? Or was he mocking her because he suspected her parents wouldn't show?

Jack's cell phone rang. He picked it up and glanced at the screen. She caught the downward twitch of his mouth before he answered. "Detective Terry…no, Lucas, no news."

She tensed and could only imagine the tension on the phone line.

"No, they haven't…no…no, he isn't here…yes, she is, but not the brother…he doesn't like the arrangement…yes, his cell phone has been tapped." Jack turned away from her slightly. "Who knows? Maybe they haven't heard, or have to make travel arrangements."

Her face felt hot—he was making excuses as to why her parents hadn't shown, but was too polite to say, "Maybe they don't give a crap that their daughter took a dive off a bridge."

His shoulders went rigid. "I know how to do my job, Lucas…yes, we can do that. I'll give him a call." He disconnected the call and heaved a sigh.

"What, Lucas is irritated that my father hasn't fallen into the tiger pit that you two set for him?"

"Hey, this wasn't my idea. I'm just—"

"Doing your job, I know. So what does he want us to do?"

"Uh, plan your funeral. I'm supposed to give Coop a call."

She pursed her mouth. "I don't suppose you could let my creditors know that I'm dead?"

He laughed and picked up the phone to make another call. After a few seconds, he said, "Coop, this is Jack…no, no sign of them yet. Just in case they don't show today, we need to put together a phony funeral for tomorrow, courtesy of the D.A.'s office. Can you handle it? Yeah, we'll be here. Can you drive something with the name of the funeral home on it to park in the driveway? Thanks." He put down the phone. "Coop is on his way over."

She frowned. "Does it make you feel weird that he walked in on us the other day?"

"No. Do you and Coop have something going?"

She bristled. "Of course not. But you work with him occasionally and I wouldn't want what happened to get you in trouble."

He scoffed. "It was a kiss, it's not like we were having sex on the floor."

Both of them averted their gaze to the floor, then back.

"Besides," Jack said wryly, "Cooper Craft is the last person to be throwing stones."

"What exactly got him fired from the M.E.'s office?"

Jack hesitated. "I don't know the entire story, but the word was that Coop was off-duty, came up on an accident scene and pronounced a woman dead. But she wasn't."

Carlotta gasped. "Did she die?"

"No, but she was left in pretty bad shape. Coop was drunk and blamed himself for not getting help sooner. And so did everyone else."

"But he's sober now."

"As far as I know, yeah. He and the new coroner butt heads sometimes, but the fact that Dr. Abrams contracted with Coop to haul bodies for the morgue tells me that he wants to keep him close in case he needs him. And I know for a fact that he calls on Coop for VIP body retrievals and for the more difficult cases."

"Like the bridge jumper?"

"Right."

She hugged herself, shaking her head. "I'm not sure this is the right line of work for Wesley. It's so…gruesome."

"It's reality," Jack said. "And not a bad thing for him to see considering some of the choices he's made."

She set her jaw. "Is that an indictment of my parenting skills?"

"It has nothing to do with you. Wesley is old enough to

take responsibility for his own choices. I think spending time with Coop will be good for him."

His phone rang again and while he talked business to a colleague, she finished her bagel and tackled the florists again. Peachtree was in at least half the business names in Atlanta, with Buckhead and Midtown being close runners-up. Letter combinations were popular names for florists, but after a while, the L&Ps, B&Gs, and K&Ds started running together. Michael Lane might remember the name on the card, but she couldn't call him without revealing the fact that *voilá* she was alive after all.

The ringing of the doorbell was a welcome distraction considering the task at hand. On the monitor, Carlotta noticed that Coop had parked a conspicuous Motherwell Funeral Home SUV in the driveway.

Carlotta steeled herself to face Coop, telling herself that there was nothing to be embarrassed about. Jack was right—it was only a kiss. It wasn't as if they'd been writhing on the floor naked, greased with herbed massage oil and having hot jungle sex, screaming each other's names and howling at the moon until the break of dawn.

It was just a kiss.

Coop walked into the living room and like a good girl, she waited until the door was closed before she left the kitchen to greet him. He was tall and lean, with the casual, funky look of a rock star, complete with longish, neat sideburns and glasses. He wore dark overlong jeans, an open-collar shirt that she'd bet was vintage and a pale-colored four-button sport coat. When she met his warm, light-brown eyes, her smile wavered a bit. His gaze wasn't critical, but the twinkle was gone.

Or maybe it was her imagination.

"Hi, Carlotta."

"Hi, Coop. I hear we have a funeral to plan."

The twinkle came back as he smiled. "A phony funeral— the best kind."

She lifted her hands. "Where do we start?"

Coop patted a satchel he was carrying. "We have a strict budget, but I just want to go over a few things with you, to make sure it's as believable as possible."

"Take your time," Jack said, moving past them. "I'd like that vehicle to sit in the driveway for a little while."

She gestured for Coop to sit on the couch and he began to spread books over the surface of the coffee table. She noticed that he took in the sheets and pillow that Jack had used last night stacked in a chair.

"Do you want something to drink?" she offered. "Jack made coffee."

"No, I'm fine, thanks."

"Are you and Wesley working today?" she asked, sitting next to him.

"Not today. I have some business at the funeral home and I want to get things ready for tomorrow." He smiled. "It's going to be hard to pull off a funeral without a body under my uncle's nose."

"How was Wesley...yesterday?"

"Angry for a while," he said, averting his gaze. "But he'll get over it. I guess it's hard for him to think of you as a woman."

Her cheeks warmed. "I want to thank you again for being so kind to Wesley the night before last."

"It's okay…it was a difficult night for anyone who cares about you." He gave her a little smile, his expression forthright and honest, his affection for her obvious.

"Doing okay in there?" Jack asked from the kitchen.

"We're planning *your* funeral, Jack," Coop called, then grinned at Jack's guffaw.

"Have you done this before?" she asked. "Planned a fake funeral?"

"No, but this is about as exciting as it gets in the mortuary business."

Carlotta laughed and, having heard the story of his fall from grace, marveled at his seemingly unending good nature. Cooper Craft seemed to be at peace with himself.

"I just need to know a few basics," he said. "Things that people who know you would expect your brother to choose."

She bit into her lip. "Then we're not talking about my parents, because even if they do show up, they wouldn't know what to expect. They don't know me anymore."

His eyes shadowed briefly, then he winked. "So what will your friends expect?"

"Is there such a thing as a designer casket?"

His laugh—a rich, mellow sound—made his eyes crinkle in the corners.

She spent the next couple of hours becoming acquainted with casket styles and colors, flowers sprays, and "In Memoriam" card formats. Coop noted her selections on a legal pad.

"This is all a little surreal," she murmured.

He nodded. "I'll need a current photo of you. And what would you like in the eulogy?"

"Oh…something generic. It doesn't really matter, does it?"

He shrugged. "I guess not. Who would you like to give the eulogy?"

She couldn't put any of her friends through that kind of trauma and Wesley would be a hard sell. "Would you mind doing it, Coop? Is that too much to ask?"

"No," he said quietly. "I think I can manage—since it's not the real thing."

"Let's hope we don't need to go through with it," Jack said from the doorway. "There's still a chance that the Wrens will show before tomorrow afternoon. But meanwhile, I want you to put the funeral announcement in the newspaper, on your information phone message…anywhere you can, to get the word out."

"Will do." Coop returned the books and pamphlets to his satchel.

"Have you heard anything about an ID on the Jane Doe?"

Coop hesitated. "You should talk to the coroner, Jack."

"Just asking."

"They don't keep me informed," Coop said, standing.

Jack put his hands on his hips. "I know that look, Coop. You know something."

But Coop only shook his head. "I'm just a body mover, Jack. I'll let the professionals handle this one." He looked at Carlotta. "I guess I'll see you when this is all over."

"Oh, no, I'll be there tomorrow," she said.

Both men looked surprised. "How?" Jack asked.

"In disguise, of course. Don't worry—no one will know me."

Jack looked dubious as he walked Coop to the door, but maintained his silence until the other man had left. "I don't think you should go tomorrow."

"Why not? It's my funeral!"

Jack lifted his finger until it almost touched the tip of her nose. "Because with your penchant for trouble, something's bound to happen."

"Nothing you can't handle, I'm sure."

He frowned. "I'm starting to doubt that."

"Besides, don't you think I'll be safer there than here alone?"

He didn't respond, but from the look on his face, she knew she had him. "Even you won't recognize me," she promised.

"Don't you have more yellow pages to look through? I'm going to call the coroner to see if anything else has turned up on our Jane Doe."

Carlotta called Wesley's cell-phone number and when he didn't answer, she left him a message about the memorial service tomorrow, wondering if the words sounded as strange as it felt to say them.

"No developments here, but I'd like to talk to you if you get a chance to call me today." But when she hung up, she felt his absence, his distance as surely as if he were in another country. He was making it clear that this was her deal with the D.A. and he wanted nothing to do with it.

Catching her kissing Jack Terry had only added fuel to Wesley's fire.

She glanced over the top of the thick yellow pages volume

to steal a look at Jack sitting across the room, engrossed in something on his computer screen. Unfortunately, she had her own fire to contend with, an internal blaze that seemed to be taking on a life of its own.

"No matter what, this will be over tomorrow?" she asked.

He looked up. "Yeah, no matter what."

So...their last night together.

The unspoken words hung in the air all day as they maneuvered around each other. Three flower deliveries were left on the stoop for Wesley—one from his probation officer, one from Neiman's and one from Walt & Tully. It made her think of Peter and wonder how this situation would affect their relationship—if it would be too much for him and he'd cut bait before he got pulled deeper into the Wren-family train wreck.

Jack spent most of the day on his cell phone, following up with the car shop, the bank and the coroner, who had no news. Mixed in with the weird sexual fantasies Carlotta was having about Jack was the sickening realization that her worst fear was on the verge of coming true. Two days after the announcement of her death, her parents had not come to mourn their daughter or console their son.

And if they didn't show up at the funeral tomorrow, the whole world would know just how little her parents cared. She blinked back sudden tears.

"You okay?" Jack asked, his gaze leveled on her from the breakfast bar.

"Fine," she murmured, blinking rapidly. "Listen, if you don't mind, I'm not feeling well. I think I'll go to my room and rest."

"What about dinner?"

"I don't think I can eat anything. I guess nerves are setting in."

"I understand," he said quietly. "I'll wake you if anything happens."

"We both know that isn't likely."

As she was leaving the room, Jack said, "Carlotta."

She turned around.

"I'm sorry." He set down his pencil and ran his hand down his face. "I'm sorry."

Sorry that her parents hadn't shown, that they were the kind of people that he would have to hunt down and put in jail.

"Good night, Jack."

The fact that she fell asleep as soon as she crawled in her bed was testament to the mental gymnastics she'd been doing for two days. But her dreams were dark—snatches of her own funeral playing out, with friends lamenting her sad, loveless life of mediocrity…her parents were there, but when she reached for them, her hands went through them….

She started awake, breathless and perspiring. The clock displayed a few minutes past midnight. The house was completely quiet, no fan drone, no television, no air conditioning hum. Carlotta lay in the dark, listening to her thudding heart, the vestiges of the bad dream remaining in the corners of her mind.

She felt so fragmented and out of control—and utterly alone. Throwing back her sheet, she swung her legs over the side of the bed and turned her head in the direction of the living room.

Jack was awake, she could feel his body calling hers.

She pressed her lips together, wavering. But if faking her own death had taught her anything, it was that she needed to live in the moment. And there was at least one aspect of her life over which she still had control.

Carlotta went into the bathroom and rummaged in the cabinet below the sink, way in the back, until she found what she was looking for. She blew the dust off a box of condoms and removed one. Then she shrugged and grabbed a couple more.

She straightened and pulled purposeful air into her lungs, then marched in the direction of the living-room couch.

24

By the time Carlotta had padded into the living room, she had lost her nerve. The low light from a table lamp revealed Jack sprawled on the couch wearing a white T-shirt and boxers. Her stomach clenched at the sight of his big body and the reality of what she'd been planning now seemed ludicrous. Humiliation zinged through her—some seductress she was.

But before she could retreat, he turned his head and sat up. "Carlotta?"

She put the condoms behind her back. "Sorry to wake you. I was just going to get a glass of water."

"Oh."

But she couldn't bring herself to move. Even in the dim light, she could feel the power of his gaze. Beneath her cotton camisole, her nipples budded. Sexual energy bounced around the room, looking for an outlet. He couldn't come to her, she knew, because his job forbade it. If this was going to happen, she had to go to him.

She wet her lips. "Jack."

He stood and she could sense his restraint. She walked to him, stopping within arm's reach. The sexual vibes rolling off his body brought dormant desire to the surface in a rush of blood that had her heart galloping. She looped her arms around his neck and held her breath in anticipation.

"Carlotta, are you sure you want this?" he demanded, even as his massive arms hauled her to him.

"Yes, Jack. Make me feel alive."

He did. His kiss was a hungry assault on her senses, the stubble of his beard grazing her face, his lips hard and firm on hers, his tongue thrashing into her mouth, a promise of what was to come.

They undressed each other in fervent tugs, their clothes tossed to the floor with impatience. The shock of his warm muscular body against hers caused a warning light to go off in Carlotta's head, but when his hands closed over her bare breasts, her brain pushed aside rational thought in favor of the incredible sensations coursing through her body.

Her moan of pleasure seemed to stoke Jack's own fire higher. His raging erection was in proportion to the rest of his big body and felt formidable against her stomach. She kneaded the wall of muscle that was his back, reveling in the firm contours, then clasped his thick cock, stroking him with a sense of urgency. It was as if they both understood that they needed to do this quickly—sexual blitzkrieg.

He guided her to the floor and dropped kisses on her neck and shoulders while coaxing her knees apart. When his fingers found her feminine heat, she gasped and clung to his neck. "I want you now, Jack."

He fumbled for one of the condoms that had landed on the floor and sheathed himself. As hurried as his movements were, when he levered his body above hers, he hesitated a split second, his gaze locked with hers, before thrusting his rigid length into her.

Carlotta cried out and rocked her hips against his, overcome with the deluge to her senses. They found a frantic rhythm and the friction instantly began to coax a long overdue orgasm from the depths of her body. His male scent, his powerful body, his fierce lovemaking heightened her every sense. She could almost feel each strand of carpet that ground into her skin as he plunged into her, deeper, harder.

When she climaxed, her body contracted around his like a spring. She shrieked and sank her teeth into his shoulder as the spasms grew in intensity and spread through her body in one of the most satisfying orgasms she could recall. He pumped into her furiously, then his body convulsed with his own release. He groaned against her neck and twined his fingers in her hair as they both pulsed with latent tremors.

Neither one of them spoke for several long seconds. Only the sound of their recovering lungs filled the air. Carlotta closed her eyes, waiting for the remorse to set in. But it didn't. She felt good—satisfied.

Jack rolled over, but pulled her with him until she lay on

his chest. After another minute of silence, he expelled a noisy breath. "Want to talk about this?"

"No," she murmured.

"Good," he said in his deep baritone and simply stroked her arm. They lay like that for a while, then he sat up and pushed to his feet and removed the spent condom. She thought he was going to get dressed and told herself not to be disappointed, but instead he extended his hand.

"Let's take a shower and try that again."

25

Wesley opened the door of Chance's BMW and swung out. "Thanks for the ride, man."

"Don't mention it. Uh, dude, about your sister's funeral today...that's not really my scene, you know?"

"Yeah, I understand. No problem."

"Hey, I just thought of something. Do you think it's possible your parents might show up?"

No one had ever accused Chance of being quick-minded. "Anything's possible, I guess."

"Well, don't sweat it. Now that you're alone, we're going to make that poker dream of yours happen, man. I mean, not to speak ill of the dead, but your sister was a bit of a drag, always riding you about playing cards."

"Yeah. See ya." As Wesley turned toward the house, anger sparked anew in his stomach. Carlotta was always telling him what and what not to do, but when their father had called, she'd told Hannah instead of him. She'd probably told the cop too and the D.A. Maybe that's why they'd cooked up this trap for his dad.

He'd spent all night on his computer equipment at Chance's tapping into Carlotta's cell phone records—with the right equipment and a little cash, anyone's records were available. She'd told him her phone had broken Sunday. The last call had come from one of those Internet calling cards—impossible to trace.

Their father calling explained why she'd been in a funk for the past few days—the reason he'd been willing to believe that she'd killed herself—but it didn't excuse her from telling him about the call or siding with the D.A. against her own family.

And taking up with that jerk cop.

Remembering the detective's warning that he might be approached when coming in or out of the house, Wesley glanced around for any signs of persons loitering or sitting in cars. Their little portion of the neighborhood was quiet and nothing seemed out of place. But he turned at a noise behind him.

"Wesley, there you are," Mrs. Winningham said, walking toward him on her side of the fence, holding a casserole dish.

"Hello, Mrs. Winningham."

"I heard the tragic news about your sister. I'm so sorry."

"Uh, thanks, Mrs. Winningham."

The woman tsked-tsked. "I always thought she was a troubled young woman, and she kept such odd company. The girl with the belts and chains attached that horrid black wreath to the door."

Wesley tried not to roll his eyes. What a waste of taxpayers' money to have Jack Terry doing surveillance, when Mrs. Winningham did it for free.

"Do you think your parents will come back, dear?"

"I don't know." He hoped not…hoped they could smell a trap…hoped his dad would follow him and approach him when he was alone to find out what was going on.

"Have you thought about selling the house?" his neighbor asked hopefully.

"No ma'am, I haven't."

"Well, you should consider it."

When he didn't respond, she lifted the casserole dish over the fence. "I made you this nice chicken casserole."

Southerners grieved with mayonnaise and cream of mushroom soup. "Thank you."

"I'll need my dish back."

"I'll make sure you get it." He waved goodbye, then climbed the steps, unlocked the front door and pushed it open.

The first thing he noticed was the makeshift bed on the couch, but his relief that maybe the cop had done the right thing was erased when he saw the clothes strewn everywhere, and the condom wrappers. Fury pulsed through his body. While he stood there, shaking, Carlotta's bedroom door opened and Jack Terry emerged, freshly showered and pulling on his suit jacket. When he spotted Wesley, he pulled the door closed behind him. "Morning, Wesley. I didn't know you were here."

"Yeah, so much for your *surveillance,* Detective."

"I'm not going to discuss this with you, Wesley."

"Creep. I should report you."

"That would hurt Carlotta too. And I didn't force her, Wesley."

"Shut up."

"You have to realize sooner or later that your sister can't spend the rest of her life taking care of you. She needs a life of her own."

"Oh and you're going to give her that life?" Wesley sneered. "Are you going to tell me that you're in love with my sister?"

Jack's mouth tightened.

"I didn't think so." Wesley headed toward the kitchen where he shoved the casserole into the refrigerator. He slammed the fridge door and leaned into the sink, wishing he were big enough to pummel Jack Terry.

He heard the man enter the kitchen, and spoke through gritted teeth. "Is my sister dressed?"

"Yes."

Wesley wheeled around and strode to Carlotta's room where he knocked loudly. "I need to talk to you."

"Come in," she said.

She was dressed in jeans and a tank top, making her bed, an image that made him nauseous as he closed the door behind him. But when she straightened and turned to him, his anger dropped a notch. The expression on her face—she looked... happy. The worry lines in her forehead were gone, and she appeared younger. Her cheeks were pink and her eyes sparkled. She'd been sad and stressed for so long, he'd almost forgotten how beautiful she could be—as beautiful as their mother.

"Why haven't you called?" she asked and just like that, the little pinched look reappeared between her eyebrows. Worry lines over him. "Never mind, I'm just glad you're here."

"Why? From the looks of the living room, you and Jack Terry seemed to enjoy being alone."

She straightened a pillow sham. "I'm sorry about the mess, but you said you weren't coming back."

"That's all you have to say?"

She smacked the pillow. "Wesley, I'm not going to discuss my personal life with you."

"Carlotta, he's using you! He's cozying up to you to bring in Dad!"

"This was the D.A.'s idea. Jack is only doing his job."

Wesley guffawed. "Right. So did you tell him that Dad called you?"

She jerked her head up, her mouth open. "How did you know about that?"

"Hannah. She thinks you're dead, remember? She thought I should know."

Carlotta sat down on the bed and heaved a sigh. "No, I didn't tell Jack. And I'm sorry I didn't tell you. I got the call on my cell phone while I was at work Sunday. When he told me who he was, I dropped my phone and broke it. I had convinced myself it wasn't him and then…"

"Then?"

"Peter showed up before I ended my shift. Dad had called him, too."

Wesley gaped and dropped onto the bed next to her. "Why would he call Peter?"

She lifted her hands. "I guess he knew that Peter would get the message to me. And he asked Peter to help him."

"Help him, how? Where are they? Are they okay?"

She told him everything she could remember that Peter had told her about the call.

"I knew it!" Wesley whooped. "I knew he was innocent!"

"Wesley," she admonished, "just because Dad says he's innocent doesn't make it so. If you haven't noticed, he's not the most honorable man."

Wesley frowned. "Don't say that. Has he called Peter back?"

"Not that I know of."

"And you haven't told any of this to the cop?"

She shook her head.

Wesley grinned. "I think I like you again."

Carlotta gave a little laugh. "What a pair we are. So, do you think Mom and Dad will put in an appearance at my funeral?"

"Do you?"

"I have no idea. I try not to think too far into the future these days." She clapped her hand on his knee. "You'd better get ready if you're going to play the bereaved brother."

"I guess I have to, don't I?"

She nodded. "I gave my word to the D.A. that we'd go along with this. I expect you to keep up your end of the bargain."

"Okay," he said reluctantly.

"I'm going too—in disguise."

"No kidding?"

"How many chances does a person have to watch their own funeral?"

Wesley smiled, feeling excited about the prospect of his

family being reunited someday. And from knowing that, despite what Carlotta said, if she truly believed their father was guilty, she would've told the cop she was sleeping with about the calls.

At the door he turned. "Carlotta?"

"Hmm?"

He jerked his thumb over his shoulder. "I don't like him, but I figure you must have your reasons, so for now I won't thrash him."

"Thank you, Wesley."

26

Carlotta walked into the living room, gratified when Wesley and Jack both stared at her in disbelief.

"Wow, sis, that's the best makeup job you've ever done."

She smiled behind the small glasses and patted her gray wig. "I thought so."

Jack shook his head. "What happened to the space between your teeth?"

"Retainer with a bridge," she said, tapping her tongue to the contraption that disguised her telltale smile. She wore green contact lenses, one of her mother's now-dated long dresses, a boxy jacket and shoes with a sensible heel. She was a very convincing sixty-something-year-old Southern woman, complete with conservative bag and jewelry.

A horn sounded in the driveway. "That's Hannah," Wesley said, jumping up. "I'll see you there."

"Wesley."

"Yeah?"

"I'm supposed to be dead. Do you have to be so cheerful?"

"Oh. Sorry." He poked himself in both eyes and blinked up a few tears. "How's that?"

"Better."

Jack stepped forward. "Just so you know, a camera will capture the face of everyone who enters the funeral home and we'll have people in the back watching a monitor. Wesley, I'll be in the chapel along with two plainclothes officers. When you get there, one of them will let you know where to sit or stand. If you see either of your parents, let someone know."

Wesley frowned. "Look, man, I'm going along with this because Carlotta asked me to, but I'm not going to do your job for you, got it?"

"Wesley," Carlotta said, giving him a pointed look, "let's just get through this, okay?"

He pursed his mouth, then nodded and left.

Carlotta watched through a tiny slit in the curtains. Hannah had her head down on the steering wheel. Carlotta's stomach pinched. It wasn't fair that she had to put her friend through this. Hannah would have been so happy to help plan a fake funeral.

When the van left the driveway, Carlotta turned to Jack and wondered if every time she looked at him, she would always think of their night together. She smoothed a hand down her costume. "So, what do you think?"

"I think I'm feeling a little pervy right now. You're pretty good at changing your appearance."

"Yeah, but I usually don't go for the middle-aged look. It's typically a wig, makeup, contact lenses, outfits, accents."

"Accents?" He grinned. "So you could be a Swedish flight attendant if I asked?"

She hit him in the arm with her purse. "Like I said, let's get this over with. Although I'm not sure how eager I am to get back to my life."

"You're convinced that your parents won't be there, aren't you?"

She nodded.

"No matter what, this could be a traumatic experience for you. Are you sure you want to go?"

"Yes."

"All right." He hefted the bulky duffel bag in one hand. "I'll back the car out of the garage, then come back for you."

She watched him leave and felt a bittersweet pang that their time playing house was over. Or was it? Would Jack still want to see her? And would it be on the sly or could they have a relationship out in the open? Then she frowned. Hanging the word *relationship* on their intense physical chemistry was a bit premature. What if they were only good between the sheets?

"Ready?" he asked from the doorway.

Carlotta looked up and nodded, then took his arm, remembering to bow her shoulders a tad and slow her step.

Jack seemed amused. "I think you missed your calling as an actress. You could go undercover."

"That's sort of what I do when I crash parties."

"You're a little scary."

She smiled. "I've been told that before."

Jack's department-issue sedan sat in the driveway. He opened the door for her and she slid inside, a little surprised at its cleanliness, considering the one time she'd been in the man's office it had been a slovenly mess.

After he slid into his own seat, she felt as if she was privy to some sort of subconscious checklist that he went through when he got inside. He checked the rearview mirror and the side mirrors, then started the ignition, turned on the police radio and patted the bulge at his waist. She found it all very arousing, and marveled at how sex changed the way you viewed a person.

But Jack was all business, calling the precinct to get messages and let them know where he'd be for the next couple of hours. Carlotta studied his profile and told herself she could not fall for this man. They had simply shared a night of great sex—to work out the mental kinks, as Hannah had said. She sank her teeth into her lower lip. Jack was a physical guy. He probably had multiple lovers and made booty calls when the urge struck him.

But she wanted to believe that this was different, maybe even a little special. The kind of sexual synergy they had wasn't typical, at least not in her world. She was pretty sure that at one point last night, she had levitated off the bed.

Plus ten points.

Maybe they could overcome the obstacles between them after all. Maybe her father would reveal himself and be taken into custody and the case would be passed to an investigator in the D.A.'s office. Then she and Jack could fornicate until the cows came home without it being a conflict of interest.

She could go to every awards dinner on his arm, beaming with pride as he accepted his distinguished-duty statues.

All you have to do is tell him about the phone calls, her mind whispered. *You could help end this ten-year ordeal and you and Jack would have a fair chance to explore whatever this is.*

But was she willing to take that risk for something that might turn into nothing? Sacrifice her father and close herself off from other relationship possibilities for Jack Terry just because he could make her hit a high-C note?

"Awfully quiet over there," Jack observed.

"Actually, I was thinking about your awards dinner and that I'd very much like to go—as your date."

In the ensuing silence, Carlotta instantly wanted the words back.

"I'm sorry, Jack. I thought you were trying to ask me to go with you the other day."

He shifted in his seat. "Uh...I don't think that's such a good idea after all."

Beneath the pancake makeup, her face burned. "Okay, no problem."

"Look, I asked you last night if you wanted to talk about what happened between us—"

"It was...fun."

He gave her a sideways glance. "That's not what I meant. And I don't think I can talk to you about sex while you look like my grandmother."

Tell him what he wants to hear. "I don't have any expectations, Jack. With all the tension between us, I think it was bound to happen sooner or later."

He raised an eyebrow. "It wasn't my intention. Not that I regret it," he added quickly. "But I'm still working your father's case and what we did…well, it was a one-time thing."

"Funny—I counted four and a half."

"Carlotta, it can't happen again."

She looked him dead in the eye. "Fine."

"You said you didn't want complications and neither do I."

"Right," she said, nodding. "I agree totally. Besides, we have nothing in common, really. Well, there's that one thing with the scarf that we both liked—"

His phone rang and he glanced at the screen with irritation. "I have to get this."

She clamped her mouth shut and told herself to stop talking and let Jack give her the polite brush-off like he was trying so hard to do. It was classic the-chase-is-over behavior. He'd sampled her goods and it wasn't worth any more trouble.

No biggie. She'd known it was the likely outcome when she'd gone to him last night. It wasn't like she was in love with him or anything.

Still, it smarted a little to be rejected just before your own funeral.

Minus ten points.

Carlotta sighed and turned her attention to the passing scenery. It was the first time she'd been out of the house in over two days and it was a bit of a shock to her system to see that in the wake of Carlotta Wren's dramatic suicide, nothing in Atlanta seemed to have missed a step. The sun was high and hot; heat wafted off the roads in distorted waves. Traffic was intense and drivers were honk-happy. Pedestrians hurried along, defenseless against the temperatures and the tempers of commuters.

The world had marched on without her. Had anyone even noticed she was gone?

Her stomach was churning by the time they arrived for the service at Coop's family's funeral home, Motherwell's. At the sight of the crowded parking lot, she felt a ridiculous surge of happiness.

"They're all here for me?" she asked, surveying the knots of people who were headed toward the entrance.

"Looks like it," Jack said, pulling up to the entrance. "I'll drop you off and I'll see you inside. I want to sit with you so you can help me ID your parents if necessary. But let's not make it look too obvious."

She looked at him over the top of her glasses. "Detective, I'm a pro."

He gave her a dry smile. "Sorry, I forgot I was talking to the woman who is crashing her own funeral."

27

Carlotta merged with the crowd to make her way into the funeral home. She looked up to find herself next to Peter, who was in conversation with his boss, her father's former partner, Walt Tully. Next to Walt was his daughter, Tracey Tully (Mrs. Dr.) Lowenstein, who had gone to school with Carlotta and had reveled in her subsequent tumble from the social register.

Neither one of them saw through her careful disguise.

"I knew this was going to happen," Tracey was saying to Peter. "Carlotta always *was* strung a little too tight, you know what I mean?"

"I'm not sure I do," Peter said, and Carlotta felt a burst of affection for him taking up for her.

"You know that her mother Valerie had a nervous breakdown," Walt offered in dramatic undertones.

"No, I don't remember that," Peter said.

"Well, back then there were code names for it, but we all knew what Randolph was going through with that woman. We let a lot of mistakes slide and covered for him when we shouldn't have because we felt sorry for him. And look where it got us."

Peter frowned. "The firm seems to have recovered, Walt. By the way, I saw Ray and Brody go in ahead of us."

"They wanted to pay their respects, too," Walt offered in defense of the other partner in the firm and the chief counsel.

But from the dubious look on Peter's face, he was thinking the same thing she was—the partners had come here thinking that Randolph Wren might show. She glanced around to see a news crew in the side lot, extra security officers, D.A. Kelvin Lucas and his groupies....

With a start she realized that most of the people were probably here for her father instead of her.

"I still can't believe Carlotta would take her life like that," Tracey said, flipping her stiff blond bob. "It's just so vulgar, stopping traffic and all. I don't mean to be crass, but at least you don't have to deal with her anymore, Peter."

Carlotta leaned in closer.

"What do you mean?" Peter asked.

"Well, everyone knows that she threw herself at you after poor Angela's death." Tracey touched Peter's arm in a way that Carlotta found very suspicious for a happily married woman. "I hope you don't blame yourself, Peter."

"Why would I?"

Carlotta frowned. *Yeah, why would he?*

"Well, it's obvious that you put her in her place and she had to face the fact that her life had hit rock bottom."

Carlotta fumed—the bitch!

Peter removed Tracey's hand. "For your information, Carlotta turned *me* down." He glanced from Tracey to Walt. "It was nice of you both to come and pay your respects. If you'll excuse me."

Carlotta pretended to lurch sideways and stomped down on Tracey's foot, clad in a Dolce and Gabbana patent leather sandal.

"Ouch!" Tracey yelped and Carlotta felt bad—for the sandal.

"I'm so sorry," she said in her best older-lady voice. "I'm a little unsteady on my feet today."

"Let me help you, ma'am," Peter said, offering his arm. It was clear from his expression that he didn't suspect she was anyone other than who she appeared to be.

She smiled up at him and tucked her hand in the crook of his elbow. "Aren't you just the nicest young man."

And he was, she realized suddenly, taking in his kind blue eyes. She'd harbored so much resentment toward Peter over the years. It was easier to think that he'd turned into an unlikable person because it made her miss him less. And in the back of her mind, she'd assumed he was nice to *her* only because he thought it would help win her over, but had suspected that he might not be so generous toward other people. Yet she'd just observed that that wasn't true.

It warmed her heart.

Not to mention made her feel a little guilty for jumping

the bones of Jack Terry for a meaningless night of sex when Peter would have been more than obliging....

And would have offered her a future.

"May I help you to a chair?" Peter asked as he ushered her over the threshold of the entryway.

"Thank you."

In the foyer, Cooper stood with his uncle greeting guests as they arrived and passing out the In Memoriam cards. She made eye contact with him, expecting to get the requisite polite nod, but instead, Coop latched his gaze on her and his mouth curled up in the merest smile. Either Wesley had let him know about her costume or he'd seen right through it.

She suspected the latter.

Carlotta allowed Peter to lead her inside the chapel. Low hymnal music reached her ears. Her gaze went to the front of the room where a deep red sample casket sat resplendent on a white pedestal, covered in white roses. A shudder passed over her body; this was, admittedly, pretty creepy. Flanking the casket were dozens of baskets and wreaths of flowers—all for her. Sudden tears gathered in her eyes.

Peter guided her through a throng of people to a chair. "There you are, ma'am. It looks like a full house, so I'll probably stand."

"Thank you," she said, patting his hand and holding on a second longer than necessary.

"You're welcome, ma'am."

She smiled as she watched him walk away, then set her purse in the vacant aisle-seat next to her and looked at the in memoriam card curled in her hand. Centered under a photo of her that Wesley had taken on some unremembered occasion were the words *Carlotta A. Wren, Beloved Sister and Friend*. Another shiver overtook her, as if someone were walking on her grave. Maybe this whole fake-funeral thing was tempting fate a little too much.

She shoved the eerie card into her purse and began canvassing the room for anyone who might resemble Randolph or Valerie Wren.

At times, she had to concentrate to remember what they looked like—older versions of her and Wesley was about the most she could conjure up. Wesley stood in the front of the room, positioned, no doubt, by the plainclothes officers nearby who stuck out like sore thumbs to her. Wesley looked solemn and nervous, which came across as completely genuine. She felt sorry for him because she had thrust him into a difficult situation.

Correction—their parents had thrust them *both* into a difficult situation.

In the front row sat Hannah dressed in what could only be described as vampire attire. She looked weepy and hollow-eyed and everyone was giving her a wide berth. The only thing that kept Carlotta from rushing forward and revealing herself to her friend was imagining the glee on Hannah's face when she realized what Carlotta had pulled off. She hoped the fact that she was still alive might help to make amends.

She swept her gaze over others near the front, spotting a composed Michael Lane and—she made a face—that odious Patricia Alexander. A few other familiar faces from the store were with them and she again felt guilty for the time and trouble that people were going through on her behalf.

While an unidentified woman lay in the morgue—*her* friends and family unaware that she was even dead.

She concentrated on every face, stopping when she spotted June Moody from the cigar bar. The poor woman must think that she left the bar, found her car, then leapt off the bridge. Carlotta felt another tug of remorse.

The next face she recognized caused her to gasp—Jolie! Jolie Goodman Underwood and her husband Beck. Hannah must have gotten in touch with her. They must have come all the way from Costa Rica. She winced inwardly and felt petty because she hadn't given thought to how many people would rearrange their schedules—their lives—to attend her funeral in good faith.

And she should enjoy it because after crying wolf once, she might not get this size crowd the next time around.

"Is this seat taken?"

She looked up to see Jack standing there. Moving her purse, she gestured for him to sit.

As he settled his big body into the chair, he murmured, "Anything?"

"No. Other than I'm totally creeped out."

"I warned you," he said out of the corner of his mouth.

She watched while he made discreet eye contact with other officers around the room. All of them gave imperceptible shakes of their head. Randolph Wren had not been spotted.

The increase in music volume signaled to everyone that the funeral was about to start. Under the wig, Carlotta was sweating profusely. People quieted and took their seats. She was still scanning faces row by row, but couldn't see everyone from her vantage point, so she settled back in her chair. Jack's leg touched her and she silently cursed him. He had to know by now that his touch was the equivalent of setting her underwear on fire—and she was wearing granny panties under this getup.

Coop walked to the front of the room and stood behind the podium, managing to strike a balance between approachable yet reverent in his deep brown suit. He adjusted the microphone for his considerable height, then gave a sweeping nod to the room and she felt his gaze pass over her. "Welcome. We're here today to celebrate the life of Carlotta Wren, a beautiful, vibrant woman who impacted the life of everyone she met."

In the chair next to her, Jack shifted. A few rows ahead and to the right, she saw Tracey Tully nudge the Buckhead clone sitting next to her. A flush bloomed at the base of Carlotta's throat and started working its way up her neck.

"Carlotta Amelia Wren was born to Randolph and Valerie Wren in Atlanta, Georgia…"

She found herself smiling as Coop chronicled her life in sound bites, conjuring up happy memories of her parents that she hadn't thought of in a long time. She bit into her lip to stem the sudden tears and felt Jack's leg press against hers in silent support.

"She was a long-time employee at Neiman Marcus where I'm told she usually topped the sales charts."

That was outdated information, she thought wryly.

"From the sheer number of friends who are here today, I can see that she will be missed. I am lucky enough to have known Carlotta myself," Coop said, once again moving his gaze in her general direction, "and I know firsthand that she was a unique and special lady."

Jack coughed lightly and she nudged his knee.

"Carlotta's brother Wesley would like to say a few words and then we'll conclude the service with a music selection."

Carlotta blinked. Wesley was going to talk? About her? She sat slightly forward in her chair.

Wesley walked up to the podium and her chest swelled with pride. He looked so handsome and grown up.

"My sister Carlotta," he began, "has been the single most important person in my life. For the first ten years of my life, she was the older sister I adored and tagged along behind. For the past ten years of my life, she was everything—mom, sister, friend." He gave a little laugh. "It wasn't easy—we didn't have a lot of money and I wasn't exactly a model kid."

A ripple of chuckles came from the audience.

"But Carlotta was always there for me, even when I got into trouble or did something stupid. I knew I could always count on her to hug me and tell me everything was going to be all right."

Carlotta's throat clogged with emotion and sniffles sounded in the audience. Hannah was wailing outright.

"And if Carlotta was here right now—" his gaze landed on her, then moved on "—and I happen to think she is—I would say to her that even though I never told her enough, I love her. She would be glad to see you all here today."

Tears were running down her face—not good for the makeup. Wesley stepped down and to her surprise, Coop took a seat at the piano and began to play James Blunt's "You're Beautiful." Wow, on top of everything else, the man was musical.

"Oh, brother," Jack muttered under his breath.

She nudged his knee.

Employees of the funeral home walked into the chapel and stopped next to pews, a signal for the attendees to exit. She kept her eye on Jolie as she walked down the aisle, dabbing at her eyes. When Carlotta saw her veer off in the entryway, she whispered to Jack, "I'm going to the ladies' room."

"Hurry back, I'm your ride," he murmured, standing to let her out.

Getting up as quickly as she dared, she threaded her way through the crowd to the near-empty ladies' room. She glanced down to see that Jolie was standing in one of the three stalls, blowing her nose. Carlotta pushed open the door, bumping into her from behind.

"Excuse me," Jolie protested in a teary voice, "this stall is taken—"

"Shh!" She stepped inside and closed the door behind her. "Jolie, it's me, Carlotta."

Jolie's eyes widened, and she stumbled backward and would have fallen into the toilet if Carlotta hadn't caught her. "Carlotta? You're alive!"

They embraced, laughing, then Jolie pulled back. "But how? What's going on?"

"Long story," Carlotta said. "Someone stole my identity

and my car, then jumped off the bridge. The police thought it was me and by the time they realized their mistake, they had already declared me dead. And they asked me to go along with it."

"But why?"

Carlotta bit into her lip. "I…kind of lied to you about my parents."

Jolie squinted. "You said they were traveling around the country."

"That's true. The part that I left out is that they're traveling because they're fugitives. My father is wanted for investment fraud."

"So this funeral?"

"Was a ploy by the D.A. to try to smoke out my parents."

"And did they come?"

She shook her head.

Jolie looked mournful. "I'm sorry, Carlotta."

"It's all right, I expected it. What I didn't expect is for so many people to come to my funeral. I certainly didn't expect you and Beck to come all the way from Costa Rica."

"You're my friend, Carlotta. The only friend I had when I worked at Neiman's. You took me under your wing during the day—and taught me how to be a party crasher at night."

"And nearly got you arrested for murder."

"Well, that's true," Jolie said, laughing. "But it all worked out. And I have Beck."

"And you're happy?"

"So happy. And what about you? Do you have someone special in your life?"

Carlotta hesitated, then shook her head. "I'm still working on it. I have to go now, but I couldn't let you leave without knowing the truth. Everyone else will know soon. It's so good to see you."

Jolie laughed. "It's a miracle to see *you*."

They hugged again, then Carlotta slipped out of the stall and exited the bathroom. She glanced around for Jack and heard the door open behind her. She turned to give Jolie another smile, but did a double-take to see Patricia Alexander coming out of the bathroom looking like someone had just peed in her hairspray.

Carlotta frowned. Where had she come from? And had she overheard her conversation with Jolie?

Out of the corner of her eye, she spotted Jack standing near the entrance. As she walked toward him, she saw Liz Fischer coming the opposite way. Moving at her slower old-lady pace meant that Liz got to him first.

Her father's former attorney was a blonde with sharp edges—except for the store-bought boobs. She stood so close to Jack that they could've been wearing the same pair of pants. From the possessive way that Liz looked at Jack, she didn't care who saw them, and certainly didn't pay any mind to an older lady standing nearby. Jack, apparently hypnotized by the woman's undulating bosom, didn't notice her either.

"Come by tonight, handsome, and I'll fix you a big, juicy steak."

Carlotta arched an eyebrow. The woman obviously knew what he liked.

"I've been on assignment for a couple of days, Liz. I really need to go home tonight."

A sly smile slid onto Liz's face. "I'll meet you there. I'll bring the steaks and *you* bring the meat." She laughed and undulated away, then looked back. "By the way, I bought a killer dress for the awards dinner. Can't wait."

Jack watched her walk away, an unreadable expression on his face, which became more telltale when he turned to see her standing there.

Carlotta gave him a flat smile. "Don't worry—I'll find another ride." She turned toward the door and bumped into an elderly gentleman in her haste to get away. The man gave her costume an appreciative look as she apologized profusely. She was almost to the door when Jack's hand encircled her upper arm and brought her up short.

"Wait."

She frowned. "You're manhandling an old woman."

"Is there a problem here?" the older man asked, eyeing Jack suspiciously.

Carlotta gave Jack a wide-eyed smile of innocence.

"No, sir," Jack said, poking his cheek out with his tongue. "I have to escort this lady back to the psych ward. They let her out only long enough to attend the funeral."

"Oh." The man glanced at Carlotta, then hurried away.

She crossed her arms. "Was that necessary?"

Jack frowned. "Lucas is waiting in the office. He wants to see you and Wesley."

Her pulse spiked. "Did my parents show?"

"No."

"Then what for?"

"Some sort of debriefing. And I assume, to discuss how you will miraculously be brought back to life."

She sighed. "Okay, let's go."

"Have you seen Wesley?" he asked.

"No," she said, glancing around and wondering who—other than her parents—could have shown up that would have captured her brother's attention.

28

"Thank you for coming," Wesley said when E. stopped next to her car.

"You're welcome." She shielded her green eyes from the sun. "It was a nice service. You said some wonderful things about your sister."

"I meant all of them," he said. Girls loved that mushy stuff.

She smiled. "I'm so sorry I didn't get to meet her."

"Oh, well, maybe someday."

She squinted. "Hmm?"

"Uh...in heaven." Where had *that* come from? He crossed himself for good measure and E. gave him a perplexed little smile.

"You can skip our meeting this Wednesday if you want," she offered. "I figure you'll need some time to regroup."

His stomach dove. And miss seeing her? "No, that's okay.

I think it's good if I stay on my regular schedule. I'll be there."

"Okay, I'll see you Wednesday."

This was his opportunity, and Wesley was going to take it. "Thanks again." He opened his arms for a hug and just as he'd hoped, she walked into them. As he wrapped his arms around her, he buried his face in her luxurious red hair to fill his lungs with the scent of her shampoo. Her full breasts crushed against his chest, but before his body could even react, she had pulled back.

"Bye, Wesley. Call me if you need anything."

He nodded and stood there until she drove away, then murmured, "One of these days..."

"She's cute."

Wesley turned to find Liz Fischer walking toward him in that loose-hipped gait that women with great legs seemed to master. A stunner who tied his tongue into knots, the hot blonde had helped him when he was arrested for hacking into the courthouse computer system because she had been his father's attorney.

"Is that your girlfriend?" Liz asked.

He shook his head. "Probation officer."

She laughed. "Well, I guess she makes your punishment a little more bearable."

"A little."

She reached up and adjusted his collar. "When you were up front today, all I could think about was how much you look like your father."

"That's what I'm told," he stuttered. Her perfume enveloped him and his cock jumped.

"Well, I should know," she said. "Your father and I were very good friends." A sad smile crossed her face. "I thought he might even put in a guest appearance today."

"I guess we all did."

"I'm sorry about your sister," she said, running her finger down his lapel. "I guess that means you're all alone."

Wesley wet his lips, getting a decent woody now. "Yeah."

She angled her head. "You know, Wesley, I have a guest-house that I rarely use. You're welcome to use it sometime if you ever get lonely."

He swallowed. "A guesthouse?"

"Yes. Actually, it's more of an office. Your father and I used to work on his case there. In fact, all the files are still there."

At the spike in his pulse, his erection sprang to life. "Really? I'd like to see them."

"Then come over sometime."

"Wesley!"

He turned his head to see Jack Terry standing in front of the funeral home, legs wide, hands on hips—his pissed-off-cop stance.

"What?" Wesley shouted back.

Jack gestured for him to come back to the funeral home and Wesley tamped down the urge to return a gesture of his own. "Guess I'd better go," he said to Liz.

"Okay," she said silkily. "Just keep my offer in mind. Do you still have my card?"

"Yeah."

"Good." She turned and walked to her red convertible Jag. Wesley exhaled slowly. Her car alone could make him come.

Reluctantly, he walked back to the funeral home. Jack was standing there, watching Liz drive away, his mouth set.

"What do you want?" Wesley asked.

"Lucas wants to see you and your sister inside for a debriefing," the detective said, biting off his words. "We're waiting for you."

29

While Jack went in search of Wesley, Carlotta went in search of Hannah. She found her still sitting on the front pew in the now-empty chapel, staring at the red casket. She looked ghoulish with black eye-liner running down her face. Carlotta settled into the pew next to her.

"She must have been a good friend of yours," she said in her older-lady voice.

Hannah glared. "The bitch didn't even say goodbye."

Carlotta bit back a smile. "Sometimes people hurt the ones they love for reasons that can't be explained."

"Do you write for Hallmark or something, lady?"

"No. But I can tell that you're upset."

Hannah pulled at a shredded tissue in her hand. "She's the only person I could be myself around."

"She probably felt that same way about you."

"It's my fault."

Carlotta frowned. "What do you mean?"

"I knew she was depressed. You wouldn't believe the things she's been through—her brother didn't tell the half of it. If I'd been her, I'd have killed myself ages ago."

Carlotta's powdered eyebrows arched.

Hannah blew her nose noisily, piercings clinking. "But she hung in there through a lot of bad shit. I thought things were getting better. Her brother was starting to be more responsible and she'd met this guy who was crazy about her."

"Oh?"

"Yeah." Hannah's shoulders fell. "I just didn't see the signs."

"It's true that sometimes we don't see what's right in front of us."

Hannah squinted. "I'm sorry, who are you?"

Carlotta reached up to remove the retainer that fixed her gapped grin. "Hannah, it's me."

Hannah's eyes widened and she scrambled back on the pew. "Carlotta—you're back! I always made you promise that if you died first, you'd let me know what it's like." She frowned at the costume. "Was that the only body available?"

Carlotta rolled her eyes. "Hannah, you idiot, I'm not dead. I never was. It was all a hoax."

As realization dawned, Hannah's face revealed disbelief, then surprise, then anger. "You bitch! I can't believe you did this to me!"

"I'm sorry. I didn't want to—let me explain." She told Hannah in as few words as possible what had transpired in the last few days, leaving out the part where she'd had sex with Jack.

Hannah pointed to the casket. "So who's in there?"

"Nobody. Coop pulled it from the sample room."

"So Coop was in on this? And Wesley?"

"Yes, but not willingly. And Peter knew, but only because he was there the night I came home and found out everyone thought I was dead."

"So the woman who jumped…"

"We still don't know who she is or why she killed herself."

"Amazing. What about your job?"

"I, uh, kind of got suspended before this all happened. But Detective Terry let Lindy in on it so she'd keep my job open."

A movement in the back of the chapel caught her attention. She looked up to see Jack and was relieved to see Wesley with him.

"I have to go meet with the D.A.," she said to Hannah, then winced. "How mad at me are you?"

Hannah glared. "Superbly." Slowly her glare turned into a smirk and she sighed. "But I'll wait to take you and Wesley home."

Carlotta smiled. "Thanks. Oh, and you said some pretty nice things just now."

The glare returned. "You know, I could kill you and then this funeral wouldn't have been wasted."

Carlotta laughed as she walked back up the aisle, but sobered by the time she reached Jack and Wesley. "So we've been summoned."

Jack nodded curtly and led them to an office where Kelvin Lucas and a couple of assistant D.A.'s were waiting. Lucas looked at her and frowned. "Who's this?"

"It's me, Lucas. Carlotta."

He squinted, then looked at Jack, who looked at the ceiling. Lucas frowned, then cleared his throat. "I thought you should know how we'll be proceeding."

"Since you didn't trick my dad into giving himself up?" Wesley asked in a bored tone.

"Your father is a criminal," Lucas spat out. "And I guess I gave him more credit than he deserved when I thought he might care enough about his own daughter to come to her funeral."

Carlotta hugged herself, glad for the heavy makeup to hide behind. A lump of emotion lodged painfully in her throat as all eyes in the room darted to her, then away. Jack shifted and wiped his hand over his mouth.

"My father cares," Wesley said angrily. "He probably knew it was a trap."

Lucas gave a dry laugh. "Your father isn't smart, kid, just heartless."

"He's smart enough to have outwitted you this long," Wesley returned.

"Wesley," Carlotta admonished, trying to salvage the situation, "not now." She turned to Lucas. "We had a deal."

But Lucas was staring at Wesley with loathing—pent up hatred for their father, no doubt. "The deal's off."

"Lucas—" Jack began.

"I said they could have the reward money if they helped to lure in their father and if he was captured. He wasn't, therefore no reward."

Carlotta had expected as much, but struggled to contain her

disappointment. Besides, she hadn't done it for the reward—she'd done it to buy Wesley some breathing room. "What about my brother's probation and fine?"

"Unchanged," Kelvin said, eyeing Wesley triumphantly.

She gripped the edge of the table for support. "But you said—"

"You should talk to your brother, Carlotta, and convince him to be as cooperative as you are."

He might as well have slapped her. Lucas made it sound as if she were on his side, but she'd done this for Wesley. And all for nothing. How stupid was she not to get Liz involved, not to get the D.A.'s offer in writing?

"What gives you the right to play games with my family?" she said to the smug, odious man, her voice shaking.

"My job title," he said simply, cracking his knuckles with a casual sweep of his hands. "And the fact that your father and brother both committed crimes in my jurisdiction."

"Lucas, with all due respect," Jack broke in, "you owe Carlotta and Wesley *something* for their assistance. Carlotta allowed her friends and family to think she was dead, for God's sake."

"A press release will be issued from my office in time for the eleven o'clock news stating that Ms. Wren had checked herself into a clinic for exhaustion. Her car and purse were stolen by some desperate woman who took her own life and who has yet to be identified. It was all a case of mistaken identity." Lucas pushed to his feet. "This meeting is over."

She looked at Jack, panicked that everything was falling apart. He gave her an almost imperceptible shake of his head.

"Lucas," he said. "Someone stole Carlotta's identity. The least we can do is to use the power of the D.A.'s office to help get her financial records straightened out."

Lucas gave him a strange look. "Have the Wrens become a charity project of yours, Detective?"

A muscle jumped in Jack's jaw. "That was out of line, sir."

"Not if it keeps you from going *over* the line, Detective." Lucas swept out the door, his assistants scrambling behind him.

"Fucking asshole," Wesley muttered, then looked at Carlotta. "Told you so."

Carlotta blinked back tears—the entire charade, for nothing. Oh, unless she counted making a fool out of herself with Jack Terry. She looked at Jack and betrayal flooded over her in waves. He was the one who'd convinced her to go along with Lucas.

"Wesley," she said through gritted teeth, "Hannah's waiting in the chapel to take us home. Let's go."

Wesley stomped out and as she followed him, Jack reached out to clasp her arm. "Carlotta, wait."

She stopped and stared up at him wearily. "What do you want, Jack?"

"I'm sorry."

"For what?"

He lifted his hands. "For…everything. I'm sorry for going along with Lucas."

"You were just doing your job," she said, parroting him.

A shadow fell over his gold-colored eyes "And I'm sorry that your parents didn't show. I know how that must make you feel."

She gave him a flat smile. "Don't presume to know how I feel about anything, Detective. See you around."

Feeling defeated but determined not to let it show, she walked back through the entryway to where Wesley stood talking to Coop, figuring out their week's work schedule. She slowed as she approached, noting the men's body language— Wesley gravitated to the older man, unwittingly mimicking his movements. They seemed to click on several levels and for that, she was grateful to Coop.

Coop turned and took in her costume. "I thought that was you."

She frowned, indignant. "How could you tell?"

"When you look at someone as much as I've looked at you, you just know."

Wesley gave his boss a withering look. "I'll go get Hannah."

Carlotta bit back a smile as they followed Wesley into the chapel. "Thank you for all the trouble, Coop."

"I was paid for my services," Coop said. "You were the one who had to go through all the trouble." His eyes suddenly clouded with concern. "Carlotta, I'm sorry your parents didn't show."

The sincerity in his face dissolved the offhand joke that sprang to her tongue. "Thank you," she murmured instead. Then she angled her head at him. "I didn't know you played piano."

A smile curved his mouth. "There's a lot about me you don't know." Then the smile disappeared. "Unfortunately, not all of it is good."

She studied his light-brown eyes and realized that despite

his peaceful exterior, Coop was still haunted by things in his past. "Perfection is boring," she said lightly.

"You think?" He looked as if he wanted to say more, then changed his mind. She wondered if the memory of her kissing Jack had stopped him.

Gesturing toward the front of the chapel, she asked, "Is there something that can be done with all the flowers that people sent?"

"I have a gentleman to bury who is indigent; I can send the flowers to his gravesite."

"That would be wonderful. Thank you."

"Sis," Wesley called, "I thought you said Hannah was in here?"

Carlotta looked around the empty chapel. "She was—" She spied the casket and noticed that the white roses on top had been displaced.

Hannah *wouldn't*.

But as she rushed to the casket, she knew that Hannah *would*.

She yanked up the lid and sure enough, Hannah lay inside in all her Goth glory.

"Hannah!" Carlotta shouted.

Hannah's eyes popped open, her expression reverent. "This could possibly be the best day of my life."

"Get out."

"Okay, okay. Give me a hand, would you?"

It took all of them to get Hannah out of the casket, then Carlotta shepherded her toward the parking lot before she could do any more damage. When they reached the graffitied van, Hannah suddenly gave her a fierce hug. "Don't ever scare me like that again, okay?"

Carlotta smiled and nodded, then expelled a long sigh. What a day! She climbed into the van, feeling as old as she was made up to be. While Hannah and Wesley chatted about his latest body retrievals, she leaned her head back and tried to forget what had transpired over the past few days. As they pulled out of the parking lot, they passed Jack's car, and he was sitting in it. In the few seconds that their gazes locked, she tried to telegraph the betrayal she felt over the way things had turned out—and that she never wanted to see him again.

Minus ten points, Jack.

30

When Hannah dropped them off—and retrieved her black door wreath, thankyouverymuch—Carlotta's first thought when she walked into the townhouse was that it felt empty. Of course, Jack was a big guy, he'd taken up a lot of room in their small place. So naturally it *would* feel empty.

"Whew, it's nice to have our place back to ourselves," Wesley said, dropping onto the couch and reaching for the remote control.

"Right," she said. "I think I'm going to go take off this getup."

"Okay," he said absently.

"Wesley."

He looked up. "Yeah?"

"You didn't have to say all those nice things that you said today at the service."

He nodded. "I know."

"Thanks."

He gestured to her costume. "Don't mention it, Grandma."

"And I'm sorry that I let Kelvin Lucas talk me into this whole charade. I should've listened to you. And I should've told you about Dad calling."

"Yeah, I should be in the loop on family stuff."

"So do you think Dad knew the funeral thing was a trap?"

"Yeah."

"But how?"

He shrugged. "I don't know. Maybe he has the house bugged."

Carlotta pursed her lips. "I hadn't thought about that." Then she winced. If so, her parents had been privy to some pretty harsh things she'd said about them…not to mention her sexcapade with Detective Terry.

"Or maybe he did something low-tech, like call."

"But Jack wouldn't let me answer the phone, I could only call out."

"Did anyone call between the time Jack left that night and came back the next morning?"

She shook her head. "Wait—there was a phone call just before he rang the doorbell the next morning."

"Do you remember who it was?"

"It was one of those Internet calling-card numbers."

"Like the one Dad used to call your cell phone."

She squinted. "How do you know that?"

"When Hannah told me that Dad had called you, I, uh, tapped into your cell phone records online."

Her eyes bugged. "Is that legal?"

"In some countries."

"Wesley!"

"So it was probably him that called the house that morning. When you answered, he knew you were okay, so he ignored the news reports."

She frowned. "It sounds a little James Bond-y. Lots of people use those calling cards. It could have been a wrong number or a telemarketer."

"It was him. Now we just wait until he calls again. You plan to stay in touch with Peter, don't you?"

"I thought you didn't like Peter."

Wesley's expression was one of pure innocence. "I never said that."

"Hypocrite."

"Hey, helping Dad is the least he can do to make amends."

"You mean for dumping me?"

"Yeah."

"So you want me to pretend to like Peter so he'll help Dad."

"I thought you *did* like Peter."

"I do, but not in that way...I don't think...yet."

He rolled his eyes. "Whatever. Just keep it in mind."

"Okay. Meanwhile, no more secrets?"

"No more secrets."

Carlotta went to her bedroom and closed the door. She started peeling off the costume, then used the heel of one shoe to dismantle the fire alarm and sat on the toilet to smoke two cigarettes. She managed to hold off the tears until she climbed in the shower to rid herself of the makeup on her face and neck and hands. And then she succumbed because she felt so damned sorry for herself.

Given the choice between the wrong decision and the right one, she always managed to make the wrong one. What was it Lucas had called her in front of Jack? A charity case. God, that cut to the bone. Well, starting tomorrow she was going to get her life in order and back on track. By the time she returned to Neiman's, she'd be ready to focus on reclaiming her spot as the store's top salesperson.

And she was going to put her father as far out of her mind as possible. Although Wesley's theory about why their parents hadn't come forward made *him* feel better, she didn't buy it for a minute. But the worst-case scenario *had* happened—her parents had rejected her even in death—and she'd lived through it.

When she emerged from her room, she felt somewhat revived. Wesley had popped corn, and they watched a dumb movie on the enormous television and laughed at the corny parts. But Carlotta kept glancing toward the kitchen where she'd become accustomed to seeing and hearing Jack. She wondered what he was doing tonight. Sharing that steak—and more—with Liz Fischer?

Later when she crawled into bed, she was bombarded with sensual images of him—the way he'd had to lie diagonally to fit on her bed, how he'd slept with his hand on the curve of her waist, the lingering male scent of him in the linens that she would wash first thing tomorrow. The memory of him standing with Liz wrapped around him was a good reminder that she simply had been a convenient fill-in. A man like Jack

Terry wasn't interested in a long-term relationship. He had told her as much and she had committed the classic female sin: thinking he would make an exception for her.

She'd be better off to turn her heart toward a man who was interested in a relationship. Like Peter.

Or maybe even Coop.

She rolled onto her back and sighed. Or maybe another man whom she hadn't yet met....

31

Sunday, Carlotta awoke mid-morning with a headache and a craving for a cigarette. She smoked half of one while she got ready in the bathroom, then followed the scent of food to the kitchen where Wesley was already eating.

"French toast," he said, pointing to the stove. "Oh and according to CNN, you're alive again."

"Thanks for letting me know. Did it come out like Lucas said, about me checking myself into a hospital for exhaustion?"

"Verbatim."

"So instead of people thinking I'm dead, everyone thinks I had a nervous breakdown."

"Pretty much."

"Great. What's on your agenda today?"

"I'm working with Coop. How about you?"

"I have so much to do, I don't know where to start." She

glanced toward the breakfast bar where only yesterday morning Jack's equipment had been spread out. Among the papers he'd left was her ghastly credit report. She passed it to Wesley. "Do you know anything about the accounts I circled?"

He scanned the pages and whistled low. "No...why would I?"

"Just checking. The woman who stole my identity must have opened these accounts. Jack said once I identified the bogus ones, I could file for some sort of affidavit to send to my creditors. Maybe I'll do that today."

"Why don't you just file bankruptcy?"

She stabbed the French toast with her fork. "Because—starting today—we are going to be on a budget and we're going to get all of our debt paid off, meaning *my* credit cards and *your* loan sharks."

"At least my loan sharks don't sell my address to junk mailers."

"Well at least my credit card companies don't make threatening house calls."

"Hey, no one's been around here in a while."

"Yeah, for at least two weeks." Carlotta tapped the table. "I mean it, Wesley, we're going to get our finances in order. And that means no more surprise purchases, like massive electronic devices."

"You seemed to enjoy the TV last night," he said sourly.

"Sure I enjoyed it, but next time you get your hands on ten thousand dollars, we need to do other things around here. Got it? That means *no* gambling."

He frowned. "So are you going to cut up your credit cards?"

She inhaled sharply and choked on a piece of toast.

"Uh-huh, that's what I thought."

"Okay, okay." She left and returned with her wallet, from which she withdrew all of her credits cards—all thirty-seven of them.

"Jesus Christ," Wesley said. "No wonder your credit is in the shitter." He got up and rummaged around in a junk drawer and produced a pair of scissors. "Here you go."

She worked her mouth from side to side. "Okay, so I need to keep a couple for emergencies."

He picked up the Sunglass Hut credit card. "Yeah, those solar eclipses can really sneak up on you."

She snatched up the card and cut it in two. "Happy?"

"One down."

Carlotta stared at the pile and sulked. They were all so bright and shiny.

"Do you need for me to hold your hand?" Wesley asked dryly.

"No. I can do this." She fished out two generic cards that she could use anywhere, then took a deep breath and began cutting like a madwoman. A few minutes later, they looked down at the colorful pile of scrap plastic.

"Wow, we could use it for mulch," Wesley said. "If we had plants."

She frowned. "That's another thing. We're going to fix this place up."

"You just put us on a budget. Fixing the house up is going to cost money."

"I'll…think of something."

She walked over to the refrigerator to get out the juice. "What's in the casserole dish?"

"Mrs. Winningham gave it to me. It's chicken something, I think."

Carlotta closed the refrigerator door. "That old bat didn't even come to my funeral."

"Would you go to hers?"

"Probably."

Wesley rinsed his dishes and put them in the dishwasher. "I'm outta here."

"Isn't Coop picking you up?"

"No...I'm riding my bike and meeting him."

She picked up her purse. "I think I'll go, too. I hope the trains aren't single-tracking today."

"When will you get your car back?"

"Who knows?"

She followed him into the living room and waited for him to pick up his backpack and jacket. Then he frowned and leaned over to pick up one of the Christmas gifts that had fallen to the floor. "Hey." When he stood, his face was red with anger. "What's this?"

"What's what?"

"You opened the gifts." He looked stricken. "You *promised* you wouldn't."

She shook her head. "But I didn't. I swear."

Wesley extended it to her. "Well, somebody did. It's been unwrapped and rewrapped with new tape." He picked up another one. "This one, too...all of them." She could tell he was holding back tears. It was the one sacred link to their parents and she'd promised never to violate it. And she hadn't.

A ball of molten fury erupted in Carlotta's chest as she gripped the small package.

She knew who had.

Carlotta marched inside the police station, through the metal detectors and stopped at the Plexiglas window. The same woman was there as when she'd come down to find out about Wesley's arrest—the first time she'd met Jack.

That seemed like a lifetime ago.

"Hey, I remember you," the woman said, eyeing Carlotta's short skirt and designer T-shirt. "Miss Too Good for the Waiting Room."

Carlotta gave her a tight smile. "And I remember you, um..."

"Brooklyn."

"Right. Brooklyn. I'm looking for Detective Jack Terry. Is he in?"

"What's your name again?"

"Carlotta Wren."

Brooklyn blinked. "The woman who was supposed to be dead?"

"That's me—alive and kicking." And looking for a target.

"I'll check to see if he's available."

Brooklyn picked up the phone and hit a couple of buttons, then turned away from Carlotta. After a few seconds, she set down the phone. "Detective Terry is in a meeting."

"Tell him this is important."

"He said he'll call you."

Carlotta poked her tongue into her cheek. "I see." She glanced at the woman's hands and smiled. "Beautiful rings."

"Thanks."

"Do you like jewelry?"

"Girl, who doesn't?"

"Good point." Carlotta fished in her purse. "Brooklyn, I have in my hand a coupon good for seventy percent off one item in the Neiman Marcus jewelry department, and it's yours if you just open that little door over there and turn your back so I can slip through."

One of Brooklyn's eyebrows arched. "Hmm. Is it valid on clearance items?"

Carlotta slid the coupon under the half-moon opening. "Oh, yes."

Brook considered the coupon, then pursed her mouth. "You're not planning to shoot him or anything, are you?"

"No. But when I'm finished with him, he might shoot himself."

"If you get in trouble, I don't know you."

"Fair enough."

Brooklyn picked up the coupon and slid it into her pocket.

"The door will be open when you get over there. Do you remember where his office is?"

"I'll just follow the smell of a rat."

"Good luck."

Carlotta walked over to the door and heard a click. She opened it and stepped inside, knowing the secret of being somewhere she shouldn't be was acting like she had every right to be there. She flashed confident smiles at everyone she passed as she wound her way back to Jack's cubicle. He was standing in the hall talking to a uniformed officer, who was distracted by her appearance. Jack's companion looked her up and down, his mouth forming an O. Jack turned to see what had the man's attention and nearly dropped his coffee cup.

"Detective," she said, walking up to him. "I need to talk to you."

"How did you get back here?"

She crossed her arms. "I was hoping we could talk in private, but the hallway is fine with me."

Jack looked at his companion. "Excuse us." Then he shepherded Carlotta into his piled-up office and dropped into his chair. "What's this all about?"

She leaned down until they were nose to nose. *"You opened the gifts under our tree?"*

He had the decency to blanch. "I...didn't look in them."

"You unwrapped them, but you didn't look in them?"

"Right."

"You're lying."

He didn't respond, only looked at her with that unreadable expression that she hated.

Her hand itched to slap him. "How dare you? I told you what those stupid gifts mean to my brother."

"Look, by rights, those gifts should've been opened and searched when your parents first went missing. They could've contained important information. Or maybe money for you and your brother to live on."

"That was *our* choice to make," she said evenly. "Mine and Wesley's."

"That doesn't make sense to me."

"It doesn't have to." She put her palm to her forehead. "I can't believe I…"

"What?"

"Slept with you!" Carlotta hissed. "What was I thinking?"

He rubbed at his eyes. "Look, I tried to talk you out of it."

"Yeah, while you were sticking your tongue down my throat."

"Look, what's done is done. Forget about it."

I have. His unspoken words hung in the air.

She gripped the shoulder strap on her purse and lifted her chin. "Well, are you going to tell me what you found inside the packages, Detective?"

Jack gave a harsh little laugh. "I thought you didn't want to know."

She bit down on the inside of her cheek to ward off sudden tears. "You're right. I don't." She removed the credit report from her purse and cleared her throat to steady her voice. "I've identified the accounts that I didn't authorize. If you could point me in the right direction to get that affidavit, I'd appreciate it."

"I can take care of it," he said quietly.

"I'd prefer to work with someone else. I'm not a *charity case.*"

He sighed. "Carlotta, please sit down. I wasn't trying to give you the brush-off, I really was going to call you. I have some updates, some pictures for you to look at."

"Regarding the woman who died?"

"Yes."

She glanced around and he quickly emptied the stack of papers from the seat of his extra chair. Carlotta lowered herself to sit on the edge. "Do you know who she is?"

"Not yet, but we're working on it." Jack pulled a grainy black and white photo from a file and handed it to her. "Do you recognize her?"

It was a woman standing in front of an ATM, wearing sunglasses, her long dark hair pulled back into a ponytail like she often wore hers.

"She looks a little like me."

"But do you recognize anything about her? What she's wearing maybe?"

"The sunglasses are Bulgari, the watch is a Rolex, the shirt is Ralph Lauren, and…" She looked up. "Do you have a magnifying glass?"

He opened a drawer and rummaged for a few seconds, finally producing one.

She held it over the photo. "And the earrings are Slane and Slane." She handed back the magnifying glass.

Jack's dark eyebrows shot up. "O—kay." He frowned. "How'd you do that?"

"Retail is my life, Detective."

He took a few notes. "I need for you to check your credit card receipts to see if anything she's wearing was charged to your accounts. We got lucky—when she tried to make a second cash withdrawal after the first one, the ATM kept the card. We're running it now for prints. And the local stations are going to air the photo and ask for phone-in tips." He handed her a photocopied form. "This is the request that the DMV processed to issue a duplicate of your driver's license. Do you recognize the signature?"

"It looks like mine."

"But you didn't fill out this form?"

"No. Where was the duplicate mailed?"

"A post office box at the mall, in your name."

She frowned. "I don't have a box at the mall."

He held up another form. "Yes, you do. And who knows how many bills you have waiting for you there. Now, *why* the thief would rent a box so close to where you work, I can't explain—it makes no sense." He shrugged. "Then again, she did jump off a bridge."

Carlotta puffed out her cheeks in a shaky exhale. "This could go on and on."

"So let me help you."

She lifted her gaze to his and was confounded by the sincerity she saw there. Her impressions of Jack revolved through her head like slot machine wheels and kept coming up with the confusing—and losing—combination of good, bad and sexy.

"Carlotta, please. I want to."

She pressed her lips together and nodded. "Okay. I'm not in a position to say no. I'm drowning here."

He set aside the papers, leaned forward and sandwiched her hand in both of his. "I'm sorry if you're angry with me. But let me tell you the view from where I'm standing. I see a beautiful, sexy, intelligent young woman who's had to fight like a tigress for everything she has because her good-for-nothing father didn't have the balls to face his failures. I see her shrinking from men who care about her. I see what his rejection has done to her. And I want to bring this son of a bitch to justice so that maybe she can get on with her life."

Carlotta sat mesmerized by his intensity, her heart thumping in her chest. Well, if he put it *that* way….

"Am I interrupting something?"

She looked up to see Liz Fischer standing there, holding a dress bag over her shoulder. Carlotta withdrew her hand from Jack's and pushed to her feet.

Jack stood a heartbeat later. "No. Carlotta and I were discussing business but we're finished."

Liz flicked her gaze over Carlotta and smiled. "You're looking good, Carlotta, considering I attended your funeral yesterday. Lucas filled me in this morning." She gave Jack a sardonic look. "Although you could've mentioned it."

"You know I couldn't," he said evenly.

She gave Carlotta a "girlfriend" eye-roll. "The man is useless when it comes to pillow talk."

Carlotta averted her gaze. "I should be going."

"Oh, stay," Liz said. "Tell me what you think of the dress I'm wearing to Jack's big awards dinner."

"Liz, I don't think—" Jack began.

"Jack is receiving an important award," Liz interrupted, unzipping the bag.

"So I've heard," Carlotta murmured.

Liz opened the bag to reveal a dazzling platinum-colored gown with beaded trim.

"Badgley Mischka," Carlotta said, nodding. "It's...stunning." She cut her gaze to Jack. "And it'll look beautiful with a gray tux."

"Won't it?" Liz gushed. "I haven't bought shoes yet though. Maybe I'll drop by Neiman's and let you help me decide on a pair."

Jack stared at the floor.

Carlotta knew when she was being put in her place. And she had no desire to compete with Liz over Jack's "meat." The woman was welcome to him. "Sure Liz, I'd be happy to." She looked at Jack. "Thanks for helping me to get this all straightened out."

He nodded, but seemed unable to speak.

"I know the way out," she said, turning toward the exit. "You two have fun."

Carlotta couldn't get out of the police station fast enough. No matter where she looked, the image of Jack and Liz as a couple loomed in front of her.

Since the mall was only a short distance away, she decided it was as good a time as any to drop by Neiman's and start working her way back into everyone's good graces. As luck would have it, the first person she ran into was Patricia Alexander, who pursed her mouth and drew herself up primly.

"Well, if it isn't the woman whose funeral I attended yesterday."

"I, um, am sorry about that," Carlotta said. "I guess you heard."

"You could say that." Patricia glared at her. "That was some trick you pulled. People were upset and took off work on a busy Saturday to attend your service. Who knows how many sales I missed out on?"

Carlotta blinked at the woman's intensity. "Like I said, I'm sorry. Is Michael working today?"

"Yes. I assume he had some commissions to make up, too." Patricia turned her back and Carlotta gave her the finger, then made her way to the shoe department. Michael was helping a customer when she caught his attention. He motioned to the stock room and she followed him inside.

"You gave everyone quite a scare, missy."

"I'm sorry...there was a mixup."

"I know. I heard it on the news this morning. Are you feeling better?"

"Um, yes."

"Sorry that I don't have time to talk but I'm kind of swamped here."

"I understand, and I heard from Patricia how everyone needs to recoup sales from being out yesterday."

He sighed. "She's not so bad—just abrupt."

A worm of jealousy worked its way through her chest. Michael and that woman were becoming friends? "I just have a question—do you happen to remember the name of the florist that delivered the roses the other day?"

"No, why?"

She gave a little shrug. "Like you said, I might have a secret admirer and I'm trying to find out who sent them."

"Sorry, I don't remember. When are you coming back to work?"

"Next Monday."

"Okay, we'll catch up then."

Carlotta nodded and left. She couldn't blame him for being irritated with her. He'd thought she was dead, after all. No wonder he was making a new friend.

She needed to give him some space, then try to repair the friendship that she'd neglected. Outside the mall she hailed a cab and gave the address for Moody's Cigar Bar. She knew it would be slow with the lounge upstairs being closed on Sunday, and she wanted to thank June for lending her shoulder the last time she'd been in.

And okay, she was craving a big, thick torpedo.

Cigar, that is.

When she pushed open the door to the quaint establishment, the bell tinkled and she was greeted with the comforting tang of tobacco in the air. The gleaming ebony horseshoe-shaped counter grounded the art-deco style showroom. The deep, narrow room was lined with glass cabinets of cigar boxes, lighters, ashtrays and canisters of loose tobacco. A smoker's paradise and the domain of June Moody, who had inherited the place from her father.

The owner herself was descending the stairs in the back of the room that led to the wine and martini bar. She was impeccably dressed as always, her blond hair and makeup perfect. But when June saw Carlotta, her step faltered and she gripped the hand railing.

"It's me, June. Alive and well."

The woman's face was a mask of disbelief. "What on *earth?*"

Carlotta smiled. "If you got a cigar, I got a story."

June walked toward her, smiling wide. "Grab a seat at the bar. What's your pleasure?"

"Something long and strong."

June laughed. "Coming right up."

Over smoldering cigars and creamed coffee, Carlotta brought her friend up to speed. "I'm sorry for deceiving everyone. I appreciate you coming to the service yesterday."

The older woman shook her head. "Honey, you do seem to find trouble."

"Trouble finds me," Carlotta corrected.

June drew on her cigar and exhaled elegantly. "So what do you make of this woman who stole your identity and committed suicide?"

"I don't know what to think. I don't know who it could be or why she picked me."

"Maybe because she resembled you."

Carlotta tapped ash into a glass ashtray. "So maybe she knew me?"

"Could be. Maybe a customer? You must see hundreds of people every day, or should I say, they see you."

"The woman rented a P.O. box at the mall in my name, so there could be a connection to my job, I suppose."

June glanced up and smiled at someone through the window. "Speaking of long and strong."

Carlotta looked up to see Coop walking in, carrying a cigar box. His face lit up when he saw her and she was equally pleased to see him in a situation that didn't involve a dead body. He looked handsome and appealing in a pair of worn jeans and a faded red T-shirt that molded to his buff chest and arms—who knew that lifting bodies could result in those kinds of guns? With his lean build, he was probably a runner, she decided.

Which was good, considering he might have to outrun Hannah some day.

"Carlotta was just filling me in on all the drama," June said. "Why don't you join us?"

"Don't mind if I do."

"I thought you and Wesley were working together today," Carlotta said.

Coop shook his head. "I wanted some time off and I thought he could use it too."

Carlotta smiled but wondered why Wesley had lied and where he'd gone today.

So much for no more secrets.

June set a cup of coffee in front of him and reclaimed her seat. "What do you have in the box?"

"It's for you," he said, pushing it toward her. "For all the cigar boxes you've given me."

June opened the lid and gasped. "Oh, Cooper, it's wonderful!"

Carlotta peered inside, and her mouth fell open. "That's this bar!"

Inside the cigar box was a miniature replica of the first floor of Moody's bar, down to the most minute detail—the horseshoe bar, the red and black checkerboard tile floor, the lettering on the windows, even tiny cigars in the tiny cigar boxes inside the tiny glass cabinets that lined the room.

"It's incredible," Carlotta breathed. "How did you do this?"

"One small piece at a time," he said.

"How long did it take?"

"I don't know. I've been working on it for months, a few hours at a time." He shrugged. "It keeps my hands busy."

"I love it," June said. "Thank you, Cooper. I'll always cherish it." She gave him a hug and a kiss, and Carlotta wondered briefly if he reminded her of the son she said was in the army. They would probably be around the same age.

"Now, if you'll excuse me for a few minutes," June said, "I'll see to those customers."

Carlotta looked at her watch. "Actually, I'm sorry—I should be going."

"Already?" Coop said, his disappointment clear.

"This identity theft is wreaking havoc with my credit. I have a lot of paperwork at home."

"Do you have your car back?"

"No, I'll grab a cab."

"I'll take you," he offered. "It's a nice day for a drive."

She smiled. "Okay. Thanks."

They said goodbye to June, then Carlotta followed Coop outside into the sunshine, wondering why she hadn't noticed before now that it was indeed a beautiful summer day, with unusually balmy temperatures and a nice breeze.

"Hope you don't mind getting your hair messed up," he said, stopping next to an immaculate white antique Corvette convertible with red leather interior.

"Wow, are you kidding? Coop, this is magnificent. What model year is this?"

"Seventy-two."

"I love convertibles."

He unlocked the door for her and opened it. "I know. I got a glimpse of your Miata inside your garage when I picked up Wesley a time or two."

She swung inside, delighting in the compact interior. "I adore that car, but it's been out of commission for a while."

He closed her door, then walked around to the driver's side and got in. "You don't like the Monte Carlo? It has pretty good engine pickup, I'll bet."

"Yeah, it's a muscle car. And it's my own fault that I'm stuck with it."

"What do you mean?"

"I bought it when the manufacturer was having a twenty-four hour test drive offer." She smiled wryly. "I needed something to drive for a special occasion and I had every intention of taking it back before the twenty-four hours expired."

Coop laughed and started the engine. "Uh-oh, I think I can guess the next part."

"I was arrested and the car was impounded and by the time I got it out, the car was officially mine."

He laughed harder and put the car into gear. "On second thought, I couldn't have guessed the next part. You are one extreme woman, Carlotta Wren. Do you care if we take the long way home?"

"Not at all." She returned his grin and lowered her sunglasses as they pulled into traffic. Coop was full of surprises and all of them so far had been good. As they wound their way around the more picturesque back roads of the city, Carlotta sneaked a peek at his profile, enjoying the relaxed way he held his body and the play of his thigh muscles beneath his jeans when he mashed the clutch.

The interior of the car was pristine down to the most tedious detail—not unlike the care he had put into the miniature vignette for June. She had heard of his exacting hobby, but hadn't seen any of his work. Allegedly, it was the hobby to which he attributed his sobriety. Indeed, it looked as if it required a steady, patient hand.

After being in the company of Jack Terry with his rough edge and unpredictable moods, being with Coop was a relaxing break from all the conflict in her life. Too soon, they were pulling into the town house driveway.

She smoothed a hand over her ponytail and sighed with pleasure. "Thanks for the ride, Coop. That was the most fun I've had in a long time."

"I'm glad." He nodded toward the closed garage. "I'm pretty handy with cars. I'd be happy to take a look at the Miata some time."

"Would you? I'd be eternally grateful."

He grinned. "Yeah?"

His flirting warmed her face, and she recalled her thought last night that she should be opening her heart to someone who seemed eager to embrace it. "Coop, why don't you have a girl?"

His eyes danced. "I'm working on it."

At the sound of a car slowing down on the street, Carlotta turned to see Peter's Porsche pulling up next to the Corvette.

"I'll let you go," Coop said with a wink.

"Thanks again for the ride." She climbed out and waved as

he backed out of the driveway, nursing the odd feeling that something unidentifiable was floating just beyond her grasp.

"Hi." Peter climbed out of his car and removed his designer sunglasses.

"Hi, yourself."

"Out for a ride?" he asked, watching Coop drive away.

"I was at a cigar bar downtown and ran into Coop. He gave me a ride home."

Peter looked puzzled. "Are you smoking cigars now?"

She angled her head, a little irritated that she felt as if she had to justify her actions. "Sometimes. The owner is a new friend who attended the service yesterday. I wanted to pay her a visit and try to explain what happened."

"Oh." He leaned forward and kissed her on the mouth, frowning slightly, she realized, at the taste of cigar smoke on her breath. "It was a beautiful service, Carly. You would've loved it."

She hid a secret smile that he didn't realize she'd been there—with him—in disguise. "I'll bet I would have. What brings you here?"

"I came to say goodbye," he said ruefully. "I have a business trip to Manhattan, and I'll be gone all week. I'm sorry—I feel like I should be here for you."

"Don't be silly. I'm fine."

"What if your father calls me again?"

"Then call me at home. The wiretap is gone. And I, uh, haven't replaced my cell phone yet."

"I figured as much," he said, then reached inside his car and pulled out a small, slick phone, still in the package. "It's on my service plan. You can use it for as long as you like."

"Peter, I can't—"

"Please, just for me. I want you to have it for emergencies."

She sighed. "Okay, just for emergencies. And only until I get a new phone. Thank you."

"You're welcome. I'll call you later this week." He turned toward his car, then snapped his fingers. "I almost forgot." A sly smile slid over his handsome face. "I have two tickets to the Elton John concert next Monday night at the Fox. Go with me. I might even be able to arrange for him to sign your autograph book."

She grinned. "It's a date."

Peter blew her a kiss, then climbed into his car and backed out onto the street.

Carlotta watched him drive away, thinking she could get used to Peter's life of travel and entertainment. For him and his family, money was no object. Take the concert tickets, for instance—they were probably the best seats in the house.

And not a bad way to keep her mind off Liz and Jack attending his awards dinner that night.

34

Liz lifted herself up on one elbow and lit a cigarette. "Want to share?"

"Sure." Wesley hated how his voice came out all squeaky. It wasn't so much the sex—which had been great—that had him reeling. It was the fact that Liz would have sex with *him*.

She took a drag off the cigarette and handed it to him. "That was great."

"Yeah," he said, taking the smoke and thinking he was going to have to brush up on his after-sex talk. He hadn't had that many occasions to practice. "So, do you do this with all your clients?"

She recoiled. "Of course not!"

"I didn't think so," he said quickly, giving himself points for a nice recovery. "You have great tits."

"Thanks. You have great stamina."

"Yeah? 'Cause I can go again if you want."

She took the cigarette from him. "Down boy. I need a drink before round three." Liz pushed herself up from the bed and shrugged into a slinky robe. "Want one?"

"Got a beer?"

"I'll see. I'll be back in a few minutes. Watch some TV if you want."

"Okay." He watched her leave the guesthouse through a set of French doors and walk across the lawn to the main house, her body perfectly outlined in the nearly transparent robe. Man, she was smokin' hot. Chance would not believe this.

Wesley got up and lit another cigarette, watching until she was inside the house. Then still naked, he went into her office and started opening drawers. She was a neat, organized woman, with her client files beautifully labeled and alphabetized. In the last drawer he found the W's, then what he was looking for: *Randolph Wren.*

After a long drag on the cigarette that got his heart pounding even faster, he opened the file and began to read.

35

Carlotta lifted her head and pulled down her beauty-sleep mask. Was that the doorbell? She squinted at the alarm clock that read 6:36. At this hour of the morning? Not again.

She climbed out of bed and stumbled to the front door, noting wryly that at least Wesley had come home last night—his fan was running. She didn't even want to think about what could've kept him out so late.

Carlotta glanced out the side window and at the sight of Jack Terry standing on the stoop, groaned loudly. She surveyed her oversize pink T-shirt and one white sock and decided she didn't care what she looked like. After fumbling with the deadbolt, she swung open the door.

"What are you, my daily wake-up call?"

He looked her up and down, then jammed his hands on his hips. "You're needed at the morgue."

"Let me guess—I'm dead after all, and this is purgatory."

He looked heavenward, then back to her. "We have an ID on the body. Get dressed. I'll make coffee."

She weighed her choices, which seemed to be few, then waved him in. When he closed the door, she noticed his suit was disheveled, his jaw shadowed. "You look worse than I do."

"I haven't been to bed yet."

"Are you bragging?"

"Hardly. Do you mind if I wash my face and hands at the kitchen sink?"

"No, go ahead."

She scrubbed her face and teeth, ran a comb through her hair and dressed hurriedly. She rummaged until she found an unopened toothbrush that the dentist had given her and carried it to the kitchen along with a tube of toothpaste. The coffeemaker gurgled and Jack was wiping his face on a paper towel, his shirtsleeves rolled back to reveal his powerful arms.

"Thought you might need these," she said, setting the items on the counter.

"Thanks." He tore open the package and squeezed paste onto the brush.

"So. The woman. Who is she?"

"I don't know yet. Abrams has the info." He wet the loaded toothbrush and began vigorously scouring his teeth.

Carlotta frowned. She and Jack had reached a disturbing level of casual domesticity. She could count on one finger the men she'd seen brush their teeth.

On the other hand, after seeing him wearing her robe, there was no place else to go.

"Was the identification made from the prints on the ATM card?"

He nodded, then turned his back and spit into the running water. "Abrams was able to lift some partials from the body—or rather, Coop was."

"Coop? He's allowed to work in the lab at the morgue?"

"I think Abrams made an allowance in this case and brought him in as a consultant or something." He resumed brushing.

From the breakfast bar, she picked up a stack of credit-card statements. "I found two of the items that the woman was wearing in the photo on my statements—the sunglasses and the earrings."

Jack spat and rinsed. "When were you going to tell me?"

"Today," she said irritably. "I was up until two this morning looking over these statements."

He wiped his mouth and hands and took the sheets from her. "This will definitely help to seal the case."

She pulled two mismatched travel mugs from the cabinet and poured coffee in them, adding a liberal amount of sugar to hers. "Ready?"

He nodded, still scanning the statements. "I'll make copies of these once we get to the morgue."

She picked up a scratch pad of paper. "I need to leave a note for Wesley." Carlotta made a rueful noise. "He still wasn't in when I went to bed. I hope he wasn't out doing something stupid."

"Me, too," Jack muttered as they went out the door.

The city morgue was about the most unimpressive building imaginable, barely noticeable to anyone driving by. "Kind of depressing, isn't it?" she said when they pulled up.

"Guess it's hard to justify great architecture on a building that people don't really want to know is even here."

She climbed out and headed for the front door. "I'm not going to have to view the body, am I?"

"No. I want you to look over the personal effects. We just need to tie up some loose ends so we can contact the family."

A receptionist directed them to Abrams's office and to her surprise, Coop was there. He had a special smile for her, then made introductions and added for the coroner's benefit that it was Carlotta's brother who worked for him.

Dr. Abrams was a slender, heavy-lidded man who looked as if he belonged in a morgue. Coop, on the other hand, looked much like he had yesterday—cool and casual. Yet utterly competent. She reminded herself that he was a physician, albeit a discredited one. But from the way Dr. Abrams responded to him, she could tell he respected Coop, if begrudgingly.

"The woman is Barbara Rook, age thirty-five," Abrams extended a photocopy of an expired Tennessee driver's license for a woman with long dark hair. "Last known address is Nashville. If she has a local residence, we haven't been able to locate it."

She and Jack studied the photo. "Do you recognize her?" Jack asked.

"No."

"But the two of you could be sisters."

"Except for the smile," Carlotta said, tonguing the gap between her front teeth.

"I like your smile," Coop and Jack said in unison, then looked at each other.

In the uncomfortable silence that followed, Coop lifted a cardboard box to the top of Abrams's desk and removed the lid. "These are the items she had with her, Carlotta. Among them, a Social Security card with your name and number, a duplicate of your driver's license and a health insurance card in your name."

Carlotta reached into the box and removed the woman's purse—Burberry. The wallet was Chanel, the lipstick case Judith Leiber. "I wonder if I paid for all this stuff."

"I'd say that's a safe bet," Jack said. "We found a complete list of your credit-card numbers in her phone."

"How did she get that much information about me?"

"Bought it online maybe. There's a credit card theft ring in the Buckhead area that we can't seem to crack."

From the bottom of the box, she pulled a tarnished keyring that looked cheap compared to the other belongings. It had some sort of symbol on it that tickled a memory chord.

"What is it?" Jack asked.

"I don't know, but it must have meant a lot to her."

"Why do you say that?"

"Because it's cheap, yet she kept it."

Carlotta scrutinized the abstract symbol. "I've seen this before, but I can't remember where."

"Is it a logo of some kind?"

"Maybe…I just don't know."

Jack's phone rang and he walked out into the hallway to take the call.

"We're finished here," Coop said. "We wanted to make sure you didn't recognize the woman and that she wasn't a relative. The personal information of yours that she had will be destroyed."

She nodded. "Did you find anything to explain why she killed herself?"

"No."

"It appears that the woman just snapped," Dr. Abrams said. "Maybe she was afraid she was about to be caught and couldn't stand it anymore."

"Or maybe she was murdered," Jack said from the doorway.

They all looked up.

"What are you saying?" Carlotta asked, her heart tripping double-time.

"We just got a tip from a woman who said she saw your car traveling toward the Seventeenth Street bridge and that another car was trying to get the driver to pull over."

Jack leveled his gaze on her. "The question is, was the car chasing her because she was Barbara Rook or because they thought she was you?"

"But who would want to hurt me?"

"How about anyone connected to the two previous murder cases you were involved with?" Jack asked dryly.

"Did the witness ID the car that was chasing the Monte Carlo?" Coop asked.

"No. She said it could've been a Mercedes."

"Maybe the person in pursuit wasn't trying to hurt any-one," Coop offered. "Maybe they thought they were follow-ing Carlotta and tried to get her attention. Maybe Barbara Rook freaked out and jumped out of the car."

Carlotta's face grew cold as the blood drained out of it.

Jack was looking at her. "What?"

Her mind raced. How many people with Mercedes tastes would follow her and try to get her to pull over? Only one person came to mind.

Jack came to stand in front of her. "You know something. What is it?"

"I can't say."

"Yes you can."

Perspiration warmed her neck as they all stared at her. "All of you have to swear not to tell the D.A."

Jack sighed. "I can't do that, Carlotta."

She turned toward the door.

"Okay."

She turned back and he looked like an exasperated man. "I won't tell the D.A."

"You swear?"

He rolled his eyes, then nodded.

She looked at Coop and Abrams. "Do you two swear?"

"He won't hear anything from me," Coop promised.

"The man's an asshole," Abrams said.

Jack jammed his hand into his hair. "For God's sake, Car-lotta, what is it?"

She wet her lips. "Well, it's possible…not probable…but the timing…"

"Spit. It. Out."

"It might have been my father trying to make contact with me."

His eyebrows drew together. "Your father? But that would've been before it was even announced that you had died. Why would you think it was him?"

Didn't she know it would somehow come down to the truth? "Because—he called me."

36

"Wesley Wren to see E. Jones," Wesley said to the old bat at the sign-in desk.

"She's running a little behind this morning," the woman said, and seemed happy about it.

"I'll wait," he said cheerfully, then took a seat in the room with a motley cast of characters. All of the men— and most of the women—were bigger than him, many sporting prison tattoos and none of them smelling particularly rosy.

From his backpack he withdrew a book about the World Series of Poker and found his place. If he were going to be playing in the big game some day, he needed to know as much about it as possible.

A few minutes later he vaguely registered that someone who reeked of cigar smoke had sat down next to him.

"Brushing up on your game?" the guy asked in a voice that sounded familiar.

Wesley turned his head to see one of the ugly meatheads who worked for The Carver, one of the two guys to whom he owed money, sitting there smoking a three-inch cigar—no doubt the same size as his dick. His intestines cramped. "What do you want?"

"What do you think, pissant?"

"I made a payment yesterday."

"A lousy four-hundred bucks? You got a ten-thousand-dollar TV sitting in your living room and all you got for The Carver is four hundred?" The man sucked his teeth. "That ain't gonna fly. Are we gonna have to start makin' house calls again?"

Wesley swallowed. "No. I'll bring more in a few days."

The guy winked. "Attaboy."

"Sir," the old bat behind the glass shouted. "You can't smoke in here."

"Sorry," the guy said.

Then he took the little cigar and brought it down on the back of Wesley's hand.

Wesley heard the skin sizzle before the pain lit up his entire arm. By the time the shock passed, the guy was gone, leaving him with an ugly raised burn. If anyone around him had seen anything, they didn't react. Wesley grimaced and sucked on the puckered skin, wondering if he'd be able to win enough in tonight's game to satisfy The Carver.

The burn on the back of his hand would be a convenient reminder of what lay in store for him if he didn't.

"Wren," the bat shouted. "You're up!"

Wesley walked to E.'s office and knocked on the door, speculating as to what kind of reception he'd get after lying to her about Carlotta being dead.

It wasn't his fault, but with women, one never knew.

"Come in," she called.

He opened the door and walked in, but E. didn't look up from her desk, just scribbled on a file. "Have a seat, Wesley."

He sat and studied her while waiting for her to stop ignoring him. She wore her great-smelling red hair in some sort of complicated braid, but a piece of it had fallen down along one ear. A pale blue shirt molded her full breasts—from their hug after the service, he knew they weren't fake. She was wearing darker lipstick than normal, a nice berry color that made her teeth look even whiter when she bit down on her lip in concentration, like now.

Did it make him a pervert that he thought of E. when he was with Liz? He wondered idly what E. tasted like and what made her feel good in bed and if she liked to smoke after sex.

Probably not. But that was okay. He wasn't supposed to be smoking anyway. He and Carlotta had a pact.

At last, she closed the file and gave him a forced smile. "How are you?"

"Okay."

She arched a thin eyebrow. "I was glad to hear that your sister is okay."

"Thanks."

"Do you want to tell me what happened?"

"Didn't you hear the news reports?"

"Yes."

Wesley lifted his hands, as if that was all the explanation she needed.

E. leaned forward in a way that squeezed her breasts together. "Wesley, I don't like the way that you and the D.A. seem to have some kind of feud going."

"Then you need to take it up with the D.A."

"I don't the care about the D.A. I care about you."

His pulse jumped.

"It's my job to make sure that you take away something positive from this experience."

Chick talk. He shifted in his seat. "I called Mr. McCormick about the community service but he hasn't called me back yet."

"He will. He's eager to have someone with your apparent expertise helping them with security." She looked over his file and made a couple of notes. "Is anything else going on that I should know about?"

He was gambling regularly, one of his loan sharks was getting antsy, his fugitive dad had made contact with Carlotta, he was balling his attorney and he was finally making headway in understanding his dad's case.

"Nope."

E. pressed her berry lips together. She didn't believe him. She put her glasses on in a dismissive motion. "Let me know when you hear from McCormick. Get out of here."

At the door he turned back. "No matter the circumstances, E., I appreciate you coming to the memorial service. That was really sweet of you."

She looked up and her expression softened. "So maybe I can meet your sister sometime after all."

He nodded. "You'd like each other."

E. hesitated, then opened her top desk drawer. "Wesley, I was wondering if you had plans next Monday."

He took the tickets she extended. "Elton John? Yeah, he's cool." He grinned, his chest flooding with happiness. "We'll have a great time."

Her eyebrows went up and there was an awkward pause. "Wesley, I can't go with you to the concert. I was offering you both tickets. We sometimes get complimentary ones around the office."

His disappointment was acute. "Oh. You're not going to use them?"

"I already have tickets. I'm going with my boyfriend."

His gut clenched. She had a boyfriend. Damn, he should've seen that coming.

"So do you want the tickets? Maybe you and a friend can go."

Wesley nodded. He'd like to get a look at this guy she was seeing. "Thanks."

She squinted at his hand. "Nasty burn you got there."

He flexed his fist. "Nah, it's fine."

"See you next week."

He left the building feeling totally bummed and rode his bike to Chance's condo building in Midtown. He locked his bike on a rack outside, then took the elevator to the top floor—nothing but the best for Chance.

Luckily for him, since his buddy's generosity often spilled over.

But being friends with Chance had its drawbacks too, he

conceded, when his door opened and a huge body-builder type came walking out with a gym bag—much like the bag that Chance had once asked him to deliver to some guy in a bad part of town. Everything about the guy screamed bad news, from his steroid-induced arms to his surly mouth to his cagey body language.

Where did Chance meet these guys?

Chance appeared in the doorway, beer in hand, and he spotted Wesley. "Wes, dude, meet Leonard. Leonard, this is my poker buddy, Wesley."

"Hi there," Wesley offered.

"Hey," the big man said, but his demeanor couldn't be mistaken for friendly. "I'll be in touch," he said to Chance, then strutted toward the stairwell, a beefy hand situated possessively on the top of the gym bag.

Wesley followed Chance inside. "Man, I don't even want to know what that was about."

"No, you don't," Chance agreed. "Ready for a game?"

Wesley hid his burned hand behind his back. "Yeah. You got one lined up?"

"Don't I always?" From the top of the refrigerator, Chance retrieved his pistol and jammed it in his coat pocket.

"Whoa dude, what's up with the heat?"

"My business is growing, man. I decided I needed to start being more careful is all." He clapped Wesley on the shoulder. "So tell me about this lawyer chick you're banging. And I want all the nasty details."

37

"Jack hasn't spoken to me in three days," Carlotta said to Hannah. They were on the back deck, drinking margaritas, their feet stuck in a kiddie pool.

"Fuck him," Hannah said.

Carlotta winced. "I did."

Hannah's eyes rounded and she gaped. "When?"

"When he had the house under surveillance. Wesley refused to stay here and we were alone." She glared at her friend. "It's your fault. You were the one who said I needed to have a night of hot sex to work out the mental kinks."

"Girl, you can't do that with someone you have feelings for—that only works with strangers."

"Wait a minute. I *don't* have feelings for Jack Terry."

"Uh-huh. Whatever. Doesn't matter anyway if the jerk isn't talking to you. What do you care? Just let him do his detecting crap to make sure that someone wasn't trying to hurt *you* when they threw that poor woman off the bridge."

"He did look into people involved in the previous two murder cases to see if anyone has a vendetta against me."

Hannah gave her a pointed look. "For someone who sells clothes for a living, you've been involved in some pretty dangerous shit."

"Thankfully, the culprits in those cases are in custody."

"But they could have someone on the outside working for them. The detective must be concerned for your safety if he has a uniform cruising the house." Hannah grinned. "See, he really does care, even if he's giving you the silent treatment."

Disgruntled, Carlotta sipped from her icy drink. Okay, so Jack had a right to be angry with her for not telling him about her father's phone call—and would be incensed if he knew about the call to Peter—but it wasn't right for him to simply ignore her. She was involved in this case whether he liked it or not.

Besides, after the way he'd behaved—using her for casual sex and opening her family's Christmas gifts—*she* shouldn't be speaking to *him*.

The back door opened and Wesley poked his head out. "Coop's here. I'm leaving."

Hannah was on her feet before Carlotta could blink. "Take us with you!"

Wesley held up his hands. "You're going to have to talk to Coop about that."

Hannah shoved her tattooed feet into flip flops and grabbed Carlotta's hand. "Come on."

"Hannah—"

"Hey, you owe me. I *cried* for you. Now get off your suspended ass and let's go move a body."

Carlotta toed her wet feet into sandals and followed Wesley and Hannah through the house and out to the driveway where Coop sat behind the wheel of his big white van.

"We want to go with you," Hannah said without preamble.

Coop looked at Wesley and Wesley shrugged. "Dude, don't look at me."

Carlotta gave Coop an apologetic look.

He must have seen the determination in Hannah's face, because he jerked his thumb toward the backseat. "Get in, but you have to do what I say."

"I can be submissive," Hannah purred. "Where are we going?"

"House call," Coop said. "Accidental death."

"Oh, goody."

Carlotta elbowed her as she climbed in. She made contact with Coop in the rearview mirror and mouthed "Sorry," but he just winked.

She'd taken Wesley to meet Coop a couple of times for body-moving jobs and had to admit that the first time had been gruesome because she'd known the victim. But by the second time, she had already steeled herself to look past the condition of the body. If a person was already gone, the best way to honor their death was to handle their body with care.

Still, it wasn't something she wanted to see every day.

Then she pursed her mouth. Maybe she and Hannah could do it one day a week for some extra cash that could help her get her credit back on track. She glanced sideways at Hannah and decided to wait and see how her friend handled the situation before mentioning it.

"So Coop, how do you find out that a body needs to be picked up?" Hannah asked from the backseat.

"Someone from the morgue calls me. If it's a residence or an accident scene and the police and an M.E. are there, I try to get there before they leave. If it's a pickup from a morgue, such as a hospital, I can schedule those."

"Can anyone do this?"

Coop grinned. "Not usually. The morgue contracts with funeral homes to pick up bodies when they can't handle the volume. I'm actually contracted through my uncle's funeral home, but I have the leeway to hire anyone I think is responsible and presentable enough to help me do the job."

"I'm very responsible," Hannah said.

The rest of them silently chimed in, "But you're not presentable," although Hannah seemed clueless, bouncing excitedly when Coop turned into a subdivision.

"Murder in the suburbs." Hannah rubbed her hands together.

"Coop said it was an accidental death," Carlotta reminded her.

Hannah glared at her. "You're determined to ruin this for me, aren't you?"

In the front seat, Coop shook his head, then double-checked street addresses. He pulled the van alongside the curb in front of a small house where a police car and a car from the M.E.'s office sat side by side. Before he could shut off the engine, Hannah was out of her seat belt.

"Girls, stay put. We'll be right back."

Hannah opened her mouth but Carlotta squeezed her knee. "Don't blow this," she whispered.

That settled her down a bit. Coop and Wesley went to the door and were let inside.

"They're having all the fun," Hannah complained.

"If you don't take it down a notch," Carlotta said, "Coop will never hire us."

Hannah's face lit up. "You mean you'll do it?"

"I'll *think* about it. *If* you go easy on the caffeine."

After several long minutes, Coop and Wesley reappeared with the M.E., who shook Coop's hand and headed toward his car. A uniformed police officer emerged and went to his car, apparently to use his radio. Coop and Wesley came back to the van and Coop leaned in the window. "They're finished, so we can remove the body." He pointed to a pile of pale blue clothing stacked in a corner. "You two, find some scrubs to throw on."

They were garbed in short order, and standing next to the gurney that Coop and Wesley had removed and elevated.

"One more thing," Coop said.

"What?" Hannah asked excitedly.

"Don't touch anything and don't talk."

She pouted, but nodded. They each took a gurney handle and moved into the house like a body-removal SWAT team.

Hannah, who was in front, promptly tripped over the body lying at the foot of the stairs and went down with a thud. While Wesley picked her up, Carlotta sent another look of apology to Coop, who had pushed his tongue into his cheek and seemed to be calling on some source of inner strength.

"Who is she?" Carlotta asked to distract him.

He checked the clipboard on the gurney that held a picture of the woman's driver's license. "Jennifer Stevenson, forty-one."

Carlotta squinted. "I used to work with a Jennifer Stevenson, but this isn't her."

"It says this lady lives alone. Her dog walker found her. Looks like a simple fall."

"What killed her?"

"Broken neck, basically, like most falls of any consequence."

"Wonder why she's wearing a wig," Carlotta murmured.

Coop crouched for a closer look. "Didn't realize she was."

"It's a good one," she said, crouching with him. "Real human hair, expensive."

He pulled on latex gloves, then tugged the blond wig a half inch to reveal dark hair underneath. "Hmm, her driver's license lists her hair color as blond."

"Maybe she used to be…or maybe that's not her real driver's license. Did the cop find anything else around here with her name on it?"

"He wouldn't have had a reason to look for anything else."

Carlotta stood and scanned the garments hanging on pegs in the entryway. "Do you have another set of gloves?"

Coop handed her a pair, no questions asked, while Wesley

and Hannah stood back and watched. She snapped on the gloves, then picked up the edge of a red silk scarf with the letters *TW* monogrammed on the edge. "I thought you said her name was Jennifer Stevenson."

"That's what it says. That scarf could belong to someone else."

"You said she lived alone."

"Maybe someone left it here."

She fingered through the garments and found a blue scarf, this one with the initials *JS*.

"That one must be hers," Coop offered.

But then Carlotta found a black one with the initials *PB*, and an ivory-colored scarf with the initials *BT*. She held it out. "Those are the vic's real initials—*BT*."

Coop frowned. "How can you tell?"

She turned over the corner to expose the tag. "It's Hermes. The other scarves are discount store quality." On the table beneath the hooks was a ball of plastic bags—probably for the dog walker. Then she spied a small drawer.

"Carlotta," Coop warned.

But she slid the drawer open a few inches. Inside were four wallets monogrammed respectively with the initials *TW, JS, PB* and *BT*. She removed them one by one and opened them to reveal four driver's licenses of women with names matching the initials, all of whom resembled the dead woman except for hair color and style.

She raised her eyebrows at Coop, who pursed his mouth. "Maybe we should give Jack a call."

Carlotta peered into the bowl of keys sitting on the table

and used forefinger and thumb to pull out a keychain that was the same as the one she'd seen in Barbara Rook's personal effects. "Yes, I think you should call Jack."

38

Carlotta followed Jack to his car when he went to get evidence bags from the trunk. "So do you think the woman is connected to Barbara Rook, that they both were identity thieves and that they were both murdered?"

He wouldn't make eye contact. "I'm not talking to you."

She put her hands on her hips. "That's pretty childish, don't you think?"

"No, it's self-preservation. The more you talk, the more trouble you cause me."

"But a woman named Jennifer Stevenson used to work at Neiman's. There has to be a connection to the mall."

"I already told you that most of the identity theft victims worked or shopped at the mall. Stop trying to do my job."

"But this means that Barbara Rook was killed because she was messed up in something bad—like this woman—not because someone thought Barbara was me."

"It doesn't mean anything for sure."

"Which absolves my father—not that I really thought he was involved in the first place. So honestly, Jack, you can forget all about that phone call."

Jack slammed the trunk lid. "Stop. Talking." He pointed. "Go sit in the van until Coop is ready to leave." His nostrils flared in anger, his eyes glittering like metal.

Carlotta put up her hands. "Okay."

She went to sit in the van with Hannah, who had long ago been banished there by Coop.

"This isn't fair," Hannah complained. "You were brilliant in there. They should give you a damn badge instead of making you sit at the little kids' table."

"It doesn't work like that," Carlotta said, leaning her head back. "I got lucky is all. Right place, right time, right training in designer accessories."

Hannah turned her head. "Life is all about timing, isn't it?"

"I guess so. Where you are, and when, determines what you're doing."

"And who you're doing it with."

She thought about Jack and wondered how much of the fact that they'd slept together could be attributed to being in proximity to each other and being alone. If she'd spent that much time with another man—Peter, for instance or Coop—would they have wound up in her bed instead?

She frowned. And shouldn't love be about more than just good timing?

"There they come with the body," Hannah said morosely. "Without us."

"We can at least get the doors for them."

They scrambled out, opened the back doors and waited until Coop and Wesley wheeled the sheeted body around. The men lowered the gurney, then picked it up by the handles and slid the body inside. When the doors were closed, Coop rolled off his gloves.

"How strong do you have to be to do this job?" Carlotta asked.

Coop raised his eyebrows. "It's a two-person job and one of the two had better be able to dead lift about two-hundred pounds."

"Check this out," Hannah said, flexing her arm until a baseball-sized biceps popped up. "I could bench press you, Coop."

His smile was tight. "I'll keep that in mind."

They all climbed inside the van. "I'll take you girls home before we make the drop-off."

"No," Hannah whined. "I want to go to the morgue!"

"We'll stay in the van," Carlotta promised Coop. "Did they find her real identification?"

"Beverly Tucker," Coop said. "And that's all I'm allowed to tell you."

Carlotta frowned. Blast Jack!

When they arrived at the morgue, Coop avoided Hannah's eyes. "Wesley, why don't you stay here with Hannah? I think Carlotta and I can handle this one."

Wesley shrugged and looked at his watch; he'd been antsy all afternoon, Carlotta had noticed. "Sure."

Coop met her gaze in the mirror. "Okay with you?"

She nodded because she was afraid she would lose her nerve if she spoke.

He smiled. "Let's do it."

Carlotta had always assumed that when a young, buff, handsome guy said, "Let's do it," he would be referring to something other than moving a body.

Her life was officially weird.

She followed Coop's lead and as long as she didn't think too much about their cargo, she could concentrate on moving the gurney safely. When they reached the door, Coop used an intercom to give his name and the name of the deceased. A buzzer sounded and they were allowed entry.

"Now what?" she asked.

"In this case, we're taking the body straight to autopsy. Normally we'd deliver to the crypt."

"Why straight to autopsy on this body?"

A small smile curved his mouth. "Because of your observations, the M.E. had to return to the scene and change his ruling from accidental death to homicide. Abrams doesn't like it when his M.E.s miss things. He wants to do the autopsy himself."

"Is someone in trouble?"

"No. But congratulations, you made a difference."

Satisfaction surged in her chest. Coop had once told her that she was smarter than she wanted people to believe. At the time she'd thought he was simply flirting with her, but now she wondered if he saw something in her that even she couldn't see.

After they delivered the body, they wheeled the empty gurney back to the van. "That wasn't so bad, was it?"

"Not with you," she conceded and he smiled.

When they arrived at the town house, Wesley jumped out and jogged toward the garage. A couple of minutes later, he zoomed by on his bike. "Later, sis."

She frowned and yelled, "Where are you going?"

"Don't wait up," he shouted over his shoulder.

"I have to go, too," Hannah said miserably. "A catering gig in Vinings." Then she smiled up at Coop. "When can we do this again?"

"I'll call you."

"You'd better," she said, dead serious. She waved to Carlotta, then climbed into her graffiti-covered van and left.

He whistled low. "She's…intense."

"I know, it's part of her charm."

"What about you? What's the sudden interest in body moving?"

She shrugged. "Well, it's no secret that my finances are a wreck. I've been thinking about getting a part-time job around my hours at Neiman's."

His eyebrows climbed. "And you're interested in helping me?"

"I know that Wesley will be starting his community service soon. I just thought if you needed someone temporarily—and on the more tame pickups—that you could give me a call."

Coop scratched his head. "I could certainly get used to your company, Carlotta, but this isn't what I had in mind in order to get to know each other. Body moving isn't the most romantic way to pass the time."

"Okay. Well, you can always call Hannah."

"Do you work weekends?"

Carlotta laughed. "I can let you know my work schedule a week ahead of time."

"Okay. I'll keep it in mind."

She lifted her hand in a wave and began to walk toward the town house.

At the sound of car tires squealing, she jerked her head around. A darkish vehicle was tearing down the residential road at a terrific speed.

"Carlotta," Coop yelled and something about the tone of his voice made her muscles seize in terror. A popping noise sounded and she heard the crash of glass breaking before being tackled from behind. She landed hard, with Coop on top of her. The air was forced out of her lungs, leaving her paralyzed and sucking wind like a beached guppy.

"Stay down," he said in her ear, and seemed to be fumbling in his pocket.

Her lungs finally expanded and she gasped to fill them with oxygen—sweet, sweet oxygen. Her mouth was full of grass and her tongue stung from where she'd bitten it when she landed. Her mind was still trying to process what happened.

"This is an emergency," Coop said, and Carlotta realized he was talking into his phone. He rattled off the address. "Shots fired from a dark vehicle in a drive-by shooting, send the police. And notify Detective Jack Terry of the APD."

39

"I don't need to go to the hospital," Carlotta said, cradling a cup of coffee at the kitchen table. The town house was full of police officers. Jack was barking at someone to get the broken window secured and sealed. It was dark outside but with all the police lights in the yard, it was as bright as day.

"Are you sure?" Coop asked.

"Absolutely."

"Did you call Wesley?"

"Yeah, I left him a message on his cell phone."

"You don't know where he went?"

"No, but I'm afraid he's out gambling."

Coop frowned. "I've been trying to counsel him."

"I know and I appreciate it. But I'm not sure there's anything worse than the judgment of a nineteen-year-old boy."

"Man," Coop corrected gently.

She nodded, then gave a dry laugh. "He's going to be upset that his TV took a bullet." She winced at the goo that had oozed onto the floor.

"I'm sure he'll just be relieved that you're safe."

She reached over and covered his hand with hers. "Thanks to you."

Jack strode into the kitchen. When his gaze darted to their hands, Carlotta pulled hers back and lifted her cup. "Are you finished, Detective?"

"For now." He looked at Coop. "Did you think of any more details about the car?"

"No, sorry. I really only got a look at the wheels—maybe a BMW or a Mercedes."

Jack frowned. "Where have we heard that before?"

"Do you think this is related to the two murders?"

"I don't know. I don't see the connection, but it's awfully coincidental not to be."

The front door burst open and Wesley came charging inside. "What happened?"

His shirt was misbuttoned, leaving one shirttail hanging low. She caught a whiff of a noxious perfume wafting off him. From the way Jack stepped back, he must have smelled it too. Here she was afraid he'd been gambling and it appeared that her brother finally had a girlfriend.

"Carlotta and I were outside," Coop said, "and someone drove by and fired two shots."

"One bullet imbedded in the siding," Jack explained. "The other one shattered the window and struck the television."

"The TV?" Wesley looked stricken.

"Sorry," Carlotta said dryly.

Wesley turned his back and wiped his fist across his face.

"Wes man, it's just a TV," Coop said.

Wesley turned back to Carlotta. "Are you okay?"

"I'm fine."

He looked relieved but a little desperate around the edges. "Coop, can you take Carlotta home with you or spend the night?"

She frowned. What was her brother up to?

"Sure—" Coop began.

"I'm staying." Jack's voice brooked no argument. "And I'll have an officer posted at the curb for the next twenty-four hours."

Wesley seemed to mull Jack's words. "Okay. I'm going to crash at Chance's," he said, backing out of the room. "See you tomorrow, sis."

Carlotta nodded, a little hurt that he'd leave her alone at a time like this but she couldn't pretend to understand how his mind worked.

While Jack cleared the cops out of the house, Coop stood. "I guess that's my cue."

She smiled up at him. "Thank you again."

"Being around you is the most excitement I've had in a while."

Jack returned in time to overhear the remark. He gave her a disparaging frown. "She can't seem to help herself."

Coop stuck out his hand. "Take care of her, Jack," he said in a mild tone that contradicted the way he squeezed Jack's hand.

Jack looked him directly in the eye. "I intend to. Thanks for your help."

The handshake lasted a few seconds longer before Coop retreated.

Carlotta walked him to the door and waved goodbye, postponing the moment when she'd have to face Jack's wrath. He would, no doubt, lecture her on withholding information and sticking her nose where it didn't belong and generally making his job harder than it already was.

When she turned, it was worse than she'd expected. The big man looked like he was on the verge of flying apart—hair ruffled, suit rumpled, pilled orange tie hanging loose. And the look on his face was a barely contained rage—directed toward her.

"Jack—"

"Can't you stay out of trouble?" he bellowed. "In the space of a few days, you've taken ten years off my life!"

She crossed her arms. "*I* didn't do anything."

He pulled his hand down his face, seeming to grapple for control. Then he shook his head. "How many lives do you have, woman?"

Carlotta shrugged, then smiled.

Wordlessly, he wrapped his arms around her and pulled her down with him to lie on the couch. He cradled her head to his warm shoulder and released a long, shuddering breath.

"Jack—"

"Shhh," he murmured against her hair. "Don't talk. Just let me hear you breathe."

40

"What did I tell you." Chance pointed to a red Ferrari in the valet parking lot of the Golden Glove. "The Carver is here almost every night of the week."

"You know your strip clubs," Wesley admitted.

A whimper sounded in the backseat. "I'm not so sure about this," Cherry said in a whispery voice.

"Shut up, drag dude," Chance said over his shoulder. "This is more money than you'll make in a month turning tricks in Piedmont Park, so find your balls, okay?"

"You're so mean." Cherry sighed wistfully.

But Wesley too, was beginning to doubt that they could pull this off. A skinny computer geek, a chubby small-time drug dealer and a drag queen—it sounded like the setup for a bad joke.

And if things went bad, they could all wind up hurt— or worse.

Still, he kept the picture of Carlotta dodging bullets in his mind as they drove Chance's SUV past the valet stand in favor of a pay-and-park lot. Chance pulled into the back where there were almost no cars. Only a swag of chain hung between posts separated them from a side road. Wesley cut through the links with a folding pocket saw in less than a minute, then he reconnected the broken chain by wrapping it with a clear piece of packing tape. Meanwhile Chance had removed his license plate and tossed it onto the floor board.

"What are you guys, some kind of cat-burglar team?" Cherry asked, giggling. "This is so exciting."

The prostitute was dressed in a short skirt and halter top, with big hair and high heels. Other than having a flat ass, Cherry was pretty believable as a woman. Scarily so.

Chance looked Cherry up and down. "Are you sure you're a dude?"

"Why don't you check me out?"

It was just the kind of dare that Chance lived for. He grabbed Cherry in the crotch and Cherry squealed.

Chance frowned. "Okay, he's legit."

"Do it again," Cherry said.

"Look, woman dude, I only yank mine as a last resort, why would I want to yank yours?"

"I can do things to you that a woman can't," Cherry purred.

"Couldn't be less interested." Chance shook his head. "But I like your initiative. How much do you pay your pimp?"

"Dude," Wesley broke in. "Let's get this over with."

"Okay. Everyone knows what to do," Chance said. "Let's go even a score."

Cherry put her arms around their shoulders and after paying a cover, they walked in like a threesome. Almost immediately, Wesley spotted The Carver sitting in a corner booth with five women—three of them completely nude—draped over him or lounging within reach. A gorgeous black woman with enormous tits danced on his table. The man looked like he'd been eating and drinking for hours, which boded well for their plan.

At the next table sat his henchmen, but luckily they seemed equally marinated in booze and T & A.

The three of them ordered drinks at the bar and stayed within sight of each other, but blended with the crowd. Wesley kept The Carver in his peripheral view. After about thirty minutes, the man made the move Wesley was hoping for—getting out of the booth and heading toward the men's room. Sweat beaded on Wesley's forehead as he watched the table of cronies. Although one looked up when The Carver stood, the guy apparently decided that licking a salted nipple and doing a shot of tequila was more fun than escorting his boss to the john.

Wesley looked for Chance to give him the signal. To his consternation, Chance was mesmerized by the blonde dancing on stage, stuffing bills into the only clothes she wore— her schoolgirl knee socks. And Cherry had disappeared.

He abandoned his drink and got Chance's attention with a poke. "The Carver's gone in—you have to find Cherry."

Chance nodded, slammed his drink and went off in the other direction.

Wesley walked toward the men's room, sweating profusely now. When he got to the bathroom, he removed an Out of

Order sign from under his shirt and tacked it on the door, then slipped inside. As Chance had described, the men's bathrooms were really like small changing rooms with toilets. He saw The Carver go into the one on the end, and all he could do at that point was pray that Chance and Cherry got there soon. Two men exited their booths and left without washing their hands. Wesley shook his head. Some men were such pigs.

Finally the men's room was empty except for The Carver. Just when Wesley had given up hope and was ready to abandon the plan, the door opened and in walked Cherry and Chance. Wesley pointed to the occupied booth and motioned for them to hurry.

A slim-jim tool got them inside the booth before The Carver could react.

"What the hell?" was all he had time to say before Wesley slapped a piece of duct tape on his mouth and Chance tied his wrists with a cable tie. The middle-aged man looked almost pathetic sitting on the john with his pants around his ankles. His eyes rolled wildly and he moaned against the tape. "Hmm hmm hmm?"

"Who am I?" Wesley interpreted. "My name is Wesley Wren. I owe you money, which I intend to repay. But one of your guys took a couple of shots at my sister today and I need to make sure that never happens again."

He motioned to Cherry, who lifted his skirt—and pulled out a massive dick, which he laid against The Carver's cheek. The older man tried to recoil, but had to maintain his balance on the toilet with his bound hands. Chance snapped a few pictures on his cell phone.

"That's good," Wesley said. Then he got up in the man's face. "If anything happens to Carlotta, these pictures hit the Internet, got it?"

The man nodded. They left the booth, exited the bathroom and made their way to the entrance as quickly as they could without raising suspicion. Wesley spotted one of The Carver's guys strolling toward the bathroom. Once they hit the parking lot, they broke into a sprint with Wesley half-dragging the high-heeled Cherry. They vaulted into the SUV.

Cherry turned to look through the back window. "Here they come!"

Sure enough, The Carver's men were in a full run, scanning the parking lot, obviously determined to retrieve the phone with the pictures on it and then beat them all to a bloody pulp.

"Hurry, man!" Wesley yelled.

Chance churned the ignition and gunned the gas, breaking through the taped-up chain and jumping a curb to get onto the side street. After they'd gone a couple of blocks, he turned on his headlights and whooped. "That was awesome!"

Wesley high-fived Chance, loving the feeling of having the upper hand for once in his life. Now that they'd escaped with the pictures, he held all the cards. He sat back in the seat and laughed at Chance's retelling of every detail, even sweeter now because they'd pulled it off.

A haughty smile crawled over his face. Maybe he wouldn't even pay The Carver the rest of what he owed. The man had almost killed his sister; he was getting off light.

Wesley folded his hands behind his head. He could get used to this power thing.

He only wished his dad could see him now.

41

Two days after the shooting, Jack still called or stopped by every few hours to make sure Carlotta was okay. After spending the night platonically in each other's arms, they seemed to have reached some sort of unspoken pact—a relationship between them was impossible.

At least for now.

Wesley had returned from his overnight stay with Chance in a suspiciously good mood and had been so attentive that she'd forgiven him for leaving the night of the shooting.

Coop too, had called to check in, but had seemed a little distant, as if he were afraid of treading on claimed territory. The professional relationship between him and Jack that predated her was going to make things sticky between her and Coop, she suspected.

Which made her thoughts swing to Peter. She'd kept the

phone he'd given her in her purse, grateful for its comforting presence. And she knew it was unreasonably selfish of her, but she was a little irritated that she hadn't heard from him all week. Carlotta realized that she wasn't even sure when he would return and she wondered if that's how life with *him* would be—leading parallel lives that ran side by side, but rarely intersected.

When he did call later that day to say hello, he sounded so harried that she was instantly remorseful. She had to keep reminding herself that he'd been through the trauma of losing his wife and was probably struggling to regain footing and focus at work. Plus, he was giving her the space *she* had requested.

"I miss you," he said. "I wish I had brought you with me. We would've had fun in the city."

"Sounds like you haven't had any down time."

"Not much," Peter admitted. "But it's been nice to get out of Atlanta for a few days, to be away from everything. Everything except you, of course."

"Sounds like a change of scenery is just what you needed."

"I was thinking that when I get back, maybe we could plan a weekend away somewhere, to get, you know…reacquainted."

"That sounds nice. I'll think about it."

"Great," he said, sounding relieved and happy. "Anything exciting going on there?"

A positive ID on the bridge jumper, the suspicion that it was murder, a second murder linked to the first and a drive-by shooting that had her still picking grass from her teeth. "No, not a thing."

"Good. I'll be back Monday afternoon and I'll pick you up for the concert around six. I made reservations at Eno's."

"Sounds wonderful. I can't wait."

"Me, either. Bye, Carly."

When she hung up the phone, the doorbell rang. She jumped—loud noises seemed to make her do that now—and groaned when she saw Mrs. Winningham on the stoop, holding Toofers.

She took a deep breath and opened the door. "Hello, Mrs. Winningham."

"So you're not dead after all." Toofers just snarled.

"So they tell me."

"I came to get my casserole dish. I told Wesley that I needed it back."

"Right. Let me get it for you. Would you like to come in?"

"Well, all right."

Carlotta stepped back and the woman walked inside, her nose crinkling. "I heard the shooting the other night and saw the police. I never thought I'd be living in an area where a body isn't safe in her own front yard."

"Neither did I," Carlotta lamented, walking into the kitchen and covering the waste can where the icky chicken casserole had ended up.

"Your family has brought a bad element to this neighborhood," the woman called after her.

"I'm sorry about that, Mrs. Winningham." No use denying it. She picked up the clean casserole dish and lid and returned to the living room.

"When are you going to get your front window fixed? It's an eyesore."

"I know. Soon, I hope."

The woman took the casserole dish and frowned. "And that enormous broken TV at the curb—you're only allowed to put out appliances for pickup on the third Tuesday of the month."

"I'll tell Wesley," Carlotta promised.

Toofers spotted the silver Christmas tree and took advantage of Mrs. Winningham's one-arm grip to wriggle loose and attack with the might of a rabid rat. Carlotta grabbed the tree, and Mrs. Winningham grabbed Toofers and a tug of war ensued. Ornaments and fur flew before the two were finally separated.

"My tree," Carlotta moaned, surveying the mass of bent and naked branches.

"My baby!" Mrs. Winningham cried, sticking her fingers down the dog's throat to retrieve bits of tinsel. She screwed up her face and gave Carlotta a poisonous glare. "If he has to go to the vet, you're getting the bill!"

Carlotta fumed. "What about my Christmas tree?"

"It's the middle of summer!" Mrs. Winningham shouted, retreating to the door. "You people are a bunch of freaks!" The door banged shut and Carlotta stuck her tongue out at it. Then she burst out laughing.

Carlotta spent an hour straightening out the limbs of the misshapen tree and putting the small, faded ornaments back in place. She picked up one of the rewrapped gifts, and a fresh burst of anger toward Jack erupted in her stomach. She gently shook the package and tried to decipher the indistinct rattle inside. Since he hadn't kept any of the presents or divulged their contents, they must not have contained any explosive information—or cash.

Not that she wanted to know.

The time to open the gifts, Wesley had said again and again, was when they were all reunited. And considering the fact that her father had at least called, it was the first time in years that Carlotta allowed herself to think that was a possibility.

Would they ever be a family again?

When the discarded chicken casserole began to smell up the house, Carlotta tied the trash and schlepped it outside to the garage where their Herbie Curbie resided. She lifted the lid and dumped the garbage inside, then wheeled the trash can to the curb where Wesley had carried the carcass of the once-glorious television.

A delivery van driving along the road slowed—another shipment for the couple next door, she surmised. But the van stopped suddenly and two beefy men jumped out, heading for her. She tried to scream but no sound came out. She scrambled backward and fell on the concrete driveway, but one of the men yanked her up by her arm and her ponytail.

"What do you want?" she cried.

The other guy leaned into her face. "Tell that idiot brother of yours that The Carver wasn't amused by his little stunt the other night."

"Wh-what stunt?"

"Ask *him*. The little shit is in big trouble, bigger than he knows. He has no idea who he's dealing with."

"I thought he was making his payments," she said, wincing against the pain of having her hair yanked out of her scalp.

"Not enough," the man said. "And now that he's pissed off The Carver, he can expect those payments—and the interest—to double."

The sound of a siren split the air and Carlotta's captor dropped her like a bag of potatoes. The men sprinted for the van, but Jack swerved to block their escape. He was out of the car, his weapon drawn over the top of his open door, almost before the car came to a halt. "Stay down, Carlotta!" He aimed the gun at the men who were standing next to the van, hands up. "Gentlemen, down on the ground."

"We don't want any trouble, officer."

He shot one of the van tires and the men jumped. "I said get your fat asses on the ground."

They did. More sirens screamed into earshot, then two squad cars pulled up, lights flashing. Jack motioned for the cops to cuff the men, then he holstered his weapon and went to Carlotta, who was pushing to her feet.

"Are you okay?" he asked, his face anxious.

"I'm fine," she said, rubbing her arms. "Just a little shaken up. They work for one of Wesley's loan sharks."

"I figured as much. I didn't want to say anything the other night, but from Wesley's reaction to the shooting, I suspect that was his first thought too."

"So the shooting wasn't connected to the murders?"

"That's not necessarily true. The loan sharks around here like the ones Wesley is tangled up with are into everything these days—including selling credit card numbers. It's not out of the question that they're behind the identity theft ring that we've been trying to crack."

Carlotta frowned. "Jack, I'm afraid for Wesley. Those guys said something about The Carver being pissed about some stunt he pulled the other night."

"Probably in retaliation for the shooting. Did they say what happened?"

"No."

"And I'm sure he won't be telling me," Jack said. "I'll help him if I can, but Wesley got himself into this mess with these guys. He's going to have to figure a way to get himself out."

She bit into her lip and nodded, turning back to the house, then stopped. "Wait a minute. How did you know I was in trouble?"

"A neighbor called 911. As soon as I heard the address, I beat it over here."

She looked up to see the curtains at Mrs. Winningham's fall back into place and she mentally retracted every bad thing she'd thought about the woman.

A sardonic smile lifted Jack's mouth. "Your name is all over my reports lately. I'm afraid my chief is going to think something's going on between us."

"Well, you can tell him that that's not true," she said lightly. "Besides, I'm going back to work Monday, so I'm going to be way too busy to get into any more trouble."

He scoffed. "Yeah, right."

Carlotta stopped at the base of the steps and turned. "Since I probably won't see you before then, I hope your awards dinner is nice. I'll be thinking about you receiving your distinguished duty award and looking so nice in your tux."

Regret flashed through his eyes, but was quickly replaced by resolve. "I'll be thinking about you, too."

42

"So," Carlotta said to Michael as they retrieved items from their lockers and prepared to go home, "Detective Terry thinks that one of the loan sharks could be responsible for the identity-theft ring. And maybe killed the women because they thought they were going to turn state's evidence."

Michael shook his head. "You're always in the middle of something, Carlotta. You seriously need therapy. By the way, Dr. Delray said you stood him up."

"That was the day my car was stolen. And my cell phone was broken."

"Well, I don't know if I can get you in now."

"That's okay," she said absently.

"Your mind is a million miles away."

"It's just that I can't help but think that there's more going on here, maybe right here in this mall. And it makes me furious that these thugs targeted me. My credit is ruined."

"Your credit was already ruined. Leave it alone, Carlotta."

"You know that I can't, Michael. Besides, I'm in a position to find out more than the cops can, you know, because I don't have to follow protocol."

He sighed. "You mean do something hare-brained." He closed his locker door. "You need to be concentrating on your sales."

"I know," she agreed. "And I had a great day today."

"It's a good thing. I don't believe Patricia was too happy about being booted back down to accessories."

Carlotta made a face. "I kind of hate her."

Michael laughed. "She's not so bad. We're going to the Elton John concert tonight."

"I'll be there too, with Peter."

"We'll be in the cheap seats in the rafters," Michael said dryly.

She closed her locker door. "I can't believe I'm gone for two weeks and you've cozied up to my arch rival."

He grinned. "The competition will be good for you."

Patricia walked into the break room, looking like a frazzled scarecrow. She gave Carlotta a glare of disdain.

"Speak of the devil," Michael whispered mischievously.

"How was your day, Patricia?" Carlotta asked. "Are those little doggy swimsuits still selling like crazy?"

"Yes, except now they're two for the price of one," Patricia said, "which cuts into my sales, which cuts into my commission."

Carlotta angled her head. "So that means you have to sell, what, twenty doggie swimsuits to equal one dress in my department? Wow, that sucks."

Patricia's stiff bangs blew up with her exhale. "Yes, doesn't it?"

Carlotta swung her purse to her shoulder and something on the floor caught her eye. "There it is." She crouched and scooped up the florist's card that must have fallen out of her locker. "I'll give this to Jack to see if he can find the man who sent the roses meant for the woman who was murdered. Maybe he'll know something."

"When did it go from Detective Terry to Jack?" Michael teased. "And why aren't you going to the concert with him instead of Peter?"

"Jack has a big awards ceremony tonight," Carlotta said, trying to keep the longing out of her voice. She would have fun tonight with Peter. She would.

Peter rang the doorbell promptly and whistled appreciatively at her skinny black skirt, silver metallic T-shirt and zebra-print jacket.

"You look dynamite," he said, then pulled her close for a hot kiss. "Do you have your autograph book?"

She nodded, a little surprised by his passionate kiss and the subtle change in him. He looked rested and more at peace. "Manhattan must agree with you."

"You know, Atlanta's not the only place in the world to live," he said as they descended the steps. "Have you ever considered living somewhere else?"

"I guess it didn't seem possible."

"Until now," he said lightly, helping her into his car.

Carlotta's head buzzed with the notion of how many experiences would be open if she would only let Peter back into her life.

After he climbed behind the wheel, he gestured to the front of the house. "What happened to the window?"

"Oh…neighborhood kids," she lied, thinking she might scare off Peter completely if she revealed just how many ways her and Wesley's lives intersected with what Mrs. Winningham had referred to as "a bad element."

Dinner was elegant and lovely. The restaurant's service was impeccable, the food and wine exquisite. It was a place she couldn't afford except on very special occasions, but the maitre d' knew Peter by name. The atmosphere was as romantic as a Norah Jones song, and gave Carlotta a further glimpse into what her life would be like with Peter. The best of everything, hers for the asking.

So what was stopping her?

She glanced at her watch and wondered if Jack's awards ceremony had started. She imagined him in his tux. He and Liz would be the most striking couple at the event, no doubt.

"You're checking your watch," Peter teased. "I guess that means you're eager to get to the concert."

She smiled and nodded guiltily, determined to push thoughts of Jack out of her mind and focus on the man in front of her. Peter signaled for the check and soon they were on their way to the Fox Theater, only three blocks away.

Known as the Fabulous Fox Theater, the building was a former Masonic Temple restored as an entertainment venue, with domes and turrets inspiring thoughts of romantic Arabian nights. Inside, the five-thousand-seat theater was arranged

with floor seating and a sweeping balcony under a spectacu-
lar ceiling of navy blue shot with twinkling lights. When the
house lights were down, it was easy to believe you were sitting beneath a velvety star-kissed sky. The dramatic structure
and glamorous interior made it a favorite of performers and
audiences alike and a jewel of midtown Atlanta.

They ran into Wesley in the ticket line and Carlotta
couldn't pass up the chance to tease him. "So, am I going to
get to meet this girlfriend of yours?"

He scowled. "Girlfriend? I don't have a girlfriend."

Coop walked up and said hello, his eyes lighting with appreciation when he looked at her. She reintroduced him to
Peter, then grinned. "You're Wesley's date?"

"Yeah," Coop said with a sigh, then draped his long arm
around Wesley's shoulder. "And I'm damn proud of it too."

Wesley rolled his eyes and Carlotta laughed, but secretly
wondered how much of Wesley's sour mood had to do with
problems with his lenders. He wouldn't talk to her about it
except to say that he had everything under control and didn't
need Jack or anyone else making things worse.

"Wesley, hi," said a gorgeous redheaded who made Wesley
straighten and knock Coop's arm off his shoulder.

"E....how's it going?"

"Great," she said. "I'm glad you used the tickets."

"This is my boss, Coop," Wesley said. "This is E. She's my
probation officer."

"Eldora Jones," the woman said, shaking Coop's hand.

"And this is my sister, Carlotta."

Eldora turned and smiled. "I've heard a lot about you."

Carlotta was struck by her dazzling beauty—no wonder Wesley hadn't missed a probation meeting. "It's a pleasure to meet you." She introduced Peter just as a dark-haired beefy guy walked up to Eldora.

"Everyone, this is my boyfriend, Leonard."

Everyone said hello—except for Wesley, Carlotta noted. He had a stricken look on his face that told her he was in love with this girl.

Her heart ached for him.

"We'd better get to our seats," Peter murmured, and they said their goodbyes.

Once they were inside the theater, they were escorted to their seats—center stage, second row. Carlotta gasped. "I've never been this close to the stage."

Peter winked at her. "Enjoy. And keep your autograph book handy. We might get invited backstage."

She squealed in delight. Collecting autographs was a lifelong hobby of hers, born of her father's proximity to celebrities since his investment firm had catered to VIPs. She'd gotten Elton's autograph years ago, but it had been ruined when her autograph book had gone swimming in a pool one night at a party she'd crashed.

Since her new autograph book, compliments of Jolie, was virtually empty, having Elton's autograph would be even more special. The fact that Peter had remembered and humored her somewhat frivolous pasttime meant a lot to her.

"I'll get us some wine," he offered.

"I'm going to the ladies' room, I'll meet you back here."

As she moved through the milling crowd, Carlotta hugged

her purse close, feeling the outline of her autograph book tucked inside beside the phone that Peter had given her. A few minutes later, when she exited the stall in the ladies' room, she saw Patricia Alexander washing her hands at the sink next to hers. Jesus, the woman was wearing a suit to a concert—what a tightass.

Her hope to go unnoticed was lost when Patricia caught her gaze in the mirror. Her mouth twitched downward. "Hi, Carlotta."

"Hi, Patricia."

"Where are you sitting?"

"Uh, up front."

Patricia got out her lipstick and began to apply it. "Must be nice, but our seats are decent. We're near the front of the balcony."

"Yeah, there really aren't any bad seats in this theater."

"So, Michael tells me that you had great sales today."

"I guess so," Carlotta said, taking a paper towel from the attendant and dropping a tip on the vanity tray. "You know, I started with Neiman's in accessories. It's a great training ground."

"I suppose," Patricia said. "But I'm not exactly new to Neiman's."

"No?"

"I worked there for a while last year."

A memory slid into Carlotta's mind and she froze—at the same time Jennifer Stevenson had worked there.

Her mind started chugging furiously. Patricia had access to the employee lockers. A determined thief could've broken in, gotten personal information from handbags and no one would be the wiser. Patricia could've sold her information and Jennifer's to the likes of Barbara Rook and Beverly Tucker. Maybe she'd gotten to know the women through the store somehow. As customers?

Then she remembered that Beverly Tucker's body had been found by her dog walker, which meant she had a dog.

A dog with a swim suit from Neiman's accessory department where Patricia worked? And there were all those scarves....

"What's wrong with you?" Patricia said. "You look positively green."

"Something I ate isn't agreeing with me," Carlotta murmured. "I think I'll sit in here for a few minutes. But I'll come by to say hello to Michael. What are your seat numbers?"

Patricia told her, then strutted out.

Carlotta took a calming breath, then pulled out the cell phone Peter had given her and dialed Jack's number. He was probably in the middle of his dinner, but she could at least leave him a message to come and pick up Patricia for questioning at the end of the concert.

"Detective Terry."

"Jack, it's Carlotta. I didn't think you'd be answering."

"Then why did you call?" he asked irritably. He was talking low and she could hear applause in the background.

"Because I think I know who's involved in the identity-theft ring. Her name is Patricia Alexander. I just ran into her in the bathroom at the Fox. I'm at the Elton John concert. With Peter." And what had compelled her to add that little tidbit?

He sighed. "And what makes you think this Alexander woman is involved?"

"Because she worked at Neiman's at the same time as Jennifer Stevenson. And because she works in accessories."

"And what does that have to do with anything?"

"Jack," Liz said in the background, "can't that wait?"

Carlotta's grip on the phone tightened.

"I'll just be a minute," Jack said. "Go on, Carlotta."

"It's significant because Beverly Tucker had a dog, and our bestseller right now in accessories are these adorable little doggie swimsuits—"

"You're killing me."

Carlotta frowned. "Never mind. I'll handle this myself."

"Don't you dare—"

She disconnected the call and turned off the phone, then exited the ladies' room. She wasn't about to confront Patricia here, but she did want to say hello to Michael and perhaps warn him about his companion.

He was leaning on the balcony when she found him. Luckily, Patricia wasn't around.

"Hey, I saw you in your seat down there," he said. "Pretty sweet."

She glanced down and saw Peter standing near their seats, scanning the crowd, looking for her. She waved her arm until she got his attention and he waved back.

"Michael, I have something important to tell you and I don't want you to get angry."

He frowned. "What is it?"

"I know who's involved in the identity-theft ring at the mall."

"You do?"

"Yes. And I came to warn you."

"Are the police on their way?" He shifted nervously and yanked his keys out of his pocket.

"What? No. Where are you—" Carlotta stopped when she saw his keyring. It was the same as the ones that Barbara Rook and Beverly Tucker had had in their possession. And suddenly she remembered where she'd seen the symbol—on Dr. Delray's business card that Michael had given her.

"Interesting keyring," she said carefully, belying the rush of adrenaline pumping through her body. I've seen it before recently...twice, in fact.

"It's from therapy," he said. "Dr. Delray gives them to patients when they reach a milestone."

So Michael had met Barbara Rook and Beverly Taylor at therapy—the perfect place to hook up with other people who had problems.

"If you were in therapy, Carlotta, the doctor would tell you that you're way too nosy for your own good."

She took a step backward, but Michael grabbed her wrist with an ironclad grip. "Don't make this worse than it has to be."

"I thought it was Patricia," she whispered. "I never dreamed it was you."

His laugh was sarcastic. "What, do you think I can afford my lifestyle on retail wages?"

Michael drove a nice car, she recalled. A Mercedes.

Could've been a Mercedes or a BMW.

"Why would you sell my identity?" she asked, her eyes clouding with tears of betrayal.

He snorted. "Your credit was already shot. Everything would've been fine if only you'd filed for bankruptcy like I told you. I only sold the information for people I knew were headed for chapter seven anyway."

She tried to pull away, but he only tightened his grip. *Stall.* "Did you kill those women?" she asked past the bile building up in her throat.

Michael scoffed. "Barbara was getting crazy—using your name to do everything, even pretending to be you at the mall. When you got the roses at work and didn't know who they were from, I knew she'd gone too far. Then I followed her and saw her pick up your car. She was bound to get caught and lead the cops straight to me. Stupid bitch. I pulled her over to talk some sense into her. And when I saw the interstate behind her, it was just so easy to push her."

Carlotta shuddered at his matter-of-fact tone.

He laughed. "Then when the police thought it was you who'd died, I thought I was scot-free. Figured you'd decided to leave your miserable life behind just like your parents and that I'd gotten lucky." His smile was mean. "But then you came back. And you wouldn't leave things alone."

"And Beverly Tucker?"

"She got antsy about Barbara's death. She was going to rat me out."

The lights flickered, indicating the house lights would be lowered soon.

She swallowed hard. "Were you working with loan sharks? Were they threatening you?"

"What? No. I was independent."

"Someone drove by my house. Fired shots."

"I was trying to throw off the police, make them think Barbara was murdered because someone thought she was you." His laugh was dry. "I'm not good at this criminal life. I should've been a ballroom dancer, like my mom wanted."

"Michael, let me help you. Turn yourself in. You can plead insanity, still have a life."

"After prison? Do you know what would happen to someone like me in prison?" He shook his head. "No. I'm going to wait until the lights go down and then, I'm sorry to say, you're going to take a dive off this balcony. Everyone was so ready to believe you took a dive off the Seventeenth Street bridge, this is actually a step down."

Her wrist was aching. "Michael, don't." She saw Patricia walking up behind Michael, carrying two drinks, oblivious to what was going on.

The lights flickered again, then went down.

"Goodbye, Carlotta."

She threw her head back and screamed, trying to resist him. But Michael was taller and had strength on his side. He wrestled her back over the edge of the balcony, and she felt the momentum of her body weight carry her over....

Minus ten points.

43

The bottom fell out of Carlotta's stomach as she felt the weightlessness of open air around her. She flailed wildly, then miraculously caught a handful of corded fringe—a curtain, she realized—and prayed it would hold her weight. It did, but she heard the telltale rip of fabric slowly giving way. The arm that had been holding her purse dangled uselessly and from the excruciating pain, she concluded it was broken. Her favorite Manolo Blahniks fell off her feet and from the ensuing yelps below, landed on the heads of the people sitting beneath where she swung at the end of the curtain.

She wanted to scream, but was afraid to move. Besides, people were screaming all around her. The lights came back on, blinding her. Carlotta dangled like a doll, but even the fact that she was about to plummet to her death—or at least a full body cast—did not erase the realization that everyone in the theater was getting more of a show than they'd bargained for. Her skirt was around her waist—and for some unknown reason, she had decided to wear a thong tonight. She closed her eyes.

What now?

"Carlotta!" Peter shouted above her. "Give me your hand."

Her chest flooded with relief. *Peter.* "My arm's hurt," she cried, keeping as still as possible. The fabric ripped again, dropping her a couple of inches. The crowd gasped.

"Hang on," he yelled. "I'm coming down."

She chanced a glance upward and saw that a chain of men were lowering Peter. She felt his fingers brush her hand.

"I'm almost there," he said.

Then she could feel herself slipping. The fabric was failing and with a loud rip, it gave way completely and she fell to a chorus of screams below. She mentally braced for landing on the rows of seats, knowing it wouldn't feel good.

She was right. She slammed face-first into a hard surface, then waited for either the painlessness of death or the pain of life to take over.

It was, thankfully, pain.

Plus ten points.

And then Carlotta heard the groan beneath her. She knew that groan. Slowly she opened her eyes to see that Jack had caught her—or rather, had broken her fall.

"You wore my tie," she whispered.

"Stand back, I'm a doctor!" came the distant sound of Coop's voice.

And then, fittingly for the theater, everything faded to black.

44

"**Y**ou can start next Monday," Richard McCormick said with a firm handshake. "I'm looking forward to working with you, Mr. Wren."

Wesley nodded. "Thank you." Richard was a geek of the first order, but he seemed nice enough.

"Ooh, nasty burn," the man commented on Wesley's wound.

Wesley put his hand in his pocket. "See you Monday."

He walked outside the city building, telling himself that he would be more excited about starting the community-service work if he didn't have so many other things on his mind.

Like if he was going to tell E. that her musclehead boyfriend was in cahoots with Chance.

But he'd never do anything that would cause trouble for Chance. The guy had, after all, helped him pull off the Great Strip Club Caper, which brought him to another, more pressing, problem.

With Michael Lane arrested for the murders of those two women and for firing at Carlotta to throw off the police, Wesley realized that The Carver had had nothing to do with the shooting.

He had humiliated one of the biggest loan sharks in Atlanta for no reason.

And he still owed the man a shitload of money.

Which, he realized, was probably the only reason the man hadn't killed him already. He probably wanted to collect his money first and then kill him.

Almost nauseous with fear, Wesley rode his bike to The Carver's place of business, a hole in East Atlanta with no street address and no front door. He went around to the back and leaned his bike against the building, aware that his teeth were chattering. Christ, he hoped he didn't piss himself.

The photo chip was in his shoe. All he could do was offer it up as a peace offering and tell the man that it had been an honest mistake.

And then hand him the nine-hundred bucks he'd managed to scrape together.

But before he could lower the bike's kick stand, the door flew open. Wesley didn't get the chance to react. Two beefy sets of hands clamped down on him, then dragged him inside.

45

"You have a visitor," the nurse said.

Carlotta looked up from the hospital bed to see Coop standing in the doorway, holding a bouquet of flowers.

"How's the lady who stole the show last night?"

She smiled wide. "Fine." She patted the cast on her left arm. "The doctor says I'll be as good as new in about four weeks. Speaking of doctors, I hear you're the one who took care of me before the ambulance arrived. Thank you, Coop."

He grinned and set the flowers on the table next to her bed. "Don't mention it. I haven't gotten to work on a live body since med school, so it was a treat." Then he wagged his eyebrows. "And such a nice-looking body at that."

She winced. "I hear that camera-phone pictures of me swinging bare-butt from the balcony are cropping up on the Internet."

"Not so many." His eyes twinkled as he pulled a chair next to her bed and sat down. "I checked."

She laughed. "Thanks a lot."

"That was quite a fall. You're lucky you escaped with only a broken arm."

Carlotta winced. "I think Jack got the brunt of it."

"Just a few bruises. The man wouldn't even let the paramedics check him out until he was sure you were okay." Coop angled his head. "Although why I'm making my competition sound so good, I don't know."

Her cheeks warmed. "Coop, Jack and I…we're not…we can't—"

"It's okay," he said, taking her good hand. "I know. It's complicated."

She gave him an apologetic look. "I'm sorry. It looks like I won't be able to work for you until this arm heals."

He sighed. "You're forcing me to call Hannah, aren't you?"

"You couldn't find a more enthusiastic helper."

"True."

"Hey, is Wesley with you by chance? He's supposed to give me a ride home, but I haven't been able to reach him. He had an interview this morning to set up his community service, so maybe he got hung up there." She fingered the edge of the sheet. "I hope."

"Where else could he be?" he asked quietly.

She hesitated. "Tuesdays are usually when he makes payments to his lenders. One of the thugs that came by the house said something about a stunt that Wesley had pulled and that he was in big trouble. I'm worried."

He squeezed her hand. "Don't be—I'll find him. But mean-while, I'll take you home."

"I'll take care of that," Peter said, walking into the room with a bouquet of flowers twice the size of Coop's. The look he gave Carlotta was pure proprietary. "How's my girl?"

"Fine," she murmured.

Coop released her hand and stood.

The men clasped hands. "Thank you for taking care of Carlotta," Peter said with a smile. "But I think I can take it from here."

Coop inclined his head, then looked back to Carlotta. "I'll see you around."

His eyes telegraphed that he would take care of Wesley, and her chest expanded with gratefulness. "Thanks, Coop, for the flowers and for everything."

He nodded. "You're welcome."

He left and Peter walked over to set his flowers in front of the ones that Coop had brought.

"They're lovely," she said.

"You're lovely." He lowered a kiss to her mouth.

"I'm so sorry about last night. I ruined the entire evening."

He touched his finger to the tip of her nose. "Well, there aren't very many people who can upstage Elton John. Don't worry—we have many evenings ahead of us."

Carlotta smiled up at him and nodded. "Would you mind taking me home now?"

Her mobility was compromised by the cast, but at least it was her left arm that had been broken, and not her right. Within an hour, Peter had her home and comfortably settled on the couch. He brought her a glass of water and the pain pills the doctor had prescribed.

She was touched by his patience, but a little surprised—and uncomfortable—with his attentiveness. "Peter, you must have other things to do today rather than babysit me. I'm fine now."

"I do have to get back to the office," he said with regret in his voice, "but I want to show you something." He reached into his jacket pocket and withdrew a familiar Cartier ring box—slightly faded, crumpled on one corner.

Her breath caught in her chest. "That looks like—"

"It is. It took about a hundred phone calls, but I tracked down the pawn shop where you sold it and was able to get it back. Except—" he removed the lid and opened the hinged box inside "—I had a few changes made."

She looked at the ring and gasped. The original diamond was surrounded by two more, all three of the large stones perfectly matched. "Peter...what on earth..."

"The past, the present and the future."

Her mouth opened and closed and panic infused her chest. "I can't...I mean, I'm not sure..."

"You don't have to take it now," he said, closing the lid and returning the box to his jacket pocket. "I'll keep it until you're ready."

Still stunned, Carlotta could only nod. He leaned forward and kissed her, his lips possessive. "I love you," he said earnestly, his blue eyes shining. "Call me if you need anything."

He let himself out and she laid her head back on a couch pillow, her mind reeling. Was Peter asking her to marry him?

And how did she feel about that? It just seemed so easy. Was that what scared her?

Restless, she got up and forced her mind back to immediate matters—laundry, dishes, a window repair shop and more bills to sort. The mundane tasks kept her mind off Wesley, the devastation over Michael's behavior and Peter's bombshell.

As usual, she had more than enough worries to fuel a migraine.

Later that afternoon, the doorbell rang. When she saw Jack standing on the stoop, her heart did a little cartwheel. She opened the door and smiled. "Hello, hero. Nice shiner you got there."

He gave a little laugh and ran a knuckle over his bruised eye. "You should've seen the other guy."

"Thank you, Jack. You probably saved my life—again."

"I'm just glad this big body of mine came in handy for something."

She pursed her mouth. "Oh, it's handy for a lot of things."

Jack grinned. "You're trouble."

"That's what you tell me."

He shook his finger. "I missed getting my award because of you."

"I'm sorry."

"I'm not." He extended a plastic bag. "I brought your things."

Carlotta took the bag with her good arm. "What things?"

"Your shoes, your purse."

"My shoes!" She squealed. "I thought everything was scattered to the winds. Thank you, Jack. For everything."

"Just doing my job," he said mildly. "See you around?"

She nodded and stood in the doorway watching him leave.

When she set down the bag, her pink leather autograph book fell out. She reached down to get it and it fell open to the ribbon-marked page.

To Carlotta...Get well soon. Sir Elton John

Her mind worked furiously. Get well soon? If Jack had collected the items after she'd left for the hospital....

"Jack!" she yelled.

He turned back.

She held up the autograph book. "Elton John signed my book? How did that happen?"

He grinned. "I know a guy." He climbed into his car and drove away, while Carlotta stood shaking her head. The man was so confounding.

Still marveling, she carried the autograph book to her bedroom and removed a pile of clothes meant for the drycleaner to set it on her dresser, open to Elton's autograph. She stepped back and smiled in satisfaction.

The boxy jacket that she'd worn to the memorial service as part of her costume slid to the floor. She leaned over to clumsily pick it up with one arm, and frowned at the crackle of paper.

Reaching inside the pocket, her fingers closed around a slip of paper. Bewildered, she removed it, then smoothed it out to read.

So proud of you both. See you soon. Dad.

Carlotta froze, her mind rewinding to the funeral when after turning away from Jack, she had bumped into an older gentleman....

Her heart thrashed in her chest. Her father had been there after all. In disguise, like her.

And from the note, it sounded as if he planned to surface again.

Soon.

★ ★ ★ ★ ★

Don't miss a single move!
Look for the third book in the Body Movers *series*
from Stephanie Bond and Mira Books in 2008!
www.mirabooks.com
www.stephaniebond.com

A dark new thriller from
internationally acclaimed author

PAUL JOHNSTON

Writer's block is nothing compared to the sinister
assignment novelist Matt Wells has just received. A chain
of e-mails from a fan turns deadly when Matt discovers
the correspondent is a cold-blooded killer with an agenda
for murder—and Matt's family and friends are among the
scheduled victims.

Under close surveillance, Matt is plunged into a plot more
twisted than any he has used in his novels. Cast not only
as the ghostwriter of his persecutor's terrifying story, but
as the victim, Matt needs to risk everything to protect his
loved ones. But with the police closing in and his friends
being picked off, he is running out of time. The White Devil
is out there...and he's watching.

"The Death List is white-knuckle stuff,
and like all good roller-coaster rides
it's fast, furious and twisted as hell."
—Mark Billingham

Available wherever books are sold!

MIRA®

A sleek, sly and irresistibly dishy peek at the world of TV news

JENNIFER OKO

It was a harmless human-interest story for breakfast television: who would've thought it would land her in jail? New York producer Annabelle Kapner's report on a beauty-industry job-creation plan for refugee women in the Middle East earned her kudos from the viewers, her bosses, even the network suits. But several threatening phone calls and tight-lipped, edgy executives suggest the cosmetics program is covering up more than just uneven skin.

The pen may be mightier than the sword, but the celebrity prisoner trumps both. Annabelle starts a jailhouse crusade to expose the corruption she's uncovered. But it'll take more than a few thousand Free Annabelle T-shirts to clear her name. Especially when she discovers just how high up the scandal reaches—and how far the players will go to keep their secret....

GLOSS

MIRA®

Available the first week of June 2007 wherever books are sold!

www.MIRABooks.com

MJO2442TR

New York Times **bestselling author**

ALEX KAVA

**The cover-up was only the beginning...
then came the nightmare.**

Sabrina Galloway, one of the top scientists at EcoEnergy,
makes an alarming discovery: someone has tampered with
their production process, and an eco-disaster of staggering
proportions is imminent. Toxic waste is leaking into the
Florida waterways and the Gulf of Mexico.

In her determination to expose EcoEnergy's lethal secret,
Sabrina is unwittingly drawn into a sinister plot that puts
corporate greed and corruption above human life. She
becomes the target of silent, faceless enemies—some of
whose identities reach Pennsylvania Avenue itself.

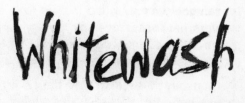

**"Kava's writing is reminiscent of
Patricia Cornwell in her prime."
—*Mystery Ink***

*Available the first week of June 2007
wherever books are sold!*

MIRA®

A heartwarming new novel
by the author of *Heathen Girls*

LUANNE JONES

MIRA®

Growing up in rural Orla, Oklahoma,
the three George cousins were as wild as
a pack of heathens. But with Bess's passing,
it's up to Minnie and Charma Deane to
remember their motto: *Live without limits.*
Love without question. Laugh without apologies.

There's not much to laugh about these days.
But as Charma Deane discovers, when you're
at the end of your rope, the ties that bind
can be a saving grace. Because nothing
soothes a tired heart like the comfort
of family....

The Southern Comforts

"Reading Luanne Jones
is like an afternoon
with a best friend."
—*New York Times* bestselling
author Deborah Smith

Available the first week of May 2007 wherever trade paperback books are sold!